Unbound

The Underhill Saga

DeAnna Jackson

Copyright© 2022 DeAnna Jackson
All rights reserved
deannajacksonauthor.squarespace.com

Title: Unbound

Cover Art by: CJ Fernandez

ISBN: 979-8-9860692-1-0

Dedication

To my mother, this book wouldn't exist without your love and support. Thank you for always being my anchor

To my grandmother, our time together was unfairly cut short, but you accepted me for who I was even if you didn't understand, and you wanted me to follow my dreams. I can only hope you're proud of me.

Chapter 1

The house knew when visitors were coming. It listened past the scampering of animals, and whispers of voices both ancient and new. The house sat in the din and waited for a different sound. Usually it was one, but sometimes it was two. This time it was three. Something new. Something strange. The house breathed and shuddered, its wooden bones creaking in the night, and awakened the one who slept within its walls.

A broom clattered to the floor. The sound resounded through the house. Alannah woke instantly. She rolled onto her side, her hands roaming across the tightly knit fabric of her blanket. The fabric was replaced by soft fur. She sunk her fingers into the fur. A small mmrp greeted her. Alannah moved closer, pressing her face into her cat's side.

"A few more minutes," she grumbled to the large bundle she was cuddling.

But he was having none of it.

He yawned and shifted next to her. Even in the dark, she saw him stretch his paws in front of him. His head butted against her cheek. Alannah grunted.

The house spoke and Alannah had to answer. Time to prepare for guests. Humans. She didn't like dealing with them. They were loud and obnoxious know-it-alls. She cooked for them, cleaned after them, and—

her mother always stressed this—she had to treat them with kindness. Even when they mocked her. Even when they never heeded her warnings about the forest.

Mr. Pinkus headbutted her again and Alannah sighed. "Damn cat," she said, rolling onto her back. She was surprised her mother hadn't come to wake her. No guests had come in months. There was much cleaning to do. And she wasn't sure there was enough time to do everything.

It wasn't until she was sitting on the side of the bed, her feet on the warm wooden floor, that she remembered. Her chest tightened and she drew in a shaky breath.

That's right. It's only me now.

The bridge of her nose began to burn as a prelude to tears. But she didn't have time for this. With her hands curled into fists, she stood, nails digging into palms. The slight twinge of pain kept her anchored to the present. Turning back to Mr. Pinkus, she beckoned for him. "Come on. I know you're hungry."

He didn't follow.

Instead, he huffed and curled back into a ball. Alannah glared at him. He didn't acknowledge her. It was her own fault. She spent her twenty-seven years spoiling him and now he was a fat, content cat who wouldn't even keep her company so early in the morning.

"Selfish," she mumbled.

Dark hallway stretched out before her when she stepped out of her room. Alannah turned on the lights in the hall reflecting off of the dozens of clocks that hung along the walls. Wooden clocks, silver clocks, gold embossed clocks. All of them ticked discordantly. A sound she was long used to by now. The stairs were to her right, a few feet from her room. Past them were four rooms. Two on each side. Across from her room was her mother's room. It had been locked up tight for a month. And it would stay that way. Behind her was her grandmother's room. Alannah didn't remember the last time she went into that room.

She turned on more lights as she navigated her way downstairs. The light revealed what she wished would remain hidden. Dust clung to the balustrade of the stairs. Footprints—both hers and small paw prints—were etched into the dust on the steps. The state of the dust grew worse the further down she went. A thin layer covered all of the wood surfaces. She patted one of the cushions on the couch and coughed as a cloud puffed up from the fabric. She hadn't cleaned anything in a month. *A whole month.* If Alannah's mother was alive, she would've been mortified at the state of the house. Grief was never a good excuse. That had been made clear when her grandmother died when Alannah was a child and her mother pushed on as if nothing had changed.

The windows slid open easily as if the house was ready to breathe in the fresh air. Alannah leaned down, her hands resting on the cushioned window seat, and stared out into early morning darkness. From her vantage point she could see the chicken coop and the goat's shed. They were silent. It was far too early for them. Her gaze moved past that to the forest that bordered her property. The forest surrounded her on all sides. Branches reached in many directions. Up to the sky, towards each other until they intertwined, and towards her. To her the forest was foreboding. A trap closed around her ankle. But humans were lured here for the promise of a mysterious and beautiful place. A place they all believed they could solve until the forest swallowed them hole never to be seen again.

Alannah dragged herself to the kitchen. A full kettle sat on the stove. She turned on the heat and selected a mug—sage green with a superficial crack down the side—from the shelf above. The porcelain was cool in her hands. She set it down on the wooden counter. While waiting for the water to boil, Alannah pulled her dark brown hair back from her face and braided it. The last thing she needed was her hair getting in the way while she cleaned.

She yawned.

The house didn't have to wake her so early. Cleaning wouldn't take her that long. The kettle whistled and Alannah pulled it off the stove.

Tiny footsteps pattered against the tile floor. She snorted. "See. I knew you would be hungry."

Mr. Pinkus' tail swatted her ankles as he weaved between her legs. He was nothing if not predictable. Alannah dropped a teabag in her cup and stepped carefully towards the fridge to avoid tripping over him. A plate sat inside with shredded chicken and cold mushy carrots from her dinner the night before.

With the plate in her hand, she looked down. "Do you want me to heat it or—"

His paw tapped her shin.

"I guess not."

Alannah set the plate down on the floor. She watched him, raising the hot cup to her lips, and wished she could be a cat. Or any creature that could eat and sleep and do little else. It would be easier. With a sigh, she set her cup back down on the counter. *This place won't clean itself.*

Simple tasks of dusting and sweeping turned into scrubbing the baseboards on her hands and knees and stripping all the beds of their linens while dust made her sneeze uncontrollably. She tottered down the stairs with the mound of laundry, barely able to see past it, and dumped it in the giant metal tub in the washroom. The breath wheezed out of her but there was so much more to do. Alannah cleaned nose prints off the glass from Mr. Pinkus, scrubbed the bathrooms until they sparkled, and mopped every square inch of floor. Even with the open windows, the house smelled overwhelmingly of lemons.

The house was correct in waking her early.

Gentle rays of sun peeked through the trees as she hung bedsheets on the clothesline. Pink clouds drifted through an endless sea of blue. Sweat dripped from her temples and instantly cooled in the morning breeze. Alannah closed her eyes, letting it ruffle the wisps of hair that had pulled free from her braid. She didn't realize how consuming it would be to have to do all this by herself. *Maybe I should stop allowing people to come here.* They could get lost and stay somewhere else. Or maybe, if she scared them enough, they would stop coming into the forest.

She picked up the empty basket and walked across the dewy grass to the porch. Leaving the basket on the porch, she walked back into the house. Sunlight brightened the rooms. Alannah turned off lights as she moved upstairs to put fresh sheets on the beds. The final touch. If she had missed anything, it was far too late.

The house had a way of knowing when company was coming and that feeling passed to Alannah. Whoever was coming, they were close. The house was poised and ready to accept them, but she was not.

Alannah drifted back to the kitchen. Her cup of tea was still sitting on the counter having grown cold. She took a sip and grimaced. Bitterness lingered on her tongue. She held the cup over the sink and overturned it. Amber liquid swirled around the white basin before going down the drain. *How apt.* She set the cup into the sink.

It was time for her to get ready. She didn't want to, but she couldn't put if off any longer. People were coming whether she liked it or not.

Mr. Pinkus was curled up underneath the windows, the forest green cushion covered in pieces of orange fur. Of course. There was no point in fixing it. He would roll around on it again with a smug look on his face. Alannah leaned down and kissed the top of his head. "Thank you for the help." Her sarcasm was lost on the cat as he purred in response and tucked his paws around his nose. She left him there.

The warm water of the shower relaxed her and she eyed her bed longingly as she dressed in soft brown cotton pants that reached her ankles and a deep purple tunic with quarter sleeves. The sweet scent of lavender and daisy invaded her senses and her fingers gripped the hem of the shirt. *A month…why does it still smell like her?* Alannah swallowed and forced her fingers to uncurl and release the fabric.

Be welcoming. Her mother's voice rang in her ears, clear as a bell. Alannah drew in a breath in the hopes of soothing the ache in her chest. It didn't work.

Yours is likely the last friendly face they will see.

Her chest deflated as she released the breath.

A knock on the door resounded through the house. The floor underneath her feet expanded and creaked as if the house drew in its own breath to ready itself. Or perhaps she was imagining things. Another knock came. She wanted to ignore it. She wanted to climb underneath the covers until they went away. It would save her from having to pretend she was a hermit who owned a quaint home in the forest and being here was her choice and her choice alone. Maybe it would save them even if they didn't know they needed saving.

The third knock came as she descended the stairs. Mr. Pinkus was still curled up in a ball. Nothing bothered him much anymore. Not even company. Alannah huffed in annoyance as she passed him.

Sunlight filtered through the clear cracked glass inlaid into the cherry wood door. She could see three amorphous blobs on the other side. *Three. Fantastic.* Too bad the house never informed her of how many beforehand. She only had two rooms prepared. The other rooms...well...she wasn't ready to go in them yet. She hoped two were willing to share.

The brass doorknob was cool under her fingers. She heard excited voices on the other side. The door swung inward and she laid her eyes on her guests. They looked around her age—twenty-seven years—give or take. Their conversation ceased when they noticed the open door. They stared at her, appraising her as she was appraising them. Two of them looked so similar, she wondered if they were brothers. However, the longer she looked, she noticed their eyes were different. One set of cerulean blue and the other a deep brown that almost matched the color of her right eye. The woman didn't look related. Dark blond hair piled on top of her head in a neat bun and dark green eyes darted back and forth between Alannah and the interior of the foyer.

Alannah stepped back. "Please come in," she said, gesturing for them. She tried her best to sound cordial, but it sounded flat.

Her greeting either didn't bother them or they didn't hear her. They walked inside.

Alannah closed the door behind them but they hardly noticed as they looked around the room in awe. From the outside, the house could seem modest and small, but the floor swelled under her feet with a sense of pride in their shock. Alannah tapped her heel against the floor to remind the house to behave. She knew little about the human realm, but she knew enough to know that their houses were dead carcasses of wood and stone built upon the bones of those that came before. A hearth with grey stones that never grew cold took up most of the eastern wall. A plush emerald-green couch and two matching armchairs were arranged in a loose semi-circle in front of the hearth. A bookshelf filled to the brim with book and knickknacks—many gleaned from previous guests—sat to the left of the fireplace and the window seat took up most of the space to right of it. Behind the couch was a long table with a record player sitting atop of it. The records lined the shelf below. More things her family had kept over the years and Alannah's personal favorite.

"I only have two rooms. I hope you're alright with sharing," she interrupted their gawking.

Three sets of eyes homed in on her.

"How did you know we were coming?" the woman questioned. "Did someone from the town call ahead?"

"There is no phone here."

They laughed, believing she was joking. When her expression remained unchanged, the laughter tapered off. Nearly in unison, they reached into their pockets and produced a small handheld device. Alannah had seen them before. Although, they used to be bigger. Unfortunately, none of the guests ever left one behind so she never had the chance to look closely at one.

"No signal," the blue-eyed man said, frowning.

"Weird," the other two echoed.

Hope sparked in her chest. Maybe they would leave. Spare themselves. Alannah knew better. Their fate was sealed the moment they stepped into her home. Her hope withered further when a gleam entered their eyes. Excitement instead of disappointment. Alannah sighed inwardly. She nodded to the stairs. "I'll show you to your rooms."

She gave them no time to ask her any more questions. Turning her back to them, she led them up the stairs. When she reached the landing, she turned right. The freshly clean rooms were right across from each other. She opened the door to each of them and stepped back into the middle of the hall to allow them to explore. Not that there was much to explore. They were simple bedrooms. Same furnishings. A wooden bed—one covered with a green quilt and the other with a red one—and a dresser with an oval mirror attached. Nothing else. There was no point when the rooms were never occupied for long.

Alannah disappeared into the background. They were too fascinated with the "quaint" décor to notice her standing in the hallway. She cleared her throat to gain their attention once more. "The bathroom is the last door on the left," –she pointed to it with her finger—

"I'm sorry it's the only one we have for guests. Breakfast will be in an hour. Midday meal is at noon and supper is at six. Feel free to roam the house and the grounds, but please remember this is my home. Some doors are locked for a reason." They could try opening some of the doors, but they wouldn't be successful. Although, she wouldn't mind a reason to throw them out.

Leaving them upstairs, she made her way back down to the kitchen. She hoped they would give her an hour of peace before bombarding her with questions. Everyone who managed to find this place was curious about it.

Mr. Pinkus jumped down from the window seat and followed her into the kitchen. No doubt in a bid for second breakfast.

Alannah opened the fridge and sighed when the shelves were empty of what she needed. "Please don't do this to me," she grumbled and closed the door. She waited a moment, whispered a silent plea for the house to cooperate, and opened the door again. She sighed in relief. Eggs, bacon, sausage, milk. It was all there, sitting on the shelf for her.

Footsteps stomped back and forth and the ceiling creaked above her. Voices filtered through the floor as they moved about. It was strange to hear people in the house again, and to hear footsteps that didn't belong to her or the cat.

"Do you need help?"

She didn't hear anyone come down, but she turned, bowl in one hand and whisk in the other, to see who snuck up on her. It was one of the men. Brown eyes and brown hair. She didn't know his name. She didn't ask. She never asked. His hands were shoved into the pockets of his dark blue denim jeans. He wore a soft red jacket that was zipped closed.

"No, thank you," she said, resuming her whisking of the pancake batter.

She expected her rejection to drive him from the kitchen. Instead, he removed his hands from his pockets and walked over to lean his elbows on the counter. Her eyes were drawn down. With her fingers tightening around the whisk, she fought the urge to smack his elbows. The thought nearly made her smile. Her elbows had seen plenty of spatulas over the years. If it wasn't her mother, it was her grandmother.

"I didn't catch your name," he said.

"I didn't give it."

"How does this place get electricity?"

The sudden shift caught her off-guard and she stopped whisking. "I'm sorry?"

He tilted his head to the side. "This place, it's pretty far out into the forest, but it has electricity and plumbing. How?"

"Is that so unusual?" she asked, setting the bowl down on the counter.

"For a place that seems off-the-grid? Yeah. I half-expected to find a dilapidated building and maybe an outhouse. But this is..." he trailed off and looked around the kitchen before his eyes settled on her once more. "Pretty."

She narrowed her eyes. "You're a very strange person."

He grinned. "Thank you..." he gestured to her with his hand.

"Alannah."

"It's nice to meet you, Alannah," he said before

pointing to himself. "I'm Elliot."

"Hello, Elliot."

"You know, the way townsfolk described you, I expected an old hag—"

She raised an eyebrow.

"A few said you were a witch. I imagined…well, you know…"

"I don't."

"So, are you?"

"Am I what?"

He leaned forward. "A witch?" he whispered.

Alannah couldn't help herself. This was by far the oddest conversation she ever had with a guest before. "Perhaps I am," she whispered back. "Perhaps I've lured you here and now you can never leave."

Elliot snorted. "That would explain it then."

"Explain what?"

"The disappearances."

Alannah sobered. She pushed herself off the counter and grabbed the bowl. She was allowing herself a distraction when she had work to do. If mother was here, Alannah would've been chastised by now. She turned her back to Elliot.

"Uh oh. I said something wrong, didn't I?"

With her focus back on breakfast, she poured batter onto the hot griddle. "No."

"I was joking, I promise."

"Why are you here, Elliot?" Her eyes focused on the batter, waiting for the bubbles.

"Well, we were going to stay at a bed and breakfast in town, but once we caught wind of this place we had to come—"

Alannah grabbed a spatula and waved it in the air. "I

mean, why did you come to the town in the first place?"

He shrugged. "The legends around this forest are well...legendary. We are into that sort of thing so we wanted to come see for ourselves. Maybe find bigfoot or something," Elliot chuckled.

"And the disappearances? They don't scare you?"

"It's mostly people who don't know basic survival skills. Sadly, they probably got lost."

She flipped the pancakes. "And you don't think you will?"

"I've camped before. Learned how to survive. My dad made sure I knew what I was doing."

Arrogant.

While he wasn't wrong, his survival skills would provide little help against what lived in the forest. There was no amount of training he could receive.

Elliot leaned on the counter a few feet from her. "You live in the forest, but you're scared of it?" His eyes followed her as she began the second batch of pancakes.

"Yes. And if you were smart, you would be too."

Chapter 2

Some guests were rude. Some were overly friendly. Usually, Alannah couldn't wait for them to leave. Maybe she was lonely, but she found herself not minding Elliot and his friends, Beverly and Sean. When Elliot relayed her message, she was surprised when they instead asked her if there was something they should prepare for. She was used to being openly mocked.

It made her wonder if they were going to laugh behind her back.

But they were so...nice. Despite her protests, the three insisted on helping her clean up after breakfast. No one went where they shouldn't. They were respectful of her animals. Mr. Pinkus was loving the extra attention. Anytime Beverly sat down, he was in her lap with his belly exposed. When midday meal rolled around, they were back in the kitchen to help her.

The nicer they were, the worse she felt.

She should make them leave. Tell them they weren't welcome. But she knew it was too late. They were ensnared now. Prey. She felt powerless to help them. It wasn't the first time she had felt this way, but it was stronger. Instead of pity, she felt something more akin to anger or maybe it was frustration. She wasn't quite sure herself. She did what could do in this situation.

She made bread.

The dough smacked against the surface of the counter. She couldn't control anything else, but she could do this. Her fingers stretched and rolled the dough over and over. Sweat dripped from her temples and she raised her arm to wipe it away with her rolled up sleeves.

"What did that dough do to you?"

Elliot's voice didn't startle her this time and she was getting used to being sought out by him. He was the friendliest of the three, and the one not in a relationship. When Beverly and Sean were the two sharing a room, she had her suspicions. It was later confirmed when she saw them kissing in the hall.

"Have you made bread before?" she asked.

He walked into the kitchen and came to a stop in front of the island. "I can't say that I have."

"Would you like to learn?" *What am I doing?*

He shrugged. "Sure." He walked around the counter and rolled up the sleeves to his black shirt.

Alannah kept still as he moved behind her to wash his hands. When he was done, he stood right next to her. Close. Closer than most have. She swallowed. "Flour your hands first," she instructed, pointing to the small pile of flour on the countertop.

"Do you teach people how to bake bread often?"

She shook her head. "No."

With flour coating his hands, she showed him the basics of kneading. He watched her in silence until she stepped to the side and let him take over. "You know...I can't quite get a read on you," he said, his knuckles sinking into the dough.

"What do you mean?"

"I mean, and no offense, but you seemed standoffish at first, then funny, then standoffish again, and now you're showing me how to bake bread. It's a little confusing."

"My apologies—"

"Oh no, you don't have to apologize," he interrupted. "I was just curious about you that's all."

"Curious?"

"Yeah, like how come you're living in a forest all by yourself."

"I'm not by myself. I have the cat, the goat, and some chickens."

"No one else?"

Alannah shook her head.

"How long have you lived here?"

"My entire life."

Elliot stopped; the dough sat forgotten on the counter. "How long have you lived here alone?"

"I don't see why that matters." She grabbed the dough and formed it into a ball.

"Why haven't you left?"

Because I can't. Alannah placed the ball into a bowl and covered it with a towel. "There's no need for me to leave. I have everything I need right here."

He didn't look convinced, but she didn't need him to. She needed him to drop it. And he did. Alannah swept the extra flour off the side of the counter into a bin while Elliot walked away to wash his hands. "So why did you cover it?" he asked.

"The dough needs time and heat to rise."

"Oh." He leaned his hip against the sink and dried his hands with a towel. "You asked me the real reason we were here and I wasn't completely honest."

Alannah stiffened.

Elliot set the towel down. "You see, the real reason we're here," –he reached into his jeans pocket and pulled out a small box— "is this." He opened the box and a small silver ring with a multicolored stone was inside. "Sean is planning on proposing to Bev."

Oh. Oh no.

Alannah leaned over to stare at the ring. The light from the kitchen bounced off the stone, throwing reds and blues and purples onto Elliot's shirt. But she was confused. "Why are you telling me this?"

"Honestly, I don't know. I've been keeping it a secret for months now, waiting for Sean to decide on how he wanted to do this. We've always loved hiking and traveling and I planned this for them. Do you think it's a bad idea?"

Alannah swallowed hard. This was her chance. She could chase them away. "There are probably better ways than a dangerous hike through the forest," she answered.

"Yeah, maybe." He closed the box and put it back in his pocket. "I want it to be a moment they don't forget."

"You care about them a lot."

He nodded. "I don't know where I'd be without them."

"Is there any chance you'll rethink this?"

His lips twisted into a frown. "What scares you so much about it?"

"I doubt you'll believe me."

"Try me." He leaned down until he was eye-level with her. But before she could answer, he tilted his head in confusion. "Have you always had a purple eye?"

"Do your people not have purple eyes?" she asked, dropping her gaze down to the counter.

"My people?"

Damn.

"I should start dinner. And I'm sure your friends are wondering where you are," she said, moving to the sink. She turned on the water full blast in the hopes that he wouldn't ask her anymore questions.

"Right..." he trailed off. "I uh, I guess I'll leave you to it."

Note to self: humans don't have purple eyes.

***

Alannah dried the last plate with a dish towel. The windows in the kitchen were cracked open to let the cool evening air in. Every few minutes, she spared a glance to the forest. The sun slowly began to sink behind the tree line.

They had not yet returned.

Not that she expected them to.

She had avoided being alone with Elliot and he didn't ask her anymore questions. After dinner, they helped her clean up and then they relaxed in the living room. With her permission, they played records and perused the bookshelves. There wasn't much else to do.

They turned in early in the evening, wanting to leave first thing in the morning. Alannah stayed up to prepare breakfast and lunch for them, and then she laid in bed for hours trying to think of a way to warn them that wouldn't reveal herself. One they might actually heed. But they were gone when she woke. They left on the kitchen counter to thank her for the food. Elliot's name was scrawled on the bottom. She had hesitated on throwing the note in the bin and instead shoved it in her pocket.

Alannah placed the dry plate on a shelf above the

sink. With a sigh, she turned the stove on to boil water in the kettle. Her eyes strayed to windows again. Nothing. She didn't know why she kept looking. There was no doubt they had been taken. It was inevitable, much like their coming to her home in the first place.

The kettle whistled and she jumped, half-expecting the sound of trumpets from deep within the forest. With the Hunter's moon moving high into the sky tonight, hunters were preparing to chase their prey. *No. They would chase Elliot and his friends.* The hunts very rarely lasted longer than a night, but she remembered once when it went on for a week. Every night she would hear the thundering of hooves and the unearthly howls of beasts.

She hated the Wild Hunts.

Alannah poured the hot water into a cup and dropped a tea infuser inside. This time she didn't leave it behind in the kitchen. She carried it to the living room. Mr. Pinkus was sleeping on the couch.

"I'm going to sit outside, care to join me?" she asked.

He opened on eye, stared at her for a moment, and then closed it again. She wasn't surprised. He was never keen to go outside during this time. None of the animals liked being outside. She always made sure to pen the chickens and goat before dinner to make them feel secure as possible. The true relief was knowing her property was warded and they couldn't come onto her property if they wished her harm.

Leaving the door open, she walked out onto the porch. Her green skirt brushed against the top of her ankles. The bright moon couldn't touch the darkness of the forest. Alannah set her cup down on the top step and sat down on the stairs. The Autumn breeze was brisk without being too cold. Soon it would be freezing and winter was bound to bring snow. The thought made Alannah wrap her arms around her middle, her fingers twisting into the white fabric of her blouse.

Once she heard the sound of trumpets, she would go back inside and shut all of the windows. Maybe even play music to block the sounds. She hoped the hunters were swift. The longer it went on, the more those being hunted would suffer. Her stomach twisted.

Alannah reached for her cup and brought it to her lips. The tepid liquid warmed her. She held the cup in her palms. Time ticked by. The moon kept rising until it loomed above her. Her teacup had grown cold when the first trumpet echoed within the forest. The sound made the hair on her arm stand up. Alannah stood up from the step and turned her back to the forest. She was nearly inside when a crashing sound made her pause. Her heart thudded against her sternum. Turning back, her gaze moved over the tree line. They never came this close during the hunts.

When she didn't hear it again, she thought she imagined it. She was tired. But the sound came closer and blood rushed to her ears. The hunters had never come here before. Were they coming for her? Why? Was it because she was the only one left now?

She wanted to bolt inside and lock the door. Hide. But the crashing sound was accompanied by a cry and a shape moving towards the house. The movements were clumsy. Jerky. And when they broke through the trees, she realized it wasn't a hunter at all.

"Alannah!" Elliot's choked cry made her stomach clench.

Impossible. No one ever comes back.

She should go inside now. She shouldn't interfere. Couldn't interfere. Not in a hunt. *Never let them see you.* But despite that, her feet carried her down the steps. *Never give them a reason to notice you.* The grass was cold under her feet. *You can't.* Her pace quickened as she neared the fence.

She reached the fence before him. What was she supposed to do? No one had ever asked for her help before. She was torn. If she helped, the hunters would target her. She would break the most important rule her mother ever gave her. But if she didn't help, then he would die. Blood would stain her hands and she would never rid herself of it.

"Alannah!"

Elliot grew closer. Blood dripped down his face from a cut on his forehead. His movements were jerky because he was trying to keep his weight on his right leg. Perhaps the other was sprained, or at worst, broken. How he managed to make it back was incredible.

Her hand moved to the latch on the gate. If she moved fast enough, she could get him inside. She would drag him if she had to. The hunters wouldn't know. She would be safe. They both would. But the thundering of hooves made her mouth dry out. Her blood raced and heart pounded in her ears.

He was so close now. His free hand outstretched towards her. Alannah found herself reaching for him, ignoring her mother's voice as it looped in her head.

Never interfere.

Never give them a reason to notice you.

Elliot crashed into the fence, his hand scrabbling against the wood to keep himself upright. The hooves grew closer. Right at the edge. There was no time. The hunters would notice her. His fingers closed around her wrist. Untrimmed nails dug into her skin. His mouth formed the word "please" but she couldn't hear him over the pounding in her ears.

I can save him.

I can finally save someone.

The first hunter crashed through the trees on a pitch-black mare. With their face obscured by a mask, they pointed at Elliot with a polished silver axe, their shout muffled. Alannah didn't need to understand to know it wasn't good. Not when the other hunters followed. They were closing distance quickly.

Elliot whimpered, his grip on her wrist loosening. Time had run out. Let Elliot die or save him? Don't interfere and live with it or give the Fair Folk a reason to see her for the first time.

The hunter raised his axe, ready to strike.

Chapter 3

The ground was cold and hard under her back. Weight pressed down on her chest and stomach. The coppery smell of blood nearly made her retch. Alannah pushed on Elliot's shoulder, but he was out cold. With a grunt, she pushed him off of her and rolled him onto his back.
Oh no.
What have I done?
Alannah pushed herself up on her feet. Her eyes flicked to the gate, to the axe embedded in the wood, and to the pissed off hunter that wielded it. Now that they stood so close, she could them more clearly. Pale slender fingers—each with an extra joint—were wrapped around the handle of the axe. A mask—craved from onyx and brushed with silver—concealed the upper half of their face. Rubies glistened where the eyes would be. How could they see? Stag antlers branched out from either side of their head. She couldn't tell if it was part of the mask or not.

The hunter straightened. They loomed over her. Even though she couldn't see their eyes, she knew they were staring at her. She didn't know if they were appraising her or glaring at her. One hand unfurled from the handle and pointed at Elliot. "Return what you have stolen." Their voice was low and seductive. It danced across her lips and lingered on her tongue like a rich wine she wasn't ready to swallow. And like wine, it made her feel light-headed.

"Stolen?" she echoed.

"The human. The trophy."

Alannah's eyes darted to Elliot. Would she really go through the risk of saving him to hand him back over?

"Interfering in the Wild Hunt is a great offense," they said, pulling her attention to them. "Perhaps no one informed you of this little witch."

"Little witch," she repeated. Their voice might be smooth, but it dripped with condescension. Anger sparked a flame in her chest. While she was ignorant of many things, she knew well of the trouble she was in. And she knew handing Elliot over would save her own skin. Yet, as the fire spread throughout her chest, Alannah found that she wasn't considering the best decision as much as she should.

"For that reason, I am willing to grant you mercy. Return the—"

"No."

She could almost imagine their eyes widening under the mask. "No?"

"No," she repeated. "I will not return him to you."

"An unwise decision." They shifted, tilting their head to the side. "Will you not reconsider?"

Alannah took in everything. From Elliot lying beside her, unable to defend himself in any way, to the hunters that lingered right outside of the tree line. The odds were stacked against her. But it was too late now. She was no coward. Squaring her shoulders, she shook her head. "I will not."

"Stop dawdling, Odhran!" one of hunters shouted. "Take them both!"

Odhran's fingers curled around the axe once more as they pulled it free from the wood with minimal effort. "Very well then," they said, taking a step forward.

They didn't get far. The barrier did not allow it.

The moment they stepped inside the gate, they froze. Alannah felt energy thrum underneath her feet. It moved towards the gate, coalescing underneath Odhran, and with a snap of energy, tossed the hunter back. The gate slammed shut and the latch clicked into place. The curse she hated so damn much, the curse that kept her from leaving, also protected her.

Alannah couldn't help the laugh that bubbled up from her chest. It was the first time she had ever seen the protective magic work. No one had ever tested it before.

The fall knocked the hunter's mask loose showing silver eyes widened in shock. It quickly morphed into humiliation and then anger when the other hunters began to laugh. "This isn't over," Odhran promised, getting back up on their feet.

That sobered her.

For now, they would retreat. If they couldn't reclaim their prey then the hunt was ruined. She had ruined it. And they would no doubt find a way to make her pay for it. One by one, hunters drew back into the forest, shadowed by the darkness. Odhran was the last, his gaze boring into her. Alannah did not feel relieved.

She held her composure until the hunters were gone, and then her knees buckled and her stomach flipped. If she didn't have a more pressing matter, she might have taken the time to vomit and pass out. Instead, she swallowed and turned to Elliot. He was out cold. She needed to get to the house to take care of his injuries. She was sure there were many.

Alannah tapped his shoulder, but he didn't stir. She was going to have to drag him then. Bending down, she hooked her arms under his armpits. "Sorry," she mumbled, pulling him across the damp grass.

He was nothing but dead weight. But pulling him across the grass was nothing compared to hauling him up the steps. Alannah huffed every step. She hoped that she wasn't hurting him. Not that she would know. When she laid him down on the porch, he didn't move. If he wasn't still breathing, she might've assumed he was dead. Alannah turned away from him.

Mr. Pinkus waited right inside the door. He meowed balefully at her, his tail twitching back and forth.

"Yeah well, I didn't have much of a choice, did I?" she shot back. He blinked at her and walked onto the porch.

With a sigh, she left him with Elliot. In the kitchen was a door. A rather innocuous looking one. Same wood as the other doors. Sometimes a knob of brushed silver protruded from the wood. Sometimes there was no conceivable way in. Tonight, the knob was there, waiting for her hand. Alannah hated this door. If she had her way, she would never walk through it again into a room that bore no name. The smell of damp, wet earth greeted her. Alannah kept her eyes away from the middle of the room. Away from the stone slab that took up most of the space. She hadn't been in the room in a month. Unfortunately, she stored her best herbs in this room and she needed them to help Elliot.

It took her less than a minute to gather what she needed. The glass bottles clinked against each other as she tossed them into a wicker basket. She fled the room and the door slammed shut behind her, the knob disappearing into the wood. Alannah drew in a breath before moving again. Dropping the basket on the counter, she grabbed fresh towels and filled a large pot with water.

Mr. Pinkus sat beside Elliot, his paw gently tapping Elliot's cheek. Alannah set the pot down beside Elliot and waved Mr. Pinkus away. "Leave him alone," she hissed.

With shaking hands, she divested Elliot of his tattered shirt. Ribbons of fabric came apart in her hands. Alannah tossed it to the side. An open slash across his chest seeped blood. *Stop the blood loss first, then focus on everything else.* Alannah pressed a towel to the wound and Elliot's eyes snapped open. A gasp tore from his throat and he tried to push her way.

"Elliot!" she cried out as he pushed her shoulder, albeit weakly. It didn't matter. She didn't think he could see her. Unfocused and addled with pain, Elliot kept trying to push her away. Alannah grabbed a glass bottle from the basket and pulled out the cork. Pulling a purple bulb out, she crushed it between her thumb and forefinger. Before he could shove her again, she pushed it past his lips. He stilled. "It's alright," she murmured, her fingers pressed to his mouth to keep him from spitting out the bitter herb. "It will help you sleep."

His eyes widened in terror. As if the very thought of sleep inspired fear. Perhaps it did. She didn't know what he experienced in the forest. But if she didn't heal him, she would never find out.

True to her word, Elliot slumped back onto the wood and didn't move again. She waited, counting the times his chest expanded and deflated. A minute passed before she attempted to stop the bleeding and clean the wound again. This time he didn't wake up.

Alannah knew how to handle minor cuts and bruises. Her mother and grandmother taught these things well. And while she knew how to handle major injuries in theory, she didn't have practical experience. Elliot was the first to come back.

Alannah finished cleaning the wound. Muscles and sinew were flayed open. She was surprised he managed to survive such a blow. And that he had made it back to her home while losing so much blood. Why had he? Was he certain she would save him? She wasn't even certain until last minute. She pressed her hand to the wound. Power stirred within her. Gentle. Warm. She so rarely called on it for anything other than tending the gardens. Warmth flowed from her core, spreading through her chest, and to her fingertips. Alannah closed her eyes to concentrate on healing the deepest part of the wound first. She would work her way from the inside out. Exactly as she was taught.

Sweat soaked her shirt. One wound was going to sap her. But there was the matter of his leg and any other injuries. Small injuries could be managed without magic, but if his leg was broken, she would need magic and she wouldn't have enough to spare without rest. These thoughts—doubts—stayed at the forefront of her mind as she worked. If she didn't get this right, she could botch any healing attempt she made. She could hurt him worse.

But what else could she do?

As she worked, Alannah was overwhelmed with the sensation of being watched. The hair on the back of her neck stood up. Mr. Pinkus' bright yellow eyes stared unflinching at the forest. She had an audience. The entire time she had lived here, they had never spared her a glance. She had been uninteresting. Just some witch who lived in the fringe. A victim of a generation curse.

Every so often she felt an itch at the back of her neck. They were getting close. Adventurous. They were testing the barrier. She didn't know if it was curiosity or maliciousness. Her mother had raised her to fear them, to never engage them. They couldn't be trusted. Alannah was supposed to remain boring so they would leave her alone.

But she had their undivided attention now.

Chapter 4

Voice clashed in the dining hall. The hunters—some sitting at the long grey marble table and others standing against the black marble wall—made their displeasure known with wild gestures at each other and at Odhran. Fists smacked against blood red tablecloth, muffling the sound but still making the porcelain dishware rattle. Wine in overfilled glasses sloshed over and splattered until the table resembled a murder scene.

The hunt had ended in disaster and it was all Odhran's fault.

Valeria sat at the head of the table, shimmery, silvery hair pulled back into a severe bun. Rubies dripped from her black lace gown. Her blood-red eyes looked on in boredom. But Odhran knew better. It was in the way her fingers were curled around the arm of her chair. The way her nails dug into the wood. And the way she refused to look at Odhran. When she held her hand up, everyone stopped speaking at once. A surprising feat given the hunters were assholes.

"What happened?" she asked. While she didn't look at Odhran, the question was directed at him.

With squared shoulders and a tense jaw, Odhran answered, "It wasn't my fault—"

"That is not what I asked."

Slamming his lips closed, he took a moment before

trying again. "The human escaped us. He made it out of the forest. We almost had him, but he made it to the fringe and found help."

Valeria's mouth twisted into a frown. "Help?"

Odhran was hesitant. How to explain the witch? She wasn't even full-blooded and had bested him. The other hunters had laughed. None lent a hand to pull Odhran out of the dirt. Even she had laughed. More out of surprise than mirth, but it looped in his mind over and over again. A constant blow to his pride.

"Odhran!"

He jumped slightly at the anger in her voice. "A witch saved him."

"Half-witch," one of the hunters—their name forgotten—snarled, correcting Odhran.

"There's a witch in the fringe?" The question came from Odhran's sister, Selanna. She sat across from him, her elbows resting on the table. Normally, a meeting about the Wild Hunts would bore her tears. She found them archaic. Cowardly. She hunted true monsters, not easy prey. But someone interfering? That was interesting. Her eyes met Odhran's over the roast pig in the center. "How did she best you?"

Odhran's mouth twitched. "Boundary protection. I...did not notice it."

Selanna raised her eyebrows. The corner of her lip twitched and he knew she was trying not to laugh which would further wound his pride and anger Valeria even more.

Percivus—the lead hunter and the man Odhran had wanted to impress—stood up from the table. Jet-black hair was pulled back into a braid and tied off at the end by a piece of leather cord. A ring was tied to the end of the cord. A human's ring. Odhran could only imagine how Percivus came into possession of it. Winning Percivus' respect was hard but doing so opened many doors. Odhran saw his own door slam shut. Percivus' dark eyes focused on Valeria. "We were promised a hunt and we have been denied. How do you intend to fix this?"

"I offer my apologies. I was under the impression that my son was ready to host such an event," Valeria said, although she didn't sound sorry at all. "I would be honored if you would allow me to plan another hunt for you. A better one."

Selanna rolled her eyes.

"Do you have something to say?" Percivus said, glaring at Selanna.

"You're acting like a damn child. Throwing a temper tantrum because your toy was snatched—"

"Selanna!" Odhran hissed.

She ignored Odhran. "Over a human? All manner of beasts exist in our world and you choose the easiest prey?"

"It is tradition," Percivus snarled.

Selanna waved her hand in dismissal. "Humans are easy sport for lazy hunters. Perhaps you're not as good of a hunter as you think you are."

Odhran had to admit, he almost chuckled at how red Percivus' face turned. Selanna was nothing if not brutally honest to those who deserved it. But Odhran's chances of redemption were plummeting by the second. It would be a feat to convince Valeria to allow him another chance to helm the hunt. They had other humans. He could do it.

"That's enough, Selanna," Valeria finally spoke up, looking rather amused herself. "You and Odhran are excused—"

Odhran stood from the table, the chair's legs scraping across the black marble floor. "Please allow me another chance, Mother. I will go to the fringe and reclaim the trophy. The witch—"

"You will do nothing!" Valeria ordered. "You will stay away from the fringe and the witch. Now go. I have matters to attend to." Her gaze didn't land on Odhran once while she spoke. That stung more than her words.

Selanna stood up from her chair and threw their mother a disgusted look. Together they departed the room. Odhran did his best to ignore the eyes that bored into his back. The heavy oak door slammed behind them when they stepped into the hall. A warning for them to stay out while Valeria was smoothing things over. Odhran scrubbed a hand down his face. None of this had happened as planned. The hunt was supposed to go off without a hitch, and then perhaps, he would garner respect with the hunters. Maybe even earn his mother's approval.

Selanna sighed. "That could have gone better."

"It could have, if you had held your tongue," Odhran grumbled.

"And let them attack you? I don't think so."

"It was unnecessary. I was fine."

"You were not," she argued, her sapphire blue eyes narrowing. "You let Mother and everyone else walk over you for approval you will never get—"

Odhran's hands curled into fists to quell the shaking.

"You may allow it, but I will not."

"You have—"

"Please don't fight," a third voice came from the top

of the stairs.

Their younger sister, Meralith walked up the last few steps of the grand staircase, hand gliding over the ornate silver banister, her black boots echoed on the marble steps. It wasn't unusual that she wasn't present at the meeting. Hunters were cruel and she wasn't one for crowds.

If anyone else were to ask them to stop bickering, they would've scoffed. But Meralith was different. At only 150 years old, she was the baby of the family. She always would be. Odhran doted on her because of that. And Selanna...well, Selanna listened because of guilt. When Meralith drew closer, Selanna's gaze dropped to the floor. She could never bring herself to look at her sister's face for long. Nor at the jagged scar that began right above Meralith's right eyebrow and ended at the right corner of her mouth. An accident. Selanna's miscalculation. A hunt gone horribly and irrevocably wrong.

Meralith's eyes—one silver like Odhran's and the other a milky white—darted between the two of them. "Selanna's right. There is no pleasing Mother."

Odhran huffed in frustration. "I am not trying to please that old wench," he argued. "But pleasing the hunters would've given me more credibility with the court."

Neither looked convinced.

"I can fix this," Odhran mumbled.

Meralith sighed. "Odhran—"

"I'm going to the fringe."

"Mother told you not to," Selanna reminded him.

"I'll bring both the human and the witch back. The hunters will be pleased and I will no longer be a laughingstock," Odhran continued as if Selanna hadn't spoken at all. "Mother will get over it."

Selanna shook her head. "This is a bad idea. Leave them be."

After the humiliation he had endured, he could not. Leaving it alone ensured a tarnished reputation that would follow him everywhere. Going to the fringe was the only way to fix it. All Odhran had to do was draw out the prey, away from the protection of the boundary spell, and capture them. Would Valeria be angry? Probably. But appeasing the hunters would smooth it over. A human and a half-witch would be an easy catch.

Nothing could go wrong.

Chapter 5

Roots twisted around his ankles. Blood dripped down his face and mixed with sweat. *Run faster!* His lungs rattled in his chest and he drew quick breaths. *I'm sorry Bev.* Tears made his eyes sting. *Sean.* Hooves thundered in the forest behind him. They were close. And he was dead. Wood under his palms. His nails dug into skin. He called her name. Wide eyes—one brown, one purple—widened in disbelief then terror. She had warned them. Tried to talk them out of the forest. She knew what lurked within. She knew what was going to happen. And she wasn't willing to save him. The axe was coming down to cleave his head from his shoulders. His chest was heavy with an intense heat, as if someone were holding a red-hot poker to his skin.

Elliot touched his chest.

No, not his chest.

Something large and furry and…alive.

Elliot's eyes flew open. *I'm alive?* A pair of large yellow eyes stared back at him. Mr. Pinkus—a ridiculous name for a cat—sat on Elliot's chest with paws outstretched to touch Elliot's chin. He breathed a sigh of relief. How? He should be dead. He was so sure he had died. Yet here he was. Having nightmares and his head still firmly on his shoulders. Trailing his hand up his bare side, he felt for the axe wound finding nothing but bandages and a twinge where a gash should be. He raised his leg—he swore he had broken it during his escape—bending and straightening until he was satisfied with its mobility.

He reached up, twisting his fingers in his hair, trying to piece everything together. It all felt like a blur. Hiking with his friends. Exploring the forest. Having fun. Then dense trees filled with shadows. He remember he felt boxed in. And then they were being dragged across the forest floor. Bev screamed. Sean called for her. And then Elliot was alone. Where were they? He had asked for them, but the men in masks didn't answer. They set him free. *No, not free.* They gave him a head start.

Looking around the room, he slowly began to remember where he was. He had made it back here. Somehow. Perhaps it was his subconscious remembering the way, but at the time it felt like something was pulling him back. There was a gate and...

Alannah.

Elliot pushed himself up on his elbows. The cat jumped from his chest and onto the floor with a vocal sound of displeasure and a thud. Alannah had brought him as far as the couch. A low fire crackled in the fireplace, but the windows were thrown open to allow in the autumn breeze.

Noise from kitchen drew his attention.

Elliot quietly sat up and swung his legs to the floor to tentatively put weight on his leg. He stood up, expecting his leg would give out, but it held up. How? Had he somehow dreamed everything? No. It was too real. Maybe he was dead and didn't know it yet.

The kitchen smelled like bread and bacon and

warm spices. He looked around the room. Two plates sat on the table, each laden with eggs and bacon. A loaf of bread sat in the middle of the table with a ramekin of herbed butter sitting beside it. Steam curled from the food. It was fresh? Did she know when he would wake?

Alannah stood at the sink with her back to him. She didn't turn around. Maybe she didn't hear him come in. He took a moment to study her. Deep brown hair was pulled back in a braid that rested in between her shoulder blades. Her shoulders were hunched inward. The lavender fabric of her blouse stretched as her arms moved. He drew in a breath and his stomach growled.

"You should eat," she said with her back to him. "I'll join you in a moment."

Elliot jumped as she spoke. She had noticed him after all. There were so many things to ask her. The possibilities were overwhelming and he didn't know where to start. "What are you doing?" he asked instead, pulling a chair out from the table.

"Trying to salvage your shirt."

He sat down. "Oh."

Despite her permission to eat, he waited for her. She could've poisoned the food. On one hand he thought it was ridiculous to think such a thing. However, his experience as live bait and her reluctance to save his life, made him feel justified in being hesitant. He couldn't write off the feeling that she could've been involved in what happened. *Sean.* Elliot's hands shook. *Bev.* They were gone. *My fault.* The trip was his idea after all. He swallowed, trying to dispel the lump in his throat.

Alannah sighed in frustration and turned off the water.

Elliot swiped at his eyes as she walked towards the

table. If she noticed the tears, she didn't say anything. "You have to eat," was the only she said when she sat down. It wasn't until she grabbed her fork that he even touched his own, but he still didn't eat.

She noticed. "Are you not hungry?" she asked.

"This isn't poisoned, is it?" he blurted out the question.

She didn't look particularly surprised at the question, but she didn't answer it right away. Maintaining eye contact, she took a bite of her own eggs and chewed slowly. Deliberately. He noticed the dark circles under her eyes. And she was paler than he remembered. She swallowed and set her fork back down. "Do you really think I would waste my time and resources to heal you only to then poison you?"

"You healed me?"

"I couldn't exactly leave you to bleed out on my porch."

"Just at your fence."

Alannah dropped her gaze.

Questions swam around in his head, eagerly awaiting their turn, but one darted to his lips first. "What are you?"

She didn't answer, but she did look at him again. One honey brown eye and one violet eye stared back at him. At first, he thought she wore a contact as a gimmick. A way to sell the strange woman living in a strange forest theme. He wasn't so sure now. He wasn't sure of anything now. The rumors that drew him and his friends here, rumors he believed were mere myths to make a small town seem interesting, were truer than he ever imagined.

"Are you a witch, Alannah?" he asked, his voice

hushed.

"Only half."

His chuckle was strangled. Devoid of amusement and filled with disbelief. The way in which she answered "only half" as if being a full-fledged witch was the most normal thing in the world.

"And the ones that hunted me, are they...?"

She shook her head. "You had a run in with the Fae. And the only human to survive as far as I know."

Fae. Witches. His friends were probably dead and he wasn't. Brought back from the brink of death by a person who almost let him die. It was too much. Too unbelievable. But here he was. Eating breakfast with her as if none of it happened. Now she was staring at him with mild concern. Like he might break apart at any moment.

He might.

He wanted to.

This didn't happen to people, did it? To have the existence of something new and frightening confirmed in the span of moments. To have the desire to go back in time and make a different decision. One that would guarantee ignorance over knowledge. Elliot wanted to go back to a moment where he thought he wanted magnificent and terrifying creatures to exist—as pure fiction—as a way to escape reality. To a moment when his friends were alive, and Sean had proposed like he wanted, and everything was perfect.

Thrust headfirst into reality—the truth—and he didn't want it.

The fork fell to the table with a loud clatter. His palms smacked against his cheeks. Tears fell down his cheeks and wrists. They splattered onto his eggs. He dug the heels of his hands into his mouth to keep silent. *This isn't right.* Elliot's nails dug into his eyebrows.

My fault.

A chair creaked and he felt her hand on his shoulder. The touch gentle, tentative, as if he was made of glass. He was. But her comfort was not what he wanted.

Her fault.

Elliot pulled out of her grasp, dropping his hands from his face. That's right. Heat filled his cheeks, turning them a deep shade of red. Lingering tears dried instantly, leaving only salt crystals behind. "You knew," he accused her, his voice raw and wet and shaky. "You knew we would die in there."

If she was surprised at his anger, his accusations, she didn't show it. That only pissed him off more. She looked so damn unbothered. People were dead and she didn't look like she even cared. She leaned back in her chair, putting distance between them.

"Didn't you?" he asked, wanting her to respond, to give a damn.

Alannah cleared her throat. "Yes," she rasped.

The answer didn't make him feel better. He was hoping she would say no. That she was ignorant of what happened in the forest. But he remembered her being scared. Her warning. A warning he had blown off because he never would have guessed what lived there. Why didn't she tell him the truth?

Would he have believed her if she had?

No.

Elliot's shoulders sagged. The anger disappeared as quick as it came and left him exhausted. His bones ached and his temples pulsed. His body cried out for sleep, for food, for energy. But he had nothing to give it. His appetite had dissipated, and he didn't know if he would ever be able to truly sleep again.

With a sigh, he pushed the plate away. Alannah remained silent. She stood from the table and gathered their plates and took them to the sink. Elliot didn't want to sit at the table any longer but didn't know where to go. Outside was out of the question. He knew he should leave, get help, but he knew he wouldn't get far feeling the way he did.

Elliot shook his head. He shuffled out of the kitchen and back into the living room, eyeing the stairs as he walked by. Going upstairs wasn't going to happen either. He flopped back down on the couch. Mr. Pinkus trotted back over to the couch, placing his front paws on the edge of couch cushion and stretching before jumping onto Elliot's chest. Without permission or encouragement, Mr. Pinkus curled into a ball.

Between the constant rumble against his chest, and sheer exhaustion, Elliot felt his eyelids drooping. He fought sleep, afraid of the dreams that lingered on the edge of his consciousness. The ones that would suck him right back into the forest. Into the fear. Into the helplessness. But it wasn't enough to keep him away. Exhaustion was dragging him into the darkness.

Right when he was at the edge, he felt a weight cover him. A soft touch lingering on his forehead for a second. Two seconds. "I'm so sorry, Elliot." The words flitted through his consciousness. He reached for them. Clung to them. And when sleep finally took him, he held them tightly in his chest.

Chapter 6

Alannah tried to go about her day as she normally would, but with Elliot passed out on her couch and Mr. Pinkus—her shadow—keeping vigil, it was impossible to pretend. The forest, usually silent, was brimming with noise. Whispers from the undergrowth made her ears twitch. The whispers melded together but Alannah could pick out a few things.

That's the witch.
How did she best the prince?
She looks plain to me.
She's as good as dead.

The whispers made the back of her neck itch. Her fingers gripped the basket until her knuckles turned white. They wanted fear. Fed off of it. She wouldn't give them a damn thing. The whispers followed her as she tended to chickens, gathering eggs and cleaning the coop, and then feeding the goat. The noise made her grit her teeth while weeding the garden.

Alannah only relaxed when she was back inside, the place the whispers couldn't reach. Elliot slept soundly on the couch. Mr. Pinkus was curled up on his chest. He blinked up at her, but otherwise didn't move. She missed him following her around while she did her chores, but she doubted he would've followed her today. He hated the forest. The whispers would've bothered him.

She warmed up the leftovers from breakfast in the skillet and ate while leaning against the counter. The eggs were rubbery, but she wasn't a fan of waste, and she wanted to finish lunch quickly. Winter would be coming and she needed to start preparing for it. And she didn't like being inside. She didn't want to be around Elliot. Every time she saw him guilt surged into her chest and leave it tight. What happened to him wasn't her fault. But her hesitation to save him almost cost him his life.

As a child, Alannah always told the unequivocal truth about what lived in the forest. The stories her mother told her, she passed on. No one ever believed. And none ever returned. Humans were stubborn and unyielding. Eventually, she stopped. No amount of warning worked. Not when they felt beckoned by it. Her mother always described it as a hungry beast. It lured. It devoured. And nothing remained. Not even bones.

She set her empty plate in the sink. Feet shuffling over the wood flooring made her turn around. Elliot stood in the entryway with hair sticking up and bleary eyes blinking in the light. "I hoped I was dreaming," he mumbled.

"I'm sorry," she said.

His eyes darted around the kitchen before he walked to the counter. He leaned on the surface with his elbows. "I want to blame you." He rubbed his red and puffy eyes. "But if you had told me the truth, I wouldn't have believed you."

"I know."

They fell into silence, neither of them knowing what to say. Alannah didn't know how to handle people in normal situations and this wasn't a normal situation. She cleared her throat. "Are you hungry?"

He nodded.

Alannah turned her back to him and sliced a thin piece of bread from the warm loaf. Since he was healing, she didn't want to give him too much at once. Soup would've been perfect, but she was running on zero energy and zero sleep. She would make it for dinner. While he nibbled on the bread, she put the kettle on the stove. A cup of tea and then she would send him right back to rest. He needed it. She did too.

"Alannah?"

"Hm?" She set two cups down on the counter.

"Do you think my friends are alive?"

She froze. She didn't want to lie to him. The odds were not good. Alannah would never know for sure. Either answer might upset him. "I don't know…maybe…" The kettle whistled and she turned the burner off while removing it.

"Can we…I can call for help…"

She shook her head while pouring the hot water into the cups. "There are no phones here Elliot."

"I can go…I'll go back to town. I can call the authorities. They can send people—"

"No one will come, Elliot. I'm sorry."

He pushed himself away from the counter. "They have to. Somebody will come. They can't abandon people. There will be a search party." He paced the length of the island.

"They wouldn't find anything." She turned back to him. "They wouldn't even make it into Underhill. Or here."

"I did. My friends did. How did we find you, but no

one else can?"

"Because you were lured here."

He gaped at her. "By what? You?"

"No—"

"Then what, Alannah?"

"I don't know, Elliot. The Fae. Underhill itself. All I know is no one ever comes here accidentally." She slid his cup across the counter. "You should drink something."

He shook his head. "How can you act like this? Like it's the most normal thing in the world? And how do you not know how it works, you live here!"

"It is normal."

"You expect me to believe that, that people go into the forest and never come back."

She raised her cup to her lips.

His elbows hit the counter and he buried his face in his hands. "So that's it. People disappear here and you don't stop them."

"There's nothing I can do."

"Bullshit, Alannah. You could've gone after them. You're a witch for Christ's sake! You couldn't save them too? Why me?"

"You're the only one that's come back."

"What does that have to do with anything?"

"I can't step foot into Underhill."

He shook his head and ran his fingers through his hair. "This doesn't make sense. How can you not step foot into a place you live in?" Before she could answer him, he was moving again, this time towards the kitchen entrance. "I'm going to go to them. I'm going to go save my friends."

"What? Elliot!" She followed him as he walked

through the living room and out the front door. "Elliot you can't go back out there!"

But he refused to listen to her. He was too focused on the forest. If he stepped foot in there he would die. She knew that without a doubt. They would be waiting. The hunter. Maybe something else. She reached for his arm but he shook her off. It shouldn't matter to her. She had no stake in his decision. And if he walked into the forest then she wouldn't have to worry about the consequences of saving him. Things could go back to normal. Safe. *Who are you kidding?* Normal was out the window.

"Elliot, stop!" She yelled as he neared the fence. The ground thrummed under her feet. The same as it did when the boundary protection kicked in. *What's happening?*

Elliot touched the fence. He almost had the latch undone before the boundary slung him back to her. Air wheezed out of his lungs as he hit the ground with a thud. He clutched his side. She was relieved when blood didn't seep through his shirt. At least her work was holding up.

Alannah stopped beside him and leaned over with her hands on her knees. "Are you okay?"

"What the hell was that?" he asked, coughing as he tried to suck in a breath.

"Boundary protection." She frowned. "But it's never tried to keep someone in before."

Laughter rang out from the trees. Multiple laughs swelled into one discordant tone.

"Are they laughing at me?" he asked.

Alannah held out her hand. "I'm afraid so."

The laughter stopped all at once and Alannah looked up. Something moved through the trees, coming towards them. Elliot's hand rested in hers, but he didn't try to get up. Antlers emerged from the tree line first. Piercing silver eyes pinned Alannah in place.

She swallowed.

While she expected to see them again, she didn't expect them a mere three days after she had saved Elliot. And she didn't expect him to show up without the other hunters. He strode out from the forest. Without the mask, Alannah studied the harsh planes of his face, her eyes roved over the sharp cheekbones and angular jaw. The face, as beautiful as it was in its harshness, would always remind her of the brutality she had witnessed. His strides made her feel as if he would walk right up to her, but he stopped a few feet away from the gate. With hands clasped behind his back, he stared at her as if waiting for something.

Everything in her screamed to go back inside. To hide away in her home. The one place that would protect her. But she knew she couldn't do that forever. She would have to come back outside eventually. And he would still be waiting. The Fae had nothing but time. She wouldn't know peace if she didn't get this over with.

Alannah squared her shoulders and swallowed the fear that sat in the back of her throat. She could do this. His eyes tracked her every move as if searching for vulnerabilities to exploit. She schooled her expression. Neutrality was best. Even when his eyes dragged over every inch of her and heat rose to her cheeks. She didn't want to give anything away. Anything that might be considered a weakness. A way to get close. A way to crack her.

"Aren't you going to invite me in?" he asked.

"No."

He raised an eyebrow. "Then perhaps you'll give me your name."

"I will not."

"Did your mother teach you to be rude to guests?"

Alannah's lip curled. "My mother taught me to be discerning about who is a guest and who is wolf. And you are no guest."

He hummed. She didn't know if he was amused or angered by her answer. So far, he seemed ambivalent, but Alannah didn't know what simmered under the surface. All she could do was hope the boundary protection would hold and she would be safe. Elliot's hand squeezed hers. *And Elliot will be safe.*

"I'm sure you know why I'm here," he finally said. "You took something that doesn't belong to you. I would like him back."

Elliot choked.

"He's a person. He belongs to no one," she answered, steeling her jaw so her voice wouldn't shake.

"He's human. That's debatable."

"Maybe for you."

"Is he worth the suffering what will befall you?" he asked. "If you turn him over to me, no harm will come to you. You will be able to go back to living quietly on the fringe with none the wiser to your presence."

Elliot was squeezing her hand so tight she winced. *I would never be able to live with myself if I did.*

"No."

The mask cracked. His face contorted in fury. Lips curved downward. Eyes were no longer cool and piercing but hot and molten. Eyebrows drew inward. "You're making a mistake. This will not end well for you."

"Why?" she challenged, unsure of where her bravery was coming from. "Because you've never been told no in your entire life? Because I snatched away your toy, and you want to throw a tantrum? Your tactics will not work. The human is not up for bargain."

The silence in the forest broke. The whispers surged. She couldn't make out what was being said, not over the roaring in her ears. But he did. It made him angrier. He wasn't expecting this response from her. "You should reconsider," he snarled.

Her mouth was dry. "I won't," she rasped.

She could've stayed and listened to another threat or two. Let him intimidate her as much as he wanted, but she wanted to get out of there. She turned back to Elliot and yanked him to his feet, wrapping an arm around his waist to keep him steady. The bravado that had driven him to the gate dwindled to nothing. He looked exhausted. Drained. Sweat dripped from his hairline. He shook. The terror swirling with in her reflected in his eyes.

Every rule her mother had drilled into Alannah about interacting with the Fae—namely that she shouldn't—had been tossed out of the window. Alannah had ripped up the rule book and she had no idea what to do now.

"If either of you leave, you're dead."

The threat made her pause, but it didn't surprise her. Leaving was death anyway. But now Elliot was trapped here with her. Alannah kept the hunter at her back, his eyes boring into her back as she walked back to the house. The door slammed shut behind them, sealing the outside, and providing a modicum of relief. All of the bravery—as false as it was—left her in one fell swoop. She slumped against the door. Elliot did the same. He slid down the door and she followed.

This can't be happening. Fear bloomed in her chest, making her heart ricochet against her sternum. *What have I done?* Elliot gripped her hand as it if it was the only thing keeping him safe. She didn't have to heart to make him let go.

What am I going to do with him?

Chapter 7

Having someone else in the house that wasn't family was an adjustment. They spent most of their time avoiding each other. Even at mealtime, they didn't eat together. Elliot was reeling from everything that had happened to him, and Alannah didn't know what to do to help. She doubted she could do anything. Two days passed by in silence. Not only in the house, but the forest was also quiet. Alannah hoped it was because they had forgotten about her once more. The third day dashed her hopes.

She woke before Elliot. He slept in his own room instead of the couch, but the creaking of the old mattress springs let her know that he spent most of his night tossing and turning. Sleeplessness and nightmares were expected. She had offered to make him something to help. He refused. He didn't trust her. She understood. Elliot had been thrust into a new world and lost his friends in the process.

Alannah left her room in the early hours of the morning. Mr. Pinkus followed her out into the hallway and walked down the hall, his tail in the air, to nudge open the door to Elliot's room as per his new routine. He would sleep with her as he always did and then spend time with Elliot. She didn't mind. Mr. Pinkus had become a source of comfort for Elliot now. Goddess knows he had always been a comfort to her.

Alannah tiptoed down the stairs, avoiding the creaky spots in the wood. She didn't want to rouse Elliot from what little sleep he would get. The lights clicked on, bathing the room in a warm glow, when she reached the bottom of the stairs. Alannah crossed to the foyer and stepped into her boots while the door unlocked with an audible click. The door opened, letting in the brisk morning air. She shivered. Time to keep her winter shawl by the door for the early mornings. Alannah grabbed a basket from the porch and stomped across the grass to the coop. The birds remained still and quiet while she collected eggs. Odd. They were usually more energetic when she walked in. Perhaps they shared in her exhaustion.

The forest remained still and silent. The lack of whispers relaxed her.

Alannah settled back into her routine. Place the basket on the counter. Put the kettle on for tea. Turn on the oven. Cast iron on the stove. Slice bread. She worked as quietly as possible. When the kettle whistled, she removed it and prepared a cup of tea for herself. It warmed her from the inside out while she finished prepping for breakfast.

The sound of feet—too loud to be the cat's—stepping into the kitchen made her turn and she watched Elliot shuffle in. As usual, his eyes were red and sunken with dark circles underneath. Seconds ticked by as they stared at each other.

"Morning," he grumbled, rubbing his eyes. It was the first words he had spoken to her in days.

"Morning." Alannah gestured to the pan. "I'm making eggs. If that's alright?"

Elliot leaned against the counter. "Sounds fine."

Having him in the kitchen at this moment was a stark contrast to first time. He introduced himself by joking and teasing her with familiarity. Now he looked as if he might fall apart if she said the wrong thing. She opted for silence. Alannah reached for the first egg and cracked it open.

Blood sizzled as it hit the hot cast iron. The yolk broke and black ichor oozed out. Alannah gagged at the smell. Rot. Infection. Using a towel, she gripped the handle and tossed the pan in the sink. But the smell lingered in the air.

Elliot had his nose pressed into his arm. "What happen—"

"Open the windows!" she cut Elliot off, trying to wave the smell away with a towel.

His socked feet slid against the floor as he raced to fling open the windows. He opened all of them in succession. Cool air seeped into the room, but the smell was strong. Alannah pressed her nose and mouth into the crook of her elbow and took a breath. So much for being left alone. None of this should be surprising to her, but it was a low, gross trick.

Elliot walked over to the sink and looked at the pan. His lip curled. "What the hell is wrong with it?"

The same thing that was wrong with all of them. Alannah grabbed a spare bowl and began cracking the eggs. They were all the same. Blood. Ichor. She dropped the shells into the bowl. *Damn.*

"It's nothing," she said, dumping the contents of the bowl into the trash. Everything was fine. She could salvage breakfast. Small parlor tricks wouldn't ruin her day. She would clean up and start over.

"It's not nothing—"

"It's fine," she snapped. "They were bad is all."

Elliot didn't believe her. She could tell by the way he narrowed his eyes and his forehead scrunched. But he didn't say anything. He backed away from the sink. A chair scraped across the floor and she knew he was sitting at the table, watching her. The smell was the worst part. It lingered the entire time Alannah scrubbed the pan and seasoned it before setting it aside for the day. She didn't want to use it right now. Not after that.

Half an hour later, she set down a plate of sausages and toast on the table. Her appetite had fled with the first egg, but she forced herself to choke breakfast down. A hard feat with Elliot watching her closely. Her dismissal of the situation wasn't good enough. He was going to ask her again. She could already see the question brewing on the tip of his tongue. And sure enough, when their plates were empty, he pounced.

"What the hell was that? And please don't say nothing," he said.

Alannah sighed into her cup. "A trick. Small magic. That's all."

"But why? And who?"

He couldn't really be asking that, could he? "Who do you think?"

Elliot frowned. "So...they messed with your eggs and that's supposed to make you hand me over. Why don't they come and get me?"

"They can't." Alannah set down her empty cup. "The magic that stopped you from leaving, stops them from entering. It's a protective boundary. Anyone wishing harm cannot breach it. It keeps my fam...keeps me safe. And apparently you now."

"Then why did it stop me?"

"I don't know. It's never stopped someone from leaving before."

Elliot ran his fingers through his hair. "If they can't get in, how did they do that?" He gestured to the stove.

"It's a small spell, not harmful. It was never meant to hurt me or the chickens. So, it slipped through. It's more annoying than anything."

"Seems pointless to have a protective boundary then."

She snorted. "Magic is not infallible."

He sat back in his chair. "So, I'm stuck here with you?"

"Yes."

"What happens if I try to leave?"

"If you can make it past the barrier, you will either be recaptured or killed on site. They were clear that you won't survive another encounter with the Fae. They are not graceful losers," she answered, cupping her empty mug as if it might still warm her hands.

Elliot sat in contemplative silence. He looked out the window. "What happens now?"

"I don't know."

"Can I ask you something?" he asked, shifting back to her.

"You can."

"You said you can't step foot into Underhill."

"That's not a question."

"Right…" he trailed off. "Underhill is the place I went to?"

"Yes."

"And it's not the same place I come from?"

"Correct."

"So where are you in this?" he asked.

"In-between." She sighed and leaned forward. "We call it the fringe."

"Because you're on the fringe of both worlds."

She nodded.

"And you've never been into Underhill?"

"Never."

"Why?"

Alannah drew a deep breath in through her nose. "There is a long answer and a short answer."

"Which one are you going to give me?"

She sighed. "I'm cursed. My entire family was. If we leave, we die."

Elliot stared at her in disbelief. Or maybe it was pity. "I'm uh…I'm sorry, Alannah."

She shrugged. "That's life."

***

The eggs were fine the next day, but the goat smelled rank. It hit her first thing in the morning when she went to gather eggs. After breakfast, she gave the goat a bath, but it barely touched the smell. Even after a second one, he still smelled. Alannah gave up. She didn't want to stress him out with a third bath.

The smell disappeared by the next morning. Replaced by dark brown patches of grass that smelled like decaying earth. Alannah found the first one with her foot. The smell hit her full force and she gagged. This time the forest wasn't silent. She heard them giggling in the tree line. If she stared hard enough, she could see eyes reflected back at her. Too many to count.

She wouldn't give them the satisfaction of a response.

Alannah carried on with her chores, clamping her

mouth shut to keep from throwing up every time she stepped on a patch. Once finished, she rinsed her boots off and left them on the porch before going into the house. Elliot didn't ask her what was wrong, and she said nothing. She knew he felt guilty even though she had promised it wasn't his fault.

While he didn't bring up anything about the curse, he didn't go back to avoiding her. He offered to help her with chores inside. He was leery about going outside. It was nice to have someone to help her with cleaning and cooking again. But he hovered. Using her presence as an anchor to keep himself from drowning. She found herself bumping into himself every time she turned around. Frustration turned into annoyance but Alannah bit her tongue.

The brown patches in the grass lingered for another day before clearing up. Then it was silence again. Alannah didn't trust it. She was afraid they would escalate and she didn't know what to expect.

She didn't have to wait long to find out.

The next morning, Alannah stood at the bottom of the steps, staring at the flower garden that wrapped around the porch. Her *mother's* flower garden. It had been filled with Gerber daisies. Her mother's favorite flowers, the ones she had painstakingly fought to keep year-round because her mother loved them so much. The last flowers her mother ever planted. The ones she couldn't plant again. They were gone. Dead. Wrinkled and brown and rotting.

Alannah knelt beside the flowers, her fingers sinking into the dirt. *I can save them.* She pulled a clump out, roots and all, but even the roots were black and shriveled. *No.* Alannah frantically pulled more out, dirt gathering under her fingernails, looking for a healthy plant she could save. One was all she needed. But they were all the same. They piled up around her knees.

Gone.

Dead.

Alannah's eyes and nose began to burn. Tears so hot they might burn her skin threatened to spill over.

"Do you concede?"

The voice rang out from the gate, clear as a bell, stoking the white-hot fury that was building in her chest. Alannah's hand tightened around the clumps she held until her hands shook. Dirt marked her steps as she strode across the yard. He was standing there with his smug smirk and quirked eyebrow. He thought he was so clever. *Damn him.*

"I suppose you've changed your—"

A wet slap against his cheek made him freeze. The clump Alannah had been squeezing in her fist, hit him square in the cheek. It fell from his face and tumbled down his dark red shirt before landing on top of his black leather boots. Dirt streaked across his pale skin. His perfect skin marred with filth would've been extremely satisfying if Alannah wasn't so angry.

"How dare you," she snarled, her voice raw.

"I—"

"How dare you take the only thing of her I had left!" Alannah wanted to throw more, throw it all, but she didn't grab enough. She wanted him to feel hurt in some way even though it wouldn't touch her pain. "You're nothing but a spoiled child. You think people are playthings because you are disgusting and vile and if I never gaze up your visage again it would be too fucking soon!"

He stared at her. Blinking in disbelief.

"I would never concede to someone as cruel and underhanded as you. Even if it kills me, you will never get what you want out of me," she vowed.

Shocked into silence, he just stared at her, his mouth opening and closing as he searched for words. What was once so terrifying to her had deflated before her eyes. He was nothing. And he didn't stop her as she turned away. No threats. No warnings. Just quiet.

Alannah stomped back up to the house, her routine forgotten. The door slammed open. Elliot jumped up from where he had been sitting on the couch. "Alannah?" he called her name as she walked by, taking in her red cheeks and watery eyes. "What happened?"

She had nothing to say. Nothing that wouldn't make her cry. And she refused to in front of anyone. She needed to be alone. To her relief, Elliot didn't follow her upstairs. Alannah slammed her bedroom door shut and leaned against the wood. Her chest heaved. She tried to catch her breath. The first wail slipped past her lips and she muffled the rest in the crook of her elbow. Alannah slid down to the floor.

A month. An entire month had passed and she didn't cry once. She didn't cry when her mother drew in a breath and didn't exhale again. Nor did she cry when she carefully prepared her mother's body. Cleaning. Anointing. Alannah had dotted her mother's skin with the lavender oil she had asked for. And she didn't cry when she carried her mother's body—so much lighter than it ever should have been—to the gate so she could be taken into Underhill. Her family could only return to Underhill in death.

Unfair.

The next morning her mother's body had been

taken just as Alannah had been told. She couldn't even bury her mother close. And now the flowers were ruined. Gone.

Dead.

Chapter 8

How dare you take the only thing of her I had left!

Odhran sat on the edge of his king-sized bed. Crimson silk sheets whispered against the fabric of his pants while his right leg bounced. His booted feet traced absent circles into the thick black rug that surrounded his bed. Stark light from the crystal on his bedside table illuminated the clumps of dead flowers she had chucked at him sat on the bedside table. Why had he kept them? He didn't know. He hadn't expected such a reaction over killing some flowers. They could surely be replanted. He had hoped she would have been inconvenienced enough to return the human. He had miscalculated somewhere.

Who was this witch?

It was apparent from the way she treated him, that she had no idea who he was. Or perhaps she did and she didn't care. Either way he wanted to know more about her. Then he might know how to handle her.

A knock at the door made him tense. If Mother knew he went to the fringe again, she would be furious. But he relaxed when Meralith poked her head into his room.

"What happened to you?" she asked as she walked into the room.

He touched the dirt smeared across his cheek. "Ah...

nothing really."

She raised an eyebrow. "Really? You look quite perturbed for nothing." She sat on the bed beside him. "You went to the fringe again, didn't you?"

He looked away and she shook her head. "You really should leave her alone, Odhran. Do you truly want to capture them and bring them here for a hunt?"

"Of course, I do," he answered quickly.

"You've never been interested in hunting before. Especially not hunting humans. Why now?"

"Everyone participates in the hunts, Meralith. It's tradition."

"That didn't answer my question."

He stood up. "Because I don't want to be trapped here like..." he trailed off, looking down at his feet.

"Like me?"

"I didn't say that."

"But you were going to. You don't want to be trapped here like your terrified little sister so you're trying to ally yourself with those repulsive people."

He clasped his hands behind his back. "Now you sound like Selanna."

"She can be brash, but she makes a good point. There are all manner of things to hunt, but they choose to hunt people. You shouldn't want to be like them."

Odhran tilted his head back and stared up at the ceiling, at the night sky projected across the surface. Incorrectly placed stars blinked in an out of existence. They tried to rearrange themselves correctly but failed every time. Odhran hadn't taken the time to fix the enchantment. Even though they were wrong, they still brought him comfort.

He didn't particularly like the hunters, but he didn't

want to remain here in his mother's domain. They were a way out. A door into the world that was far bigger than this prison. But Meralith was right. As was Selanna. He wasn't going to admit it. Selanna's ego was big enough.

"Fine," he said, a sigh escaping his lips. "If it will get you off my back, I will stay away from the fringe for a while."

"And the witch?"

"I'll leave her be."

For now, at least.

***

Alannah stayed in her room for the rest of the day and then the day after that. She left Elliot alone to fend for himself and figure out what the hell had happened. The dead flowers, rotting flower bed, and asshole hunter were the obvious culprits, but Elliot didn't understand why Alannah went nuclear over flowers. Mr. Pinkus stayed in her room for most of the time, but sometimes he would come out for food and to keep Elliot company. Every time Elliot opened the fridge there were two plates. One for him and one for Mr. Pinkus. He wondered if she snuck out while he was asleep to cook and clean, but he was certain he would've heard her making noise.

It was weird.

Elliot stretched out on the couch with only his thoughts for company in the quiet. The house was far too quiet. He missed the droning of a television or music in the background. Without it, his mind raced to places he didn't want to go. He pulled his phone out of his pocket. No bars. No service. He couldn't open any of the apps, even the ones that didn't require internet. He was completely cut off.

Elliot didn't know how she handled so much silence.

When he first arrived, he had noticed she was completely alone with only a cat, chickens, and a goat for company. He didn't think much of it. He assumed she went into town. Maybe had friends there. That the lone woman in the woods was an act. He knew now that it wasn't. How long had she been alone? Was she always? Where was her family?

He would ask her next time he saw her. She had to come out sometime. They were trapped together and they might as well get to know each other.

The silence grew maddening. Elliot pushed himself up. He needed something to occupy his mind or he needed to find a way to lure Alannah out of her room. When was the last time she ate? Maybe he could make her something. She always made eggs. Those were easy. He could do that. But that meant going outside to gather them. Elliot's eyes strayed to the door. Could he do it? It would be a quick trip. She had assured him the boundary would keep him safe. But he couldn't help the way his stomach tightened every time he stared out at the forest.

Before he could talk himself out of it, his hand was on the doorknob and he pulled the door open. It wasn't late, but it was already getting dark outside. Cool air made him shiver. The forest, cloaked in shadow, loomed beyond the fence, simultaneously beckoning to him and warning him away. A part of him wanted to go back in, to find out for sure that his friends were gone.

Elliot steeled himself. *There and back.* The basket for the eggs sat beside the door. He grabbed the handle so tight his knuckles turned white. *There and back.* The grass was cold and damp under his feet. He should've grabbed shoes. *There and back.* The chickens stirred, eyeing him warily. They didn't seem keen about a stranger, but they let him take the eggs. Only one ruffled their feathers as if they might peck his hand. *There and back.* With the eggs secure, Elliot closed the coop. The distance between the fence and the forest seemed smaller. Branches reached across the space with greedy fingers to snatch him from where he stood. Whispers from within promised to devour him whole. Elliot sprinted back to the house. *There and back.*

He didn't feel safe until he was inside with the door shut tight behind him.

Despite the chill in the house, his clothes stuck to his skin with a thin layer of sweat. His hands shook and he gripped the basket tighter to make it stop. Closing his eyes, he drew in breath after breath until his heart slowed. When his hands stopped shaking, he took the six perfectly oval eggs into the kitchen and set them down on the counter. Would that be enough? Would she be mad if he made full use of her kitchen? Would an omelet make her a little less mad?

He opened the fridge. The last time he opened the fridge, there were just two plates inside, but now it was brimming with leftovers from meals he didn't remember making, and also fresh produce, dairy, meats. He grabbed a portion of bacon wrapped in paper. There was absolutely no way Alannah had managed to sneak out and shop for this food. "Where the hell did this come from?" The question lingered in the air with no one to answer it.

Something else to ask her.

The fridge held everything he needed for breakfast. Elliot prepped everything as quietly as he could. He laid out bacon on a sheet pan, whisked eggs, and sliced bread for toast. Scents of bacon and butter filled the kitchen. But the entire time he cooked, he didn't hear her move. Maybe it wasn't enough. Elliot plated everything —bacon and cheese omelets, and toast—and set it aside. If she wouldn't come down on her own, then he would go get her.

Stairs creaked underfoot. Instead of turning right to go to his room, he turned left to the first door. Elliot approached with his hand raised to knock on her door when he noticed the door to the room beside hers sat open. Maybe she was in there. He walked over and slowly pushed the door open all the way.

Drawn curtains blocked light from coming in. Elliot reached inside, his hand moving against the wall until he found the light switch and flicked it on. Looking around, he noticed the room was empty. Elliot knew he wasn't supposed to be there, but he found himself stepping inside. A large bed took up most of the room. The green comforter was covered in a thin layer of dust. Everything was. From the dresser on his left to the desk that sat underneath the window. There was something in the corner beside the bed that was covered in a large black sheet. In the dark, it would've scared the shit out of him.

Who did this room belong to?

Unable to help himself, Elliot crossed the room to mystery item. His fingers grasped the fabric and he carefully pulled until it fell to the floor in a heap to reveal an ornate oval mirror. Dark wooden scrollwork around the edges resembled tree branches. Elliot marveled at the craftmanship when he noticed something. A shape. A shift. He turned, expecting to see Alannah catching him in the act, but no one was there. He turned back and jumped.

An older woman sat on the bed behind him. There was nothing terrifying about her appearance. In fact, she reminded him of his grandmother. Her face was adorned with laugh lines and crow's feet. Warm brown eyes looked back him. Curly grey hair hung loose around her face. She stared at him. Studied him. And he wasn't afraid. Elliot turned once more, but there was no one on the bed.

He looked back at the mirror and she stood beside him with her finger pointed at the closet door. A clicking sound accompanied her change in movement and Elliot turned to the closet. The door slowly swung open but not enough that he could see inside. Abandoning the mirror, he walked to the door and peered into the darkness. He could make out shapes, but he wasn't sure what they were. His fingers curled around the wood to open it more and—

"What are you doing?"

Alannah's voice made him jump. She stood in the doorway to the room. Wet hair clung to her neck and cheeks.

"I was just—"

"Snooping," she finished, crossing her arms over her chest. "Going into places you have no business being in—"

"It's not—"

"I asked you leave things alone. This is my home, not some attraction. Get out."

"Alannah, I'm so—"

"Get out, Elliot."

Elliot closed the closet door. Alannah moved to the side to allow him to leave and before he could attempt another apology, she slammed the door in his face. Elliot heaved a sigh. If she had given him a moment to explain...

But there was something else. Despite her interruption, Elliot made out the shapes in the closest. A staircase sat in the dark. Did Alannah know? Where did they lead? Who was the woman in the mirror and why had she pointed them out? He didn't think asking Alannah would net any results. If she did know, he doubted she would tell him. She would consider it none of his business. But he wanted to know.

Was he willing to risk her anger to find out?

Yes.

Chapter 9

Alannah sat on the porch steps in the late afternoon with a pot of cold water and potatoes beside her. She peeled the clean potatoes, cut them, and tossed him in the pot. Mundane and routine work to bring her back and tether her to the present. And it helped her prepare for dinner. Two birds, one stone. She could peel potatoes inside, but she hoped Elliot would leave her alone if she stayed outside. He had tried to apologize several times. Tried to strike up conversations. She remained unmoved by his efforts. When she caught him in her grandmother's room, she wasn't even angry. She was too tired for that. Two days of crying would do that to a person. Two days of grief pouring out of her.

The door opened and Elliot stepped out onto the porch. She didn't look at him. Didn't lift her head up. Her lack of acknowledgement didn't deter him. He sat down on the steps a few feet away from her. "I really am sorry, Alannah," he said, his fingers twitching until he dug them into his knees. "The door was already open so I thought you were in there."

"And yet you didn't leave when you saw that I wasn't."

He sighed. "I know. I was curious. And then the woman in the mirror—"

She paused and looked up at him. "Who?"

"There was a woman in the mirror. She pointed at the closet door and I was looking inside because of that. I wasn't—well I was snooping—but I wasn't doing it to be malicious or anything."

Alannah dropped potato cubes into the water, the cold water splashing back onto her wrist. "The woman, what did she look like?"

Seemingly relieved that she wasn't angry with him, he launched into a description. He described her grandmother exactly. But how? And why? Alannah had looked into that mirror many times and had never seen anything other than her own reflection. Why would her grandmother show herself to Elliot and not Alannah? Or maybe it was his eyes playing tricks on him? Somehow, she didn't think so.

"I don't know why you saw what you did, but please stay out of her room. I have certain doors locked for a reason." Alannah grabbed another potato.

Elliot fell silent. But only for a moment. "Can I ask you a question?"

"You just did."

He made a noise in his throat. "I mean…nevermind. Since I'll be staying here, I want to get to know you better. May I ask questions?"

"I have a feeling you will even if I say no," Alannah mused. She pushed the bowl of potatoes towards him and handed him an extra knife. "Help me and you can ask your questions."

Elliot grabbed the knife from her. "Awesome!" He leaned forward, picking out a potato to peel. "How do you get food? I've never seen deliveries, and you don't leave, but there is always food in the fridge. How?"

"It's magic—"

He scoffed.

"It is. Anything I need the house provides. I keep chickens and a goat more for company than sustenance."

Elliot stared at her, a half-peeled potato sitting in his hand. "No way."

She raised an eyebrow.

"So, can you get anything? Like if you wanted a pizza would one show up?" he asked.

"I have to know what it is first."

"Do you not know what pizza is?" His mouth hung open and when she shook her head, he let out a strangled gasp. "What if I wanted one? Would it show up?"

Alannah paused, her eyebrows drawing inward. "I don't know. A guest has never influenced the house before. Although, I'm not sure if you could be considered a guest anymore..." she trailed off.

"Is that how you get electricity and plumbing all the way out here?" he asked

She nodded.

Elliot looked thoughtful. "I wonder if the house could do internet."

"Maybe if you asked nicely," she said, resuming her work. She didn't find what she said particularly funny, but Elliot laughed.

They worked in silence. She wondered what question would follow up that one. If he wanted to know how the house worked, and some magic worked, she would be more than happy to answer. Those were easy things to answer.

"Are you by yourself, Alannah?" he asked, finally grabbing a second potato.

She froze a moment before nodding her answer.

"How long?"

Alannah cleared her throat. "A little over a month now."

"Who lived here with you?"

"My mother. And my grandmother, but she's been gone for many years," she said, not looking up at him.

"So, your mother—"

"Died."

"What happens if you try to leave," he whispered the question as if it would make it easier for her to hear.

"I'll die."

Elliot didn't seem to know what to say. Perhaps he didn't expect such a succinct answer or for her to be so nonchalant about it. But she grew up with it hanging over her head, and it wasn't something she gave much thought anymore.

"Like, instantly?"

"I won't drop dead, no," she clarified. "It'll be over a matter of weeks. I'll slowly get sick and waste away... and then drop dead."

"Jesus," he muttered. "What did your family do to deserve that?"

She shrugged. "I've heard stories, but I don't know if they're true. And after a while I stopped caring. I've accepted it. Like my mother did. And my grandmother before her. It's a curse. If it can be broken, no one ever figured out how."

"Damn Alannah. I'm sorry."

She dropped the last potato in the pot. "It's fine Elliot. I've come to terms with it. Now, let's make dinner."

Her answer wasn't enough for him, but he waited until after dinner to ask her anymore questions. They sat in the living room. He fiddled with the record player until he managed to get one to play. He happened to choose her favorite album, *Dreamboat Annie*. Alannah relaxed, mouthing the words to the songs. She knew them by heart.

Elliot waited a few songs in before he spoke. "What about your father?"

Alannah looked up from the chair, sewing needle in one hand and blouse in the other. "What?"

Elliot sat on the couch across from her. Mr. Pinkus stretched out beside Elliot's thigh; his purrs audible from where she was sitting. "Your father...you told me about your mother and your grandmother, but what about your dad?"

She shrugged. "I never met him. Shortly after I was born, he went into the forest and never came back."

"Didn't he know about the forest? I mean being with your mom and being here...did she not tell him?"

"Oh, he knew the forest was dangerous. He lived in town, heard the stories, but came here because he was curious. He became taken with my mother, she got pregnant with me, and you know the rest."

"You don't sound bothered by it."

"Losing people to the forest is common. And I didn't know him." Alannah picked up her sewing again. "My mother always told me it was better to keep a distance. We lose everything we love to the forest. Eventually."

"Do you think it's part of the curse?"

"It's possible. I honestly don't know."

"If it is, it sounds like it's meant to keep you as isolated as possible."

Alannah paused. "I hadn't thought of it that way, but you might be right. If it is, it has certainly worked."

"Have you ever thought about trying to break it?"

"Of course."

"When did you stop trying?"

"When my grandmother died."

Elliot leaned forward. "Do you want to talk about it?"

"I'm not sure what to say."

"There had to be a reason her death stopped you."

The needle slipped through the fabric and stabbed her fingertip. Blood welled from the tiny dot. Alannah cursed under her breath while sticking her finger in her mouth. She set the blouse on the side table. It was apparent she couldn't have this conversation and sew at the same time.

Elliot sat back on the couch, waiting for her answer. But Alannah wasn't sure what to say. She had never unpacked why she stopped thinking of ways to break the curse. For a few minutes, she stared at Elliot's hand as it moved through Mr. Pinkus fur. She was surprised he wasn't pestering for an answer. Elliot was curious, a dangerous trait sometimes, and never seemed to run out of questions. She'd answer a handful and he'd come back with more. It wasn't as annoying as she thought it would be. Sometimes it reminded her of how she was when she was younger.

"We had a guest stay for a few months. It was the longest anyone had stayed before," she finally said, leaning back in her chair. "He had no interest in going into the forest, which was a surprise for us because that's all anyone came for."

"Why wasn't he interested?"

Alannah brushed a piece of stray hair away from her face before cupping her chin in her hand. Her elbow rested on the arm of the chair. "He was a writer. Patrick Holden was his name and he wrote science fiction novels. He wanted a change of scenery and a quiet place to work on his novel." She smiled softly. "It wasn't all that quiet though. I was constantly asking him questions about the human realm and he answered all of them. I suppose he did because he felt sorry for me. Probably thought I was just some backwoods girl, but everything he told me made me want to see the human realm myself."

"What happened to him?"

Her nails dug into her chin. "The same thing that happens to all of them. He decided to go into the forest. Said he was being called. I begged him not to go, and he promised. But one morning he was gone. Left everything behind and disappeared." She hadn't thought about him in a long time. It surprised her to find embers of anger still smoldered in her chest. "I was sad. And pissed. That was when I knew I wanted to break the curse. A feeling my grandmother fostered even though my mother disagreed."

"Why was your mother against it?"

"Because she knew it's an impossible task. That I would get my hopes dashed, and how much it would hurt when it happened."

Elliot scratched underneath Mr. Pinkus chin. "And that was when your grandmother died?"

She nodded. "When we die, we can't be buried here. We have to be returned to Underhill. I don't know why. My mother never could explain it and I honestly don't think she knew herself. But we had to prepare my grandmother's body—clean her, dress her, say our goodbyes—then take her to the edge of the forest and leave her there. The next morning, she was gone. I—"

Alannah felt the familiar crushing weight in her chest. The anger, what little of it there was, burned away into raw grief. It always did. She blinked back the tears. "The place we can never step into in life," –her voice shook— "but have to return to in death. We can't even keep those we've lost. The forest takes everything."

"It doesn't seem fair."

"It isn't."

They lapsed into silence. Alannah took that time to compose herself. She hastily wiped the tears from her eyes. "My grandmother tried to find a way to break the curse and she never could. When she died, I realized that we were never meant to break it at all."

"So that's that?"

"Yes," she said, nodding. "That's that."

"I'm sorry, Alannah."

She shrugged. "I can't break, but I can end it."

"What do you mean?"

"I refuse to pass this curse to anyone else. I can't break it, but I can make sure it dies with me."

Chapter 10

Elliot couldn't sleep. First, he was too hot. He would fling the covers off and close his eyes for a few minutes. Then he was too cold. For an hour, he wrestled with the quilt in an effort to find the optimal temperature. Once achieved, the tension drained from his body and he sank into the mattress. But then his arm or leg would start to ache. Shifting his position would alleviate it for a moment, but then something else would hurt. It was the dance of an insomniac. Sleep wasn't coming easily. Not tonight.

I can make sure it dies with me.

He was beginning to understand why she was so distant. After so much loss, he couldn't blame her. Then there was the curse. She was willing remain alone and die alone in order to stop it. Elliot understood how noble it was, but it was sad to think about. And now she was stuck with him. It made him wonder what his presence here could change for her.

With a sigh, he flung the covers off once more and sat up. He wasn't sure what time it was. There were clocks throughout the house, but none of them told the same time. Elliot hadn't decided if it was a quirk of an already odd house or a feature. But he did know it was late. Alannah was probably asleep. He was as good as alone. Knowing that, he couldn't help but wonder about the stairs in the closet. He wanted to know where they led. And if she was asleep, she couldn't stop him from finding out. Was it wrong? Probably. But he was trapped here. He might as well find out everything he could about the place.

The floor warmed under his feet. His footsteps were light. The door creaked when he swung it inward and he paused, wincing at the sound, but he didn't hear Alannah stir. Moonlight barely lit up the darkened hallway, leaving it bathed in shadows. Elliot waited for his eyes to adjust before tiptoeing down the hall to grandmother's room.

Elliot held his breath as he passed Alannah's door. His heart thudded against his sternum so loud that he was worried she would hear it. *Please don't wake up.* He reached for the doorknob, but the door opened before he could touch it. Under normal circumstance—ones where he wasn't trapped in a magic house—he would've turned tail and run the other way. Doors opening by themselves was the beginning of a horror movie. But it was the least terrifying thing to happen to him lately. He stepped inside the room while his hand brushed against the wall to find the light switch. The door didn't wait. It began to close the moment he stepped into the room. He found the switch right as the latch clicked. Warm yellow light filled the room.

The sheet covered the mirror once again. He didn't need to remove it. He needed no guidance. The knob of the closet door was warm as if someone had been holding it. His heart raced, and in his excitement, he pulled the door open without caring about noise. The stairs, barely lit by the light of the room, disappeared up into the darkness. Elliot used the wall to guide him upwards up and up until shadows enveloped him. In the inky blackness, there was another door.

He wasn't given time to hesitate or change his mind. The door opened.

Moonlight filled the room from a large round window. Impossible. He had never seen the window from the outside. But here it was. It illuminated every corner of the cluttered room. Shelves lined the left side, filled to the brim with books. Most had nothing on the spines, others had gold or silver lettering, and some had symbols etched into the leather. On the right side was a large cabinet with jars and bottles littering the shelves. Purple, green, blue, clear. Some shimmered. Some were empty. Some were filled with weird substances that he didn't want to touch. Boxes were stacked beside the cabinet. Elliot leaned over to look in them. More jars and bottles and papers and trinkets.

"Magical junk," he murmured, snorting under his breath.

In front of the window sat a desk made of purpleheart. Leaves and vines were carved into its curved legs. Elliot stepped closer to see flowers etched into the surface of the desk. His fingers traced the grooves. He didn't know what kind of flower it was. While everything else was overflowing with treasures, the desk only held two things. A plain book and necklace. The black cover didn't indicate what was inside. He carefully flipped through the pages so he didn't bend them. It looked like a journal. *I probably shouldn't read this.* Elliot closed it.

Elliot picked up the silver necklace and wiped the dusty surface of the pendant with his thumb. The gem was a deep amber with a black slash down the middle. It reminded him of a cat's eye. What was it used for? He frowned, holding it closer to his face as it he could discern its function by doing so.

The pendant blinked at him.

Elliot tossed the necklace with a shout. It struck the window with a thunk before falling to the floor. The pendant shattered on impact. "Oh...*shit*," he whispered. *Shit, shit, shit.* Alannah was going to kill him. He knelt down to pick up the pieces but some were too small. Sweat beaded on his brow. How was going to explain this to her?

Maybe I can glue it together? She'll never know.

"Elliot?"

He jumped, flinging the shards back to the floor. "Alannah!" her name came out louder than he meant it to and he winced.

She stared at him, but he couldn't tell if she was mad or if she looked mad because he had woken her *and* he was snooping. Something she had asked him not to do. More than once. She stood there in her rumpled black pajama pants and lilac tank top. Wisps of hair escaped from her braid. Neither of them said anything for a minute. Both were waiting for the other to speak first. Elliot didn't want to go first.

When it was clear he wasn't going to say anything, Alannah folded her arms across her chest. "I heard you shout..." she trailed off, looking around the room as if she was noticing it for the first time. "What is this?" she murmured.

"You don't know? It's your house."

"I've never seen this room before."

He watched her spin in a slow circle before moving to the bookcase. Her fingers stroked the spines of the books. "I don't understand. How could she keep this from me?" The question was rhetorical, but she looked to Elliot as if he could give her an answer. His shrug made her lips curve downward. He didn't know what to say.

Alannah didn't stop moving around the room. She went to the curio and bent down to stare at the glass jars. All he could do was watch her in silence and give her a few minutes to take it all in.

Her eyes finally moved to the floor—to the shattered pieces of pendant at his feet—and she pointed. "What is that?"

"It was a necklace."

"Was?"

"I uh...I may have broken it," he admitted, while running his fingers through his hair.

"You may have broken it," she repeated.

"Yes."

Alannah drew in a deep breath and released it, her nostrils flaring. "How?"

"I thew it, not on purpose—"

Her eyebrow quirked.

"It blinked at me and I got scar—"

"It blinked at you. How did it blink at you?"

Elliot threw his hands up. "I don't know, Alannah, probably some weird magic shit. I've seen a lot more of it than anyone needs to in a lifetime. The point is, it blinked it at me, I got scared, I threw it. "

Alannah sighed, scrubbing her hands down her face. "Do you have any idea how ridiculous that sounds?"

"Ridiculous? Ridiculous!" Elliot's voice climbed an octave. "You're the one who lives in a magical house in the middle of a magical forest with things that want to kill me, but a necklace blinking at me is too much for you to believe?"

"You're up in the middle of the night instead of sleeping. Snooping, once again I might add, through my grandmother's things and breaking what could be an important heirloom and waking up everyone in the house!"

"Everyone in the house? Who is everyone? It's only you and me!" He gestured between them. "Oh, and I forgot, the cat! Did I wake up poor Mr. Pinkus?"

"Yes, and I was sleeping quite well, thank you."

Alannah uncrossed her arms and pointed at Elliot. "You have been nothing but trouble from the moment you came here!"

"Trust me Alannah, I wish I hadn't. I would've been fine never meeting you or coming to this damn place!"

"Would you two please stop arguing."

"No!" they shouted in unison, turning in direction of the third voice, but no one was there. Mr. Pinkus sat in the doorway.

There had been a distinct third voice. They both heard it. But there was no one else there. No one but the cat. And cats couldn't talk. Or could they? Elliot stepped close to Alannah. He studied her expression, but she seemed just as confused.

He pointed at the cat. "Did he just—"

She shook her head. "Mr. Pinkus can't talk."

"Oh, but I can." Mr. Pinkus' tail thumped against the wood floor. "And you're going to want to hear what I have to say."

***

Elliot began to laugh. Not a chuckle or a snort, but full-on belly-aching laughter. The kind of laughter that made him lean on the wall to keep upright. Tears streamed down his face. He swiped at them, but they kept coming the more he laughed.

Alannah was glad someone found it funny. It felt like someone had kicked her legs out from under her. Her only companion, the one she grew up with and confided in, spoke. And not even to her, but to Elliot too. All those times she felt alone and mourned the friends and lovers she would never have, and the one who could've made her feel differently never break his silence. She sank to her knees.

As if sensing her train of thought—perhaps he could read her mind too—he walked over to her and place his front paws on her knees. "If I could've spoken to you all these years, Alannah, I would have."

Elliot's laugher trailed off.

"Why didn't you?" Alannah asked, her voice no higher than a whisper.

"Your grandmother asked for my silence until you were ready. And when she wasn't sure if she could trust me, she locked away my voice until the time came." His eyes strayed to the pendant fragments on the floor behind her. "I did not deceive you."

Her upper lip curled and she made a noise in her throat. "How can I be sure you're telling the truth?"

"I cannot lie."

"You're of the Fae," she murmured.

"I am."

Elliot moved closer to her. "How can you tell?"

"Fair Folk can't lie. Not outright," she said. "But they can still deceive and find ways around telling the truth."

Elliot frowned. "It doesn't seem like he's lying." He knelt down beside Alannah. "You said you would be able to speak when Alannah was ready. Ready for what?"

"To learn the truth of the curse. And break it."

Alannah scoffed.

"So, there is a way?" Elliot asked.

"Possibly."

"Possibly isn't a sure end," Alannah snapped.

Your grandmother believed you would be the one. I believe her. I believe in you," Mr. Pinkus said. "I can help you, Alannah. Don't you want the truth, the knowledge, a path other than the one you believe you must walk?"

Yes.

"It can't hurt to hear him out at least," Elliot encouraged.

Alannah nudged Mr. Pinkus' paws off her knee and stood up. "Of course, it can. False hope can be just as hurtful."

She didn't want to hear anymore. She found it difficult enough to process finding Elliot in a hidden room, a room she didn't know about even though she'd lived in the house her entire life, but also the knowledge that her friend could speak and held the secret to breaking her family's curse? Too much to take in at once.

She left them in the room to talk amongst themselves. There was no point in telling them to leave. Elliot had made it clear that her wishes would be ignored. She passed her room—sleep wasn't a possibility—and trudged down the stairs. Tea might help. It wouldn't, but she could pretend. The lights flickered on in the kitchen as soon as she walked in. The house sensed her agitation.

Elliot and Mr. Pinkus entered the kitchen while she grabbed her cup. She reached for a second with a sigh. They didn't say anything to her. A chair scraped across the floor and creaked as Elliot sat down. Alannah kept herself busy measuring the tea leaves and adding orange peel to the cups. A terrible blend for sleep, but she had a feeling she wouldn't be sleeping anytime soon. Not with the possibility of breaking the curse hanging over her head.

A possibility she didn't want to hope for.

What if she couldn't? What if she listened to Mr. Pinkus and tried, and then failed? She had accepted what her life would be. That she would live in this house and die in this house. No children. No lovers. No one to prepare her body. She was going to wither and rot in this house. And she was fine with that. She was set in her choice.

Am I?

Alannah ran out of things for her hands to do. She stood at the counter with her back to them, her fingers tapping against the countertop while her mind raced. Everything she had thrown away, all of her dreams and hopes, wormed their way back into her head. The dream of simply leaving the fringe, of meeting real people, and of possibly never returning this place. It was a dream she had clung to as a child. Could she really have it again? How much would it hurt to let it go a second time?

The kettle whistled, momentarily pulling her from her thoughts. She poured the hot water into the cups, steam billowing in her face, and set the kettle off to the side. Elliot look away from her when she turned as if he had been staring at her back the entire time. Concern and curiosity warred in his eyes, but he remained quiet. Shockingly.

An inconspicuous book sat on the table in front of

him. She imagined it was important if he had brought it. She placed the cups on the table. One for her and one for Elliot. Mr. Pinkus sat beside the book, his tail swishing back and forth. She looked everywhere but at him. If he thought her hurt would subside so quickly, he was mistaken. Knowing he could speak, but her own grandmother kept him from speaking, stung. Not to mention a way to break the curse and a hidden room.

    She wanted to wake from this cruel dream.

    Elliot slid the book to her. "It's a journal. I didn't read it."

    "Why not? You seem to like getting in my family's business."

    "Please don't start again," Mr. Pinkus said, thwarting her attempt at an argument. "The journal belonged to your grandmother. She detailed as much of the family history that she knew. As well as how the curse began. She left it for you."

    Alannah dragged her fingertips over the supple leather, lingering at the edge. Half of her was telling her to open it while the other half was telling her to play it safe and never lay her eyes on it. *She believed in me.* Alannah didn't understand why. If anyone could've broken it, it would've been her grandmother. She was strong and loving and insightful. Alannah lacked those qualities. *Why me?*

    She pulled her hand back and reached for her cup. Piping hot tea scalded her lips and tongue but she kept drinking to avoid deciding. The pain anchored her to the present. She focused on it to keep her mind from wandering in circles.

    "What are you afraid of?" Mr. Pinkus asked.

    Failure.

Her grip on her cup tightened. "I don't think I should read it."

"Why not?" Elliot piped up. "This could be your chance, Alannah"

"Or it could be nothing."

"You won't know until you read it," Mr. Pinkus said. "If you don't try you will never know. Do you truly want to spend the rest of your life trapped here, wondering if you should've taken the other path?"

Alannah swallowed hard.

Mr. Pinkus tapped the journal with his paw. "Take the road less traveled, Alannah."

Her grandmother believed in her. Maybe it was time she tried to believe in herself.

Alannah set her cup down and reached for the journal. She flipped it open. Elegant script filled the first page. She recognized her grandmother's impeccable handwriting anywhere. It was a letter to her. But she didn't read it. She would prefer to read it alone. She moved on to the next page. Skimming the words, Alannah realized it was about the original village they came from. *A village. People.* If Alannah were to find them, would they know who she was? Would she be welcome there?

"What does it say?" Elliot asked.

She snorted. "You're so impatient."

"I know. What does it say?"

"Our family came from a village of healers and craftsmen. Which I suppose would explain our affinity for healing and green magic." She flipped the page. As she read, she felt Elliot's eyes on her. His knee bounced under the table as he pressed his lips shut against the tide of questions. She found joy in making him wait. But her humor began to ebb the further along she read.

"What is it?"

Alannah's forehead wrinkled and she frowned. "She writes about a woman named Moirne and her lover," – Alannah turned a page, letting out a breath when she read the first line— "her Fae lover."

Elliot leaned forward, resting his elbows on the table. "So?"

She shifted in her seat. "My mother always told me the Fae didn't like the witches, felt we were interlopers, and had rules against intermingling."

"Are you telling me your family was cursed because two people fell in love?" Elliot scoffed. "That's a little ridiculous don't you think."

"Not for the Fair Folk," Mr. Pinkus said. "But that isn't the only reason. Keep reading."

Alannah looked back to the journal. They waited in silence. Her eyes darted over the words and didn't stop until she reached another name. Valeria. She had never heard the name in her life, but as she repeat it in her head, she felt a sharp pain in her stomach before it flipped. For a name she never knew before, it certainly made her nervous. "Who is Valeria?"

Mr. Pinkus straightened. "Queen of the Ruby Court. Vicious. Cruel. And someone I would prefer not to meet again."

"Moirne's lover was also Valeria's. They were caught and punished..." Alannah's nostrils flared and she slammed the journal shut. "My family was cursed because of an affair?"

"Yes—"

"That's a little ridiculous, don't you think? Several generations bound to this place because of one mistake, one that may not even be Moirne's fault. I mean, did she even know he was with someone else?" Alannah ranted.

Mr. Pinkus sighed. "Unfortunately, it didn't matter. Valeria was a slighted woman and she used the breaking of rules to lay down punishment. Her original punishment was to kill them both, but the witches intervened for a lighter sentence."

"I'm not sure I'd call this a lighter sentence," Elliot said.

"It's not. It was overkill. A punishment that didn't at all fit the crime." Alannah opened the journal again. "Now how the hell am I going to break it?"

"You're going to try?" Elliot asked.

"This entire time I believed my family did something truly heinous to deserve this. And now I know that's bullshit. I am going to break it." She flipped through the pages, but after the story of Moirne there was nothing. "The rest of these pages are blank. There are no instructions here."

Mr. Pinkus blinked at her. "No. Your grandmother believed once you knew the truth, you would know what to do."

Alannah closed the journal with a sigh. "Well, she was wrong. I don't know what to do."

"You will." Mr. Pinkus touched her fingers with his paw. "It will come to you."

Chapter 11

Alannah rested on the porch steps watching golden rays of sun peek over the trees. A third cup of tea sat beside her. She hadn't slept a wink. Elliot and Mr. Pinkus slept together on the couch, their unburdened minds allowing them to sleep. Even with her newfound knowledge, Alannah felt as if she didn't know anything.

The forest sat still and quiet in the distance. Nothing rustled or scampered or whispered. Perhaps her previous audience had found something new to amuse themselves. Alannah stared at the trees as if she could make the forest open up to her. As if she would crack it open and see it for what it truly was. Maybe then she would feel knowledgeable. But she knew it would never be that easy.

Alannah held the open journal in her lap with her fingers resting on the first page. She was alone and it was the perfect time to read the letter, but she hesitated. She didn't want to open the wound of her grandmother's death. And she didn't want to know her grandmother's expectations of her. Especially when she might fail.

I have to.

Alannah sighed and leaned over to read.

My Dearest Alannah,

If you're reading this, then everything has fallen into place. First and foremost, I want you to know that I love you dearly and I never wanted to keep anything from you. Your mother and I oft disagreed on whether or not to prepare you for what's to come. This is why I am creating this journal for you. Do not lose it. It contains many secrets. They will reveal themselves when it is time.

Many things in this life are predetermined, but there is always room for change. I have had many visions of your future and of the future of Underhill. You will be a part of the future, but your choices will determine the part you play. I cannot tell you what choices to make. I can only hope that you succeed in creating a hopeful future.

Your first step is to break the curse. I know you. I know you are filled with self-doubt, but trust in me when I say, it was always meant to be you. Not me. Not your mother. Not the ones that came before. You. I have given you the necessary information to begin your journey. Be brave, Alannah and know that I am always with you.

Maeve

Tears dripped onto the page and Alannah reached up to wipe them away. She heard her grandmother's voice in her head as she read it, but the letter left her even more confused. Alannah couldn't imagine herself as a part of Underhill's future. What had her grandmother seen? And why had it scared Alannah's mother so much that she made Alannah promise to stay out of Underhill. She flipped through the pages again, hoping for something new, but it was the same. It was a shame she couldn't track down Valeria herself. Would such a cruel person even lift her curse if she asked? Or would she laugh Alannah out of the court? Maybe Valeria would even kill her, but Alannah doubted she would ever find out. She couldn't enter Underhill. It would kill her. *Not right away.* She froze. *Perhaps I could.*

"Alannah?"

She turned to Elliot. He stood in the doorway, rubbing his eyes. "Did you get any sleep?" he asked.

"No."

Nodding, he walked to the steps and sat down. A yawn escaped his mouth. Alannah gestured to the forgotten cup of tea sitting beside her. He picked it up and took a sip. "You really need coffee, Alannah," he grumbled. His shoulder rested against hers. "So, did you have any ideas?"

"Just one." She wasn't sure if she should tell him. She didn't think he would approve. While she didn't need it, she also didn't want to argue.

"And?"

"Remember when I told you that if I entered Underhill, I would die, but not right away?"

"I hate it already."

She nudged his shoulder with her own. "Hear me out."

Elliot took a sip of tea and side-eyed her.

"It would take weeks to drain me completely and for me to die. That might be enough time for me to find this Valeria and demand that she removes my curse."

"Let me get this right, your plan is to go into a place that you know will kill you—"

"Eventually."

"Irrelevant." He sighed. "And then approach someone that Mr. Pinkus said was horrible and ask her—"

"Demand."

"Even worse."

"*Elliot.*"

"Alannah, no offense, but this is a terrible idea. How do you know she won't kill us?"

"Us?"

Elliot rolled his eyes. "Did you really think I'd let you go by yourself?"

"You almost died last time you went in. The forest should terrify you."

"Oh, it does, but being stuck here for the rest of my life is equally terrifying. I'm going with you."

She shook her head. "I don't know if that's a good idea. They will definitely try to kill you."

Elliot set the cup down beside him. "Maybe. Probably. But it will be better than being trapped. At least if they come for me, I can find out what happened to my friends."

"You were captured together, weren't you?"

He nodded. "They kept us together for a bit, but then they separated me from them. I assume that they're..." he trailed off and looked away. "I want to know for sure. Who knows? Maybe they're alive. I'll never know if I stay here like a coward."

"I don't think you're a coward," she whispered. His friends were probably dead. The Fae would have little reason to keep humans alive. And since he escaped, his friends may have paid the price. She didn't want to say those things. Maybe it was wrong to let him keep his hope, but she also didn't want to dash it.

"Say we do this, do you even know where to go?" he asked.

"Not a clue." She tapped the journal with her index finger. "Grandmother didn't give me a map."

"I know where to go," a voice piped up behind them. They turned to Mr. Pinkus sitting in the doorway. A yawn split his face in two before her padded over to them. "I know where Valeria is. But I will not take you unless you are sure you want to face her."

"That depends. Do you think it's a bad idea?" she asked.

"Without a doubt," he answered. "Valeria doesn't take kindly to being challenged and she would hate to be reminded of your existence—"

"Thought so," Elliot mumbled.

"However, you have the right to ask for a chance to have your curse lifted. She will not deny you that as long as you approach her in court. She wouldn't defy the rules in front of an audience. It is the only chance you will get."

"It's settled then," Alannah said, although she didn't feel sure.

"Be sure, Alannah. She will not break your curse for nothing and you cannot possibly know what she will ask for the make it happen." His eyes flicked to Elliot for a moment before he looked back at her. She didn't need him to spell it out. Would she be willing to give up Elliot for a chance to end her curse? Especially after what she went through to save him. Would she be like them and use him as a pawn for her own gain?

No.

She would be better.

***

An old black backpack sat open on her bed; the fabric still sturdy despite the years of disuse. She didn't think Patrick would mind her using it. So far, she had only managed to pack several pairs of underwear. Mr. Pinkus had told her to pack light, only essentials, but she didn't know what those were. She didn't know how long they would be gone. How could one prepare for a trip with so many unknowns? Then there was the voice in her head telling her how bad of an idea this was.

"Alannah?"

She gave Elliot a brief glance as he walked into the room. "Yes?"

An armful of clothes plopped onto her bed. Long-sleeved shirts, plain button-ups, denim pants, and thick socks were strewn beside the backpack. "I didn't think you had the kind of clothes you would need for this."

"What makes you think that?"

He shrugged. "Everything I've seen you wear is flowy and light. Great for here, but not for the forest. They should fit fine. You and Bev..." he choked on the name. Elliot turned his face away from her for a few seconds before he drew in a breath. "They'll fit." He left the room.

She heard him go back to his own room, but she pretended she couldn't hear him sobbing. What could she say that would make it better? Nothing. She should talk to him again. Tell him that he couldn't come. Perhaps she should be mean to him so he wouldn't. He didn't want to stay behind, but that was a better alternative to dead. It probably wouldn't work. Elliot's survival was a testament to his stubbornness.

Tightly rolled clothes filled the backpack. She packed everything he had brought save for a pair of brown leggings, a black long-sleeved shirt, and a pair of cream-colored socks. Alannah stripped out of her clothes and kicked them off to the side. At least he was right about the fit. The leggings were stretchy enough to slide over her hips and thighs. She had her doubts for a brief moment. The fabric was warm, perfect for the weather. They would do nicely.

Alannah heard the creaking of Elliot's bedroom door and the stomping sounds of him going downstairs. Did that mean he was ready? Alannah's heart raced. She didn't feel ready. Maybe they should discuss it again. Really decide if this was worth it. The pounding in her ears made her wobbly and she sat on the edge of her bed. The familiar feeling of weight on her chest threatened to crush her. She drew in a shaky breath and closed her eyes.

I can do this.
No, you can't.
She believed in me.
She was too scared to do it herself.
Not her.
You're going to get Elliot killed.

Mr. Pinkus jumped into her lap. His back claws dug into the tops of her thighs and her mind quieted. "I know what you're thinking. You don't have to do this if you don't want, but you *can* do this."

"How do you know?" she mumbled.

"I know you. I know what you're capable of. And eventually, you will too."

Alannah took a deep breath. "Do you really think I can do this?"

"I can't lie, remember?"

She snorted. "I guess I better finish getting ready then."

Mr. Pinkus jumped off her lap and left her alone.

It took a few more minutes to grab essentials from her bathroom and pack them. She wrapped the journal in one of her mother's blouses to keep it safe and shoved it inside. Alannah moved quickly, afraid that if she stopped for a moment, she would rethink her decision once more. The time to act was now. To take her own life—her future—into her own hands.

Elliot and Mr. Pinkus were waiting in the living room. Elliot sat on the edge couch, leaning over to lace up his boots. Alannah frowned. She didn't have boots. But apparently, he had thought of that as well. He pointed to a pair of dark brown boots sitting on the floor beside him. They must have belonged to his friend as well. Alannah hesitated. While it was normal for her to use things left behind, it felt different this time. Elliot was with her, attached to these things, and Alannah felt strange accepting them.

"It's okay, Alannah," Elliot said, sitting up and patting the seat beside him. "Bev would want you to use them."

"I don't know..."

"Trust me. If Bev had gotten to know you, she would've wanted to help. They both would." He leaned down and opened the boot, beckoning for her foot. "That's who they were."

Alannah shoved her foot into the boot and grabbed the other one before he could. "Do you want to talk about them?" She pulled the boot on.

Elliot's fingers trembled while he laced her boots. "Maybe later. I...can't."

That was something she understood well. Talking about loss felt like ripping open a wound. Whether it was old or raw, didn't matter. It hurt.

Elliot finished lacing her boots and sat up. "There. I'm glad they fit."

Alannah stared at the boots that didn't belong to her and swallowed. "Thank you."

"Are you ready?"

Her laugh was humorless. "Do I have to be honest?"

"You're scared."

She nodded.

"Me too."

"Are you really sure you want to come with me, Elliot? You're putting your life on the line and I don't know if I'll be able to save you a second time," she whispered.

He shrugged nonchalantly, but his hands were shaking. "Who knows? Maybe I'll save you this time." He chuckled. "But if we don't go, then we're stuck. And neither one of us should be trapped here the rest of our lives."

"I guess that's it then," she said, standing up from the couch.

He followed her lead and they pulled on their backpacks. Elliot's green backpack was much larger and buckled around his waist. A water bottle sat snug in a holder attached to the side. She was grateful that he was coming, she hadn't even thought of food and water, and Elliot knew what he was doing. Alannah had only ever read about adventures and trekking through wilds in books and that wouldn't serve her in this situation. If she were alone, she would've walked into the forest with the clothes on her back and the wrong shoes.

The sun sat high in the sky. Warm rays of golden light provided nominal warmth amongst the chill. She closed the door behind them. The house would keep anyone from entering until she returned. But as they began to walk into the yard, she paused. "Wait."

"What is it?" Elliot asked.

"What about the chickens, and the goat? If I'm not here, who will feed them?"

"They'll be fine," Mr. Pinkus reassured her. "The house will take care of everything while you're gone. That's its function."

She threw a glance at the coop. What if she never came back? Would they miss her? How long would the house care for them? *Stop making excuses.* Alannah turned back towards the forest. Despite the brightness of the sun and lush green of the trees, the forest stretched into darkness. She didn't know what she would find inside. What if the stories her mother told were true? What if they didn't do it justice? Her blood raced in excitement and fear. She was going to know, going to learn, and it was as terrifying as it was thrilling.

They waited for her to start walking again. Her feet carried her to the gate. The wood was warm under her fingers. She hesitated once more, her eyes scanning the forest. There were no whispers, no eyes, no movement. Alannah unlatched the gate and swung it open. But she didn't move. She waited for something, anything, to stop her. The boundary remained silent.

One step and she was throwing out every single warning her mother ever gave her. One step and she would defy everything she knew.

Alannah took the step.

The air was still. Nothing moved. Everything was quiet. And then she felt it. Heard it. Calling out to her. Beckoning her forward.

One step turned into two turned into three. The ground thrummed under her feet, growing stronger and stronger the closer she got to the trees. Energy like she had never felt before reached out to meet her. It coiled in her belly and surged through her veins. All the years she used her power and it never felt like this. It was like she came alive for the first time. This is what had been kept from them all these years. This power. This feeling.

It felt like coming home.

Chapter 12

Odhran didn't know what drew him to the fringe that day, but he woke to a nagging feeling in his brain. The feeling paid off when he felt her enter the woods. Underhill reached out to her and he felt her magic respond. It was a weak response. If one wasn't paying attention, they would've missed it. He couldn't help feeling a sense of satisfaction. Perhaps, she had changed her mind after all.

Gnarled roots moved from his path as he neared her location. Leaves crunched underneath his boots. It wasn't until he grew close that he realized she wasn't alone. The human walked beside her, his eyes fearfully darting around the trees. And a cat—that Odhran realized wasn't a cat at all—was walking on her other side. She looked around the forest, but she didn't look afraid.

No.

She looked around with wide-eyed wonder. It was as if she was seeing this place for the first time. Could that be true? Had she spent her life in the fringe? Was it because she was only a half-witch? Or was there another reason? He knew she wouldn't answer his questions. Although, he did have an advantage here. Perhaps he could leverage them from her. It was the only way he would learn something about her. His mother shut down any line of questioning regarding the witch. He didn't understand it. He wanted to know.

But first, he wanted to know why she had stepped foot into his domain.

The cat that wasn't a cat, noticed him first. It stepped in front of her, laughable considering it could do little to protect her, and she stopped. The human froze beside her. Odhran watched her wide eyes turn to him. He expected a little bit of fear. He could be here to kill them both. Yet her eyes narrowed and her mouth twisted.

"What do you want?" she spat.

Not the reaction he expected. She was a strange thing. Even if people didn't fear him, they feared his mother. No one in the court would talk to him this way. Selanna would, but as his sister, she didn't count. The witch's disdain for him was palpable in the way her fists clenched and her nose scrunched in disgust. No trace of fear in her whatsoever. It would make things more difficult.

So why did he like it?

"Have you changed your mind?" he asked, ignoring her question since he didn't have a truthful answer for her. She confused him. And while before he would have wanted an earlier slight repaid in full, he didn't know if he still did. Not when she was such an interesting creature.

"I have not."

"Then why are you here?"

"That's none of your business."

Odhran tilted his head to the side. "Perhaps I can help."

"Hah! As if I would accept anything from you."

"We're here to see Valeria," the cat said, his large

yellow eyes looking at Odhran as if they knew each other. Did Odhran know them?

"Why did you say that?" she hissed.

"Because he can take us to her," the cat answered.

What did they want with his mother? How did she even know of his mother? Striking them down was definitely out of the question now. First, she stepped into the woods but wasn't giving him the human, and now she wanted to see his mother? If Odhran wasn't already curious, he definitely would've been now. He would take them to his mother. It would be interesting to see how his mother would react to the witch and whatever it was she wanted.

"I will take you," he said.

"Why? What's in it for you?" she asked.

"Amusement." Odhran turned his back to her. "Follow me."

"Wait a minute."

He stopped to look at her. "Is there a problem?"

"I don't trust you, and I'm not going to blindly follow you into the forest. I want your word first."

"My word?"

"Yes. No harm comes to me or my friends. The human is especially off-limits," she demanded.

"You think I'm leading you into a trap."

"Maybe you are, maybe you're not. I'm not taking the chance. Give me your word."

Strange thing indeed. "Very well. You have my word. No harm will come to you or your friends while you are with me. I can make no other guarantees of your safety if you wander off. I suggest you stay close."

She gestured to the forest. "Lead the way then."

Odhran didn't miss the way the human gripped her

hand. Or the sweat that glistened on his forehead. She didn't push his hand away. Instead, she gently squeezed in false reassurance. Odhran would not go back on his word, but if anyone else were to come across them, there would be nothing she could do to save the human. They were considered fair sport in this area. Hunting them was mostly ritualistic during the hunts, but humans that wandered into the forest often found themselves at the mercy of its inhabitants regardless of when.

He led them down the winding path through the trees. Smaller paths branched off, some leading to other places, some looping in endless circles. It could be confusing—on purpose—to those who didn't know it well. Every few minutes, he found himself slowing down to make sure they were following them. Odhran didn't want to leave them behind to get lost.

"How much farther?" she asked, trying to hide her labored breathing. She definitely wasn't used to covering long distances.

"Not much."

He didn't catch her grumbled response.

"What do you want with Valeria?" he asked.

"Why do you want to know?"

"I'm curious."

The statement was greeted with silence. He wondered if she intended on answering him at all and he was shocked when she did.

"She cursed my family. I've come to ask for her to remove it."

Odhran stopped in his tracks. A curse? His mother was no stranger to lobbing curses at people, and she certainly wasn't quiet about it, but he had never of her cursing a half-witch. If true, why did she hide it? And then there was the matter of what else the witch had said. "Do you truly believe she will lift your curse?" he asked.

"I don't know."

He did. He knew his mother. And Valeria would never do such a thing. Should he tell her the truth? Let her return home before she was inevitably disappointed. Or should he let her try anyway? If only to force his mother to acknowledge a curse she had hidden from her children. Perhaps even embarrass her in front of the court. A sight he would pay to see.

He chose to remain silent.

It took them a few minutes more to reach a break in the trees. And he relished her gasp when she laid eyes on his home.

The stone path to the veranda was lined with glittering red flowers. They gleamed in the sunlight and at night they exuded light. Trees obscured most of the house, their leaves providing privacy and shade. Their trunks were home to more of the red flowers. Stone columns lined the veranda and held up a balcony on the second floor. One would find it hard to tell the difference between flora and stone when they were entwined so thoroughly. Vines wrapped around columns, keeping them together even after some of the stone had worn away. They crept up the walls and framed the windows. Large red flowers grew from the vines. They glistened with dew. From afar it looked like they were encrusted with rubies. He watched her pause to run her fingers over a petal. The flower opened at her touch.

A green witch then.

Excellent healers. Could work even the harshest

earth to create life.

But could she stand up to his mother?

Odhran pushed open the doors to the foyer. Light filled every inch of the space, illuminating the stark white floors. The foyer opened to a sitting room with a grand staircase in the center. A silver balustrade continued upstairs, creating a balcony that overlooked the first floor. The vines continued inside. They grew from cracks in the wall and twined around the staircase, but they didn't touch the floor in an unspoken rule. Tripping the occupants wasn't allowed.

Heavy footsteps came down the stairs towards them.

"Where did you go—"

Selanna stopped at the foot of the stairs. Her eyes moved past him to their guests, widening and then narrowing, and she pressed her lips into a thin line. "What the hell are you doing?" she asked.

"We have guests."

"You said you were going to leave the witch alone," Selanna hissed. "Especially after she so thoroughly humiliated you last time."

The witch choked down a laugh.

Odhran grit his teeth. "Thank you, Selanna. But she came to me seeking an audience with Valeria. I am doing as I was asked."

Selanna's eyes darted back to the witch before moving to the human. "The hunters are here. Do have any idea what's going to happen if you bring them in there?"

"Yes."

She shook her head. "What are you thinking?"

"Nothing will happen. She has just cause for an audience. The hunters know the rules and will know better than to interfere."

Selanna sighed. "I hope you know what you're doing, little brother. Our mother is in a foul mood today."

"When isn't she?"

"Valeria is your mother?" the witch spoke up.

"Yes, did I forget to tell you?" Odhran answered.

She rolled her eyes. "Clearly."

"What's your name?" Selanna asked.

The witch cleared her throat, taking a moment to size up his sister before answering "You can call me Alannah."

"And your companions?"

Alannah gestured to the human first. "Elliot," –she gestured to the cat— "and Mr. Pinkus."

"Prepare yourself, Alannah. My mother is not an easy person to deal with," Selanna said, turning on her heel and walking back upstairs.

Odhran didn't move. "You never told me your name."

"That's because I don't *like* you," she responded, walking past him to follow Selanna up the stairs.

The human, Elliot, trailed behind her. His grip on her hand so tight his knuckles were white. She didn't seem to mind. They had clearly grown close in their time together. Maybe that's why she was so protective of him. Odhran couldn't fathom ever having feelings for someone with so little time in them. They would be a blip in his very long life. It didn't seem worth it.

The cat stayed in the foyer.

"Are you coming?" Odhran asked.

"No. I have no reason to show myself to your mother."

Interesting. "You must have angered her then."

"Who hasn't?"

"Fair point."

"Keep your word, prince. Let her leave here unharmed," the cat warned.

Odhran nodded. He had no other choice. Breaking his word would have disastrous consequences—he knew someone who couldn't keep down solid food for a month after breaking an oath—and he wasn't willing to risk it. He followed the others up the stairs, taking care not to sneak up behind the Elliot. Odhran didn't understand why he would risk coming here. Even with an attachment to Alannah, it would be ridiculous to put his own life on the line for her.

Selanna stopped in front of the large, gilded doors to the main hall, a cacophony of voices thundering from inside. Odhran wouldn't be surprised if they were still arguing over the failed hunt. With their prey about to walk into the room with a promise of protection, they would be even more infuriated. Imagining their response made Odhran glad that Selanna would be the one to lead them inside. She could keep the hunters at bay. She was good at being an authoritative voice amongst discord. A trait he admired her for. He would never tell her that.

"I'm ready," Alannah said, nodding to Selanna who didn't look the least bit convinced.

Doors opened inward to reveal the large main hall. The hunters lingered about the room, some stood directly in front of his mother and others leaned on the walls to talk amongst themselves. Valeria sat at the end of the room on a dais. Ruby red stained-glass windows lined the wall behind her throwing blood red light onto the white marble floor. All talking ceased the instant Alannah stepped into the room behind Selanna. The tense silence lasted all but a second before angered voices crashed over them. Alannah, who had squared her shoulders before entering the room, reeled back from the vitriol directed towards her. She no longer looked assured.

"If they see your fear, they'll eat you alive," Odhran murmured from behind her.

Percivus moved in front of Valeria and placed his hand on his pommel, ready to draw his weapon. And he would've if Selanna hadn't mirrored his action. No one could best her. A fact that irritated Percivus often. "What is the meaning of this?"

"The witch seeks an audience with Valeria. No harm can come to her or her companion while she does so. Even you know the rules," Selanna said, her voice booming. No one in the court could claim they couldn't hear her.

"What would a *half-witch* want with the Queen? She is not welcome here," Percivus snarled.

Selanna smirked. "You talk much for someone who isn't in charge here. You should remember your place. But I suppose I shouldn't expect propriety from such a piss poor hunter."

Percivus drew his sword. "You—"

"Enough!"

All eyes turned to Valeria. A moment ago, she had been seated, the boredom plain on her face while she spoke to the hunters, but now, she couldn't keep her eyes off Alannah. The ruby pendant that rested on her chest moved up and down as Valeria's chest heaved. Her nails dug into the ornate silver arms of her chair.

Odhran had seen a look of hatred in his mother's face before. It was an expression she had levied at all of her children over the years. But this was different. It wasn't just hatred—pure, unadulterated—but also fear. What was it about Alannah that scared her so much? Odhran wanted to know. If only to have something to use against her.

"I told you to leave the witch alone," she finally said, her words aimed at Odhran.

"I did as you said, mother. She entered the forest of her own volition. I simply brought her to you."

"Why would you do something like that? There is nothing here for her."

"She has a right to ask for an audience, mother. You should know that."

Valeria's nostrils flared. "She has no right—"

"I am right here," Alannah interrupted.

Everyone's eyes landed on her, but she stared at Valeria. Alannah was such a stark contrast to the others at the court. With the exception of her vibrant eyes, she was plain to look at. Her clothes were muted and earthy against the opulence of Valeria's red gown with jewels sewn into the fabric. They were two opposing forces. Alannah's mouth was set in a thin line and she held her chin high. Odhran wasn't sure if she truly was fearless or if she was very good at hiding it. Either way, he admired how readily she interrupted a leader in their own court. He doubted she knew that it was an insult or the consequences that could follow. He swallowed a laugh. Bringing her was very entertaining.

"What right do you think you have to request an audience with me?" Valeria finally asked her.

Alannah cleared her throat. "You placed the curse

on my family. I've come to ask you to remove it."

Valeria stared at her a moment, perhaps to gauge whether or not the witch was joking, but when it was clear she wasn't, Valeria began to laugh. Her silver-tipped fingers covered her lips. The laugh seeped through her fingers. Some of the hunters, including Percivus, followed suit until the entire hall filled with mocking laughter.

With red-tinged cheeks, Alannah's gaze dropped. She must've known it wouldn't be this easy, but the longer Odhran stared at her expression, the more he realized that she didn't. She truly didn't know how things worked here. And now everyone was laughing at her. The same laugh Odhran had heard over the years. The same laugh that often made him feel small.

"Did you really think you could come into my court, insult me in front of my guests, and ask me nicely to remove your curse?" Valeria asked, her voice rich with amusement.

"I—"

"If so, you are sorely mistaken. I have no desire to remove your curse."

Odhran expected that response. The best thing he could do now was remove her from the court and escort her back to the fringe before things escalated. And yet, he found the words that came out of his mouth a complete surprise. "Perhaps she should be given the chance to break it."

Valeria scoffed. "Why would I do that?"

"Why not? Unless you are afraid of her succeeding," he challenged.

"How da—"

"Bearers of curses can ask for a quest. A chance

to prove themselves," Selanna chimed in. "It is the fair route, mother. Don't you want to be fair?"

Valeria's upper lip curled. "Fine." Her eyes focused on Alannah again. "I will give you a choice then. You can both return to the fringe, live the rest of your miserable lives, and die there. Or you can accept a task. It will not be an easy task and once you accept it you must complete it or risk death. Your choice."

"What is the task?" Alannah asked.

Valeria sat back in her chair, taking a moment to think before her lips curved into a malicious smile. "Find and bring me a child of both Fae and witch blood in three weeks' time. If I remember my curses, it is all the time you will have here."

"That is an impossible task, mother," Selanna argued.

"It is. But it is the task I have given. Will you accept?" Valeria asked.

Selanna shook her head. "There is nothing fair—"

"I'll do it."

Odhran stepped closer to Alannah. "Perhaps it is best if you return home. This is not a task you can complete—"

Alannah looked at him, the determined expression on her face made the words die on his tongue. "I will not return home empty-handed." She turned her steeled gaze to Valeria. "I will complete this task or die trying. But if I succeed you will remove my curse, remove the death sentence from my friend," –she nodded to Elliot— "and release his friends if they are alive."

"I accept your terms only because I know you will not succeed," Valeria said, smirking. "But it will be entertaining to watch you try and fail."

Selanna gestured for them to leave. Once the task was accepted, the timer began. Alannah would need to begin her search. A search that would turn up nothing.

"Good luck, little witch," their mother called after Alannah. "You will need it."

Chapter 13

The witch made a swift exit with her friends in tow. Odhran didn't follow them. They would either succeed or they wouldn't. Perhaps he would check in on them now and again to see if they were making any progress. He didn't think they would. But she might surprise him once more.

"What were you thinking?"

He turned to find Selanna glaring at him with her arms crossed over her chest. If he looked hard enough, he would see the steam coming out of her ears. The tip of her nose flushed pink. "What do you mean?" he asked.

"You brought them here and threw them to the wolves!"

"She asked—"

"She doesn't know anything about this place or its people, that much is for certain. *You* should've been discerning." Selanna pointed at him. "This was low, even for you."

"I fail to see the problem."

She threw her hands up in the air. "Of course, you don't! You're so selfish and self-serving you don't see anything wrong with what you do. You shove off responsibility onto someone else." Selanna shook her head. "When are you going to learn to hold yourself accountable? Your actions, your desire to stick it to our mother, is going to get that woman killed out there."

Odhran sighed. "You're being dramatic."

"Are you kid—"

"Will you two please stop?" Meralith came down the stairs. "Fighting will get us nowhere."

Selanna slammed her mouth shut and shook her head. "Talk to him, Meralith. Maybe he'll listen to you." She turned on her heel and walked away, the door to kitchens slamming shut behind her.

Odhran shook his head. "She is being ridiculous."

"She's not."

"Not you too," he grumbled.

Meralith sat on the stairs. "Why did you even bring the witch here? Last time you wanted to kill both her and the human for hurting your pride. What changed?"

He shrugged. "The allure of catching mother off-guard was too strong." Odhran clasped his hands behind his back and began to pace in front of the stairs. "A curse we didn't even know about. Would you not be curious?"

"I would," she admitted. "However, I would like to think I wouldn't hurt others while trying to achieve what I wanted."

"Who have I hurt, really?"

"Do you remember after the incident? When mother kept bringing me suitors even when I begged her not to because I couldn't handle the constant rejections."

He didn't know what that had to do with anything, but he nodded. "Of course, I do."

"You went to her and told her that perhaps it would be better to stop humiliating the entire family by pushing me to match with someone. That every time she did, word would spread about the ugly daughter in the Ruby court."

Odhran stopped moving. How had she heard the conversation? He and Valeria had been alone. He had made sure of it. That was the last thing he wanted her to overhear even though it had been a lie. A way to stop his mother from doing the very thing that was hurting his sister. He swallowed. "You weren't—"

"I wasn't supposed to know? I know." She stood up from the stairs. "But I had gone to beg her again and I overheard."

"Meralith, I'm—"

"I know you were catering to her own thoughts. And that you were doing it for my benefit. But to hear those words come out of your mouth—the last person I would have expected them from—still hurt. Even now, it stings." She closed the distance between them. "You say and do things that hurt people and you don't take responsibility for it. You can change that now."

"I don't know what you want me to do."

"There must be—"

Crunch.

Selanna leaned against the wall with an apple in her hand. The smug look on her face already annoyed him. But he kept his mouth shut before he started another spat that would go absolutely nowhere.

Selanna finished chewing and swallowed. "It's simple, little brother. What are you going to do to help the witch succeed?"

He sighed. "Why are you set on me helping her?"

"Because it would be good for you to think about someone other than yourself." She grinned. "Besides, you won't be able to resist the allure of someone finally besting mother at something. Not for long, at least."

"We both know there is no way for her to succeed," he argued.

"Do you really think that everyone follows the rules all of the time? The quest is only impossible because mother believes it so, but that doesn't mean she is right."

"There are bound to be people who fell in love in secret," Meralith added. "Not everyone shares the same thoughts about the boundaries between us and the witches."

He rolled his eyes. "Of course, you think she will succeed. The two of you are hopeless romantics."

"I'd rather be a romantic than let her—" Selanna gestured her head towards the upstairs— "make me afraid to feel for other people."

"I'm not afraid," he said. "I don't find much use for those feelings."

"Sure," Selanna drew out the word while shaking her head. There was no use in arguing with her. "So back to the task at hand—"

Someone cleared their throat by the stairs, drawing the attention of the three siblings. One of their mother's servants, Neria, was standing on the bottom step. They looked nervous. Neria clasped their hands behind their back. "Odhran, your mother would like to see you in her quarters."

The words made his blood run cold. Odhran swallowed. He should've expected this. Bringing the witch here angered her. He knew it would. But he didn't consider what she might do after. Mostly had had hoped she would be too preoccupied with the hunters. He miscalculated. He curled his hands into fists so his sisters wouldn't see them shaking.

"Whatever it is can wait. I'm sending him on an errand," Selanna said.

"She insists."

"Then I'll go talk to her. I don't know why she wants to talk to him, this was my idea," Selanna continued. "I brought the witch here."

Neria shook their head. "My apologies, but she specifically asked for Odhran. And she asked that you keep the hunters company."

Selanna scoffed. "And why would I do that?"

"She wanted me to tell you that it's you or Meralith."

"That bit—"

"I'll go," Odhran said. He wasn't going to subject his sisters to whatever punishment his mother had planned for him. Especially not Meralith. She didn't deserve the insults the hunters would hurl at her. Selanna was better equipped to handle them.

Neria bowed their head and sighed in relief. "Thank you. She is expecting you."

Without another word to his sisters, he followed the servant up the stairs and turned left. Odhran's mind raced through the possible punishments he might receive. His mother was not known for her leniency. Not even her children were spared from her anger. After a few hundred years, he should be used to it, but the thought of her ire still made him tremble. *Why did I provoke her again?* The servant opened the door and gestured for Odhran to step inside. When he did, the door closed behind him.

Valeria sat at her vanity with her back to him and she didn't look up as he entered the room. *Oh, right.*

Valeria's silver-tipped fingers tapped a silver-handled brush on her vanity. *I hate her.* Odhran crossed the room and stood behind her. She didn't even have to ask for what she wanted. This wasn't the first time they had played this game.

First, he carefully pulled the pins from her hair until it cascaded down to right underneath her shoulder blades. Then he picked up the brush and gently brushed her hair when he didn't want to be, but if he was careless, it would anger her more. With a tight grip on the brush handle, he started at the bottom and worked his way up. His lips were pressed into a thin line, forcing him to breathe as quietly through his nose as he possibly could. The only sounds were the brush going through her hair and her fingers tapping the top of the vanity. Any other sound might set her off.

"Do you hate me, Odhran?"

Her voice made him jump and he almost dropped the brush. Honesty would cost him. "Of course, I don't, mother," he said, struggling to keep his voice neutral.

Her eyes met his in the mirror. "Then why did you bring that filthy thing into my court?"

"I was following the rules—"

She shot up before he could finish his sentence. The chair fell back and hit the floor with a thud. Her fingers dug into his cheeks as she gripped his chin. The silver tip sliced into the skin. Blood welled from the cut. Rivulets of blood dripped down the tips and stained Valeria's hand. "You could've killed them. You know I would've looked the other way. But no, you wanted to play a game with me instead."

"I—"

Her face was inches from his. "Do you feel like

you've won, Odhran?"

"Mother, please—"

"I've done everything for you," she hissed. "I dealt with your father, the havoc you wreaked on my body, and the countless years of disrespect. I bore you from my own body and you think you can treat me this way?"

He tried to swallow but his mouth was dry. The pain of his cheek was nothing. Minimal. A precursor to what would come next. Valeria never did things small.

"It's time for me to teach you some respect again, my son. Perhaps you will remember this lesson well."

"Mother—"

"And as for the witch, she won't live through the night. I've made sure of it."

***

Meralith waited in his room. The strong smell of mint made him nauseous. She waited until he made it to his bed. With shaky hands, he undid the buttons of his shirt. Fabric dragged against the fresh wounds that spanned his back, side, and arms. Valeria didn't care where she hit as long as she made contact. Hiding it was not a priority. It's not like anyone would care that she had hurt him. Odhran hissed as Meralith dabbed his back with a cloth.

"I'm sorry," she murmured.

"It's fine," he said, grinding his teeth together. He sucked in a breath when the healing poultice touched his wounds. It was cool. Icy. A balm to his hot, raw skin, but also more pain. He hunched over to rest his forearms on his legs. His hair fell around his face, hiding the tears that gathered in his eyes.

The door to his room opened and closed. He could see Selanna's boots as she walked over to him. A glass was shoved in front of his face. Deep blue liquid sloshed up the sides. "Here," she said, her voice gruff.

Odhran's hand shook as he grabbed the glass. Selanna hovered, keeping her hand underneath the glass in case he lost his grip, but he managed to choke down the contents of the glass without dropping it. A cloying sweetness hit his tongue first and then a bitter aftertaste. His lips puckered. Selanna took the glass from him and set it down on the bedside table.

"What about the hunters?" he asked.

"They're eating so they're pacified for now," she answered, moving to the couch. She crossed her arms over her stomach. "I should've gone."

"No, you shouldn't have," he said.

She pursed her lips. They could go back and forth all day about who should've taken it. But none of them should have to. This was why Odhran wanted to leave so badly. Selanna wanted to leave as well. She had briefly, years ago, but she came back. He wondered why she would, but he realized he wouldn't leave Meralith alone with their mother, and he understood then. They had to leave together and the only way they would get away from their mother, was to diminish her power.

She won't make it through the night. I've made sure of it.

"The witch, Alannah," –Odhran straightened up, wincing from the fresh wounds— "I'll help her. She will succeed. I'll make sure of it."

"Are you sure?" Selanna asked. "You risk incurring mother's wrath again."

"I'll risk it. I want to see her lose for once."

Chapter 14

All the bravado—the courage—left Alannah the moment she stepped foot back into the forest. What was she thinking? Valeria had handed her an impossible task, one that would kill her, and it angered Alannah so much that she puffed out her chest and accepted it. An action she regretted now. With a groan she leaned against a tree and gently tapped her forehead against the bark. "I'm an idiot."

"You're not," Elliot said while sitting on a log next to Mr. Pinkus.

"I am."

"I think you're pretty awesome actually."

She scoffed and pushed herself off the tree. "You're just saying that."

"Why would I do that?"

Sticks broke underfoot and dry leaves crunched as she walked back and forth. If she kept it up, she would wear a path into the dirt. She had no idea where to go. No idea where to even start. She would waste time figuring that out and then waste time looking and by then she was going to get them all killed. "I didn't think this through."

"Perhaps not," Mr. Pinkus said. "But lucky for you, I know where to find the witches. They will certainly be more help than the Fae."

"See! We're going to be fine." Elliot scratched behind Mr. Pinkus' ears, causing the cat to purr.

She narrowed her eyes. "Are you always so disgustingly optimistic?"

Elliot shook his head. "No, but one of us needs to be. Besides," –he rubbed the back of his neck— "you put yourself between me and those hunters. You stood up for yourself, for me, and for my friends. You're not an idiot."

Alannah flushed. "It wasn't that big of a deal," she mumbled.

"It was."

"Anyone would do it."

"No, they wouldn't."

She huffed. Elliot was determined to pay her a compliment and while it was nice that he appreciated what she did, it wasn't the smartest decision she could have made. Not without consulting him or Mr. Pinkus first.

"Are you going to keep beating yourself up?" Elliot asked.

"Probably."

"You might want to save it for later. We do have a deadline for this quest," Mr. Pinkus said.

Alannah sighed. "Right. A quest I can't even complete because there is no way a child with Fae and witch blood even exists." *I'm going to die.*

"Why not?" Elliot asked.

"It's against the rules. Why do you think Valeria exiled my family? It wasn't because her lover was courting someone else, it's because her lover was a courting a *witch*. She was humiliated, not just angry—"

Elliot nodded along as she rambled.

"And Underhill may be home to the witches now,

but the Fae aren't necessarily accepting of us. They see witches as interlopers—"

Elliot held up his hand. "Wait...witches don't originally come from Underhill?"

Alannah shook her head.

"And, for whatever reason, Fae and witches aren't allowed to...mix?"

She nodded.

He sighed and pinched the bridge of his nose. "The more you tell me about this place, the more I don't understand how anything works here."

"It seems obscure to most, but Underhill is really very simple. The people that inhabit it, are not," Mr. Pinkus said. "We can talk about it more on the journey, but we really must be going. We are sitting ducks here."

"You make it sound like we're in danger," Elliot snorted.

"We are. Especially you." Mr. Pinkus jumped down from the log. "Not only are the Fae not fond of humans and will have no problem stealing you, hunting you, and/or killing you, but Valeria will absolutely send assassins."

Elliot stared at Mr. Pinkus, trying to determine if he was kidding. Large owlish eyes stared back at him without blinking. There was no break in the silence, no laugh from the cat. He was very serious. Elliot slapped his thighs with his palms before standing. "I guess we better get going then."

"Wise idea," Mr. Pinkus said. "The witches are north of here. We should reach them in a few days—"

"Days!" Alannah and Elliot shouted at the same time.

Mr. Pinkus' ears laid flat against his head. "Yes, days.

We are on foot, you know."

Alannah sighed, rubbing her temples with her fingertips. "I did not think this through."

"No, you didn't. But the choice is made. Now let's go," Mr. Pinkus didn't wait for either of them to argue or ask any more questions. He began walking—in the general direction of North—leaves crunching under his paws.

With little other choice, Alannah began to follow him. She truly hoped he knew where he was going. She found it difficult to trust him after learning that he wasn't even a cat. Perhaps he was working with Valeria and he was leading them into a trap. *Don't be ridiculous.* Alannah shook her head. All those years of companionship...they couldn't have been fake. Could they? *He's still Mr. Pinkus. Right?*

Elliot bumped his shoulder against hers, pulling her out of her head. "You okay?" he asked.

She snorted.

"Sorry, stupid question."

"Do you really think I made the right decision?" she asked.

"I don't know," he answered, shrugging his shoulders. "Sometimes there are just decisions, not really good or bad, and you have to choose what you feel is best. Sometimes it isn't the best. Sometimes your heart decides for you before your head can think about it. And maybe it'll turn out for the worst, but at least you'll know."

"Yeah, we'll be dead."

He shook his head. "What I mean is, your decision was to either go back to being alone without any real connections to people or to take a shot in the dark and hope you don't die. Both suck, but one could turn out for the better."

She didn't know if he really had boundless optimism or if he was spouting bullshit to make them both feel better. She also couldn't say if it was really working, but at least she felt a little less like she had made the worst decision in the world. And he was right. It was better than sitting that home and living the rest of her life wondering if it was truly better to not try at all.

Alannah cleared her throat. "Maybe you're right. I could've been fine alone, but I would've always wondered."

"You wouldn't have been fine alone."

"Why not?"

"No one is fine alone. People need connections. Everyone needs people around them to love them and challenge them and help them. We're made that way."

"You mean humans are."

"You are half-human, Alannah. And even if you weren't, I don't believe that you would be so different that you wouldn't need community."

Community? All she ever had was her grandmother and her mother and eventually they left her. Alannah never once had a community, only a dwindling family. Was she really missing something? It sounded like a pain having so many people around. More people meant more people to answer to. Was that really necessary? She hopped over a root. "If you say so."

"Can you honestly say you weren't lonely? That you haven't craved some sort of connection with another person?" he asked.

Have I? How could she miss what she didn't really know? What did it mean to crave connection? Did that mean she wanted friends or lovers? Both? She had spent so much time knowing that she would be alone, that she would refuse companionship, that she no longer knew if her apathy towards forming bonds with others was real or an impenetrable wall to protect herself from getting hurt. No one had ever made her question it before. And she it had been a long time since she asked herself what she truly wanted. So long that she didn't know the answer anymore.

"Alannah?"

She turned her head to realize he was staring at her. "Hm?"

"I...nothing," he said, shaking his head. "You don't have to answer."

Alannah frowned. "Elliot—"

"We should catch up to Mr. Pinkus before we lose him." He cut her off and quickened his pace.

She fell into step behind him. The conversation ended but it didn't feel resolved and she couldn't help but wonder what exactly he was going to say to her.

***

Alannah couldn't form the words to describe how beautiful the forest was. Trees with trunks larger than Alannah reached skyward until it grew harder to tell how tall they were. Branches dripping with thick leaves and sweet-smelling flowers stretched towards each other, creating arches that she and her companions walked under. Green grass sprouted between rocks and tree roots. Lavender and dandelions danced in a breeze that she couldn't feel. Wisps of blue, purple, white, and pink darted between trees in the distance. Everything about it was magical. Ethereal.

And she was sick of it already.

They walked through a hallway created by trees and it felt like the same one they had walked through nearly an hour ago.

"Are you sure we're not lost?" she asked Mr. Pinkus. "Because it feels like we're lost."

He huffed. "We're not lost."

"I agree with Alannah. It feels like we came through here already," Elliot said.

"I know where I'm going. I'm from here, remember?"

"Right, but how long has it been exactly?" Elliot asked.

Mr. Pinkus sniffed. "I don't know. Time doesn't move the same between the two places. But I wouldn't forget my home and how it tries its best to trick people."

"I think it has tricked you," Alannah grumbled.

Mr. Pinkus stopped and turned towards her, sitting on his haunches. "Would you like to lead us then?"

"I don't know why you won't admit that we're lost," she said.

"Because we're not."

"Okay, but clearly, we are! We're going in circles and I don't want to die because we walked in circles for three weeks. I'd at least like to get somewhere."

Mr. Pinkus thumped his tail against the ground. "We are getting somewhere. If you knew how to tap into this place you would know that too. We are wasting time by arguing."

Alannah flung her hands up. "And how would I know how to do that? I can't even try because I am already a ticking time bomb. And you don't even take the time to explain anything to either of us! We're supposed to trust you, which forgive me, is a little hard to do lately."

They stared at each other, the silence stretching between them. Mr. Pinkus broke it first with a sniff. "That wasn't a fair suggestion."

She crossed her arms over her chest. "No, it really wasn't. You know I can't use any magic, no matter how much I really want to."

"You can't use your magic here?" Elliot asked.

She shook her head. "If I do, it'll drain me even faster. I'll run out of time and I already don't have enough."

"You conveniently skipped telling me that when we planned this."

"Sorry, I…I'm so used to the people around me knowing already. I didn't think to. I didn't even think I'd get this far," she chuckled, but it was devoid of humor.

"Well, I guess it's too late now. Why don't we rest for a few minutes? We've been walking for a few hours," Elliot said.

"And my feet hurt," Alannah added.

Elliot nodded. "Let's sit and be thankful and it isn't any worse."

"How could it get any worse?" she muttered.

The first droplet splash against her cheek. After that, the sky opened up. How could it when they were standing underneath a canopy of trees? She didn't know. It was as if it was done on purpose. To test her. To prove it could always get worse. Now her feet hurt and she was drenched. She could barely see the other two through the sudden onslaught of rain.

Elliot sighed. "Good going, Alannah."

"I fail to see how this is my fault."

"You never tempt fate. Sometimes it's listening."

"May we keep going now?" Mr. Pinkus asked.

Alannah heaved a sigh. "Please."

The rain obscured her vision. Thank goodness Mr. Pinkus was orange, otherwise she might lose him to the landscape. She trudged behind Elliot. The ground was slick under her feet. The rock came out of nowhere. At least, that was her story and she was sticking to it. Alannah felt herself pitch forward. Her stomach rose into her throat as she began to fall.

Elliot grabbed her upper arms to steady her. "Be careful!" he shouted over the noise of the rain.

"I'm trying!" she shouted back.

"Come on," he said. He let go of her upper arms only to grab her hand.

It was warm. Searing even. His palm pressed against hers and their fingers interlaced as if they had done this a hundred times. Her heart stuttered in her chest. *Do I crave connection?* No one had ever held her hand before. Not even her mother. In fact, her mother barely touched her at all. Not even a hug. *Do I want to be touched?* Elliot's hand squeezed hers as he led her through the path. *Maybe, I do.*

Elliot didn't even notice Alannah's inner turmoil. He focused on getting through the rain. Good thing he was because she was far too focused on determining whether or not she liked him holding her hand and surprised that she was leaning towards liking it.

The rain slowly let up. It took half an hour for it to stop completely. Only then did they stop. Elliot let go of her hand, but the warmth lingered. Alannah stumbled away and leaned against a tree to pull herself back together. She leaned against a tree and began to wring the water from her shirt. Her eyes looked everywhere but right at Elliot.

Mr. Pinkus jumped up onto a log and shook his head. "Please don't challenge this place anymore. It's going to take forever for my fur to dry."

"Sorry," she grumbled, squeezing the water from her hair.

"How much further do you want to go today?" Elliot asked.

Mr. Pinkus licked his paw. "It would be imperative to get close to the edge of the forest by nightfall."

"There's more than the forest?" she asked.

"Of course," the cat chuckled. "There is much to Underhill. It's a shame you'll see so little."

Elliot sat down beside him, unbuttoning his overshirt. "How big is it exactly?"

"Exactly? I couldn't say. At the very least, comparable to the size of the human realm if not bigger."

"How can it be bigger?" Elliot asked.

"We aren't bound by your...what is it called again..." Mr. Pinkus stopped grooming himself a moment. "The physical limitations of your realm or your laws of—"

"Physics?" Elliot offered.

"Yes, that."

Elliot pulled off his shirt and twisted it in his hands until water dripped onto the ground. "How do you know about physics?"

Mr. Pinkus rolled his eyes. "I didn't spend all of my time as a well-fed housecat. I know many things about the human realm. The humans that stumble their way through the forest often have such interesting things on them. And those things are often left behind." He hopped down from the log. "I would be remiss not to learn in my spare time."

"Have you ever actually been to the human realm before?" Elliot asked.

"We should get going. Night fall will be upon us soon enough," Mr. Pinkus said instead of answering and began to walk off without waiting for them to follow.

It wasn't a no. And ignoring the question made Alannah wonder. Her home didn't count as the human realm. It existed in between. A pocket. Tethered between the two worlds but didn't fully exist in either. So, had Mr. Pinkus been in the human realm before? Now she was curious. She pushed off the tree and began to follow him with Elliot trailing behind her. The cat had no intentions of answer now. She would have to wait. Maybe catch him off-guard. Elliot caught up to her and matched her stride. It seemed he had the same thought process as her if the twisting of his lips and minimal space between his eyebrows were any indication.

For now, they remained silent, letting the cat lead them further along the path.

The forest grew still. Flowers didn't move in an invisible breeze. Wisps didn't move between the trees. They had gone. Perhaps the rain had forced them away. Or maybe it was something else. The hairs on the back of her neck stood up. The sudden quiet unnerved her.

Alannah couldn't shake the feeling that they were being watched.

But she could be paranoid. After being a spectacle for over a week, she consistently felt eyes on her and in the quiet, she could feel them again. At home, the boundary kept her safe. Out here, they could get her. Whoever "they" was. A feeling didn't tell her if it was someone friendly or someone who meant harm. Given that she was still in Fae territory, it was more likely that whoever it was, wasn't friendly.

She cleared her throat. "Uh...Mr. Pinkus—"

"I know, Alannah. Keep moving," he cut her off, his voice terse.

Her hand sought Elliot's without a spare thought. With their hands intertwined, they quickened their pace to close the distance between them and Mr. Pinkus. Alannah heard a whistling sound, like a rush of wind moving through the trees, and felt a breeze against her cheek. Something landed into a tree a mere foot from her left with a hollow thunk.

She reached for it, her fingers grazing feathers. "Is that a—"

"Arrow!" Mr. Pinkus shouted. "Run!"

Elliot's hand tightened over hers and he tugged her away from the tree right as another arrow missed her by an inch, landing beside the other. *They're really trying to kill me.* When Mr. Pinkus said Valeria would send assassins, it felt like a joke. Like he couldn't possibly be serious. Why would she be worried about Alannah succeeding when it was damn near impossible?

Another tug from Elliot—this one more insistent than the first—and they were running. Mr. Pinkus stayed ahead of them, leaping over rocks and roots. He shouted back to them. She couldn't make it out. It was too hard to hear over the ringing in her ears and the thudding in her chest. The only thing that kept her from falling flat on her face, was Elliot's firm grip on her hand.

Don't trip. Don't trip. Don't trip.

The forest wasn't silent now. She heard the rustling in the trees. Above them. Behind them. How many were there?

Sweat dripped down her face. It burned her eyes. Her lungs and thighs burned. How long were they supposed to run? She doubted she had the stamina to outrun assassins. And she couldn't use her magic. There was no conceivable way to defend themselves. What was the plan? Did Mr. Pinkus have a plan? Did anyone?

This was a bad decision.

Her boots slipped on wet grass and rocks. Every step threatened to send her flying forward. Inevitable really that she would find herself falling and taking Elliot down with her. She threw her hands in front of her face. Sharp rocks scraped her palms. Dirt mixed with a blood. She sucked in a breath through her teeth. *Get up.* Her legs ached and her thighs trembled. *Get up.* Footsteps from every direction closed in on them.

Get up!

Alannah pushed herself up onto her knees. A glint of metal in the corner of her eye made her freeze. It was too late to run now. They emerged from the trees. She expected many, but only saw two. One stood tall with skin color of severe storm clouds, bright purple eyes, and black hair pulled back in a braid to reveal pointed ears adorned with silver rings. One hand curled around a recurved ebony bow. The other clutched an arrow.

The second was shorter. Pale. Opalescent scales covered their forehead, curved around their cheeks, and continued down their slender neck. Wisps of white hair framed their face and the rest was secured in a ponytail. Black eyes with no trace of color or light stared at Alannah with curiosity, much like one would look at a fascinating creature, not a person. Daggers—pearl-handled with a deep blue blade—were pointed at Elliot.

Both assassins wore the same style of leather

armor. A jet black with ruby red stitching around the edges. It covered their chest and forearms. Their boots were made of the same material, but without the stitching. Underneath the armor, clothing was a simple shirt and leggings the same color as their armor. Something an enemy wouldn't be able to discern from far away.

Valeria's wasted no time in sending her assassins. Perhaps she was afraid Alannah would succeed after all. Despite the dire situation, the thought sparked an inkling of hope. One that wouldn't last long unfortunately.

"Sorry, Elliot," she murmured.

He squeezed her arm.

The bow raised. The arrow aimed right at her.

Alannah should run. It would be better than kneeling in the face of death. But she couldn't move.

I should've stayed home.

Chapter 15

She waited for the blow. Time slowed down. Seconds felt like minutes. He drew the arrow and she drew in a deep breath. Her last one.

Something slammed into her back, knocking the air right back out. "Stay down!" Mr. Pinkus yelled in her ear. Why did it matter? Was it somehow better getting shot while lying on the ground?

But with her ear to ground she heard it.

A third set of footsteps. They were coming from the other direction. And fast. Friend or foe? Alannah desperately hoped it was a friend even though she didn't have any. Maybe Mr. Pinkus did. The others seemed to hear it too. Eyes darted away from Alannah, and the assassin aimed the arrow into the thicket of trees behind her.

She heard the whistling of an arrow, but it came from behind her. The assassins moved. Something the other person clearly anticipated. It pierced right underneath the armor of the smaller assassin. Their mouth opened and shrill cry made Alannah clap her hands over her ears. They stumbled backward, fingers clawing at the arrow protruding from their armor, their partner catching them to keep them upright.

Alannah lifted her head to see the stranger step out of the trees. Brown leather boots left impressions in the soft earth. A hood was pulled up to hide their face, but Alannah could see a hint of light from within. A bow —this one shorter than the assassin's bow with veins of gold threaded through the wood—held firm in their grip.

"I've never known Valeria to break her own rules. She always waits at least a day to send assassins," the stranger said, their voice neutral with the hint of a lilt as if they were disguising their voice.

The grey one sneered with arms wrapped around their partner's shoulders. "I know that's you, Senna."

The person—Senna, they had been called—shrugged and reached up to pull their hood back. Alannah noticed their eyes first. Gold, not the polished kind, but more like an ore with black veins running through it. Skin of dark umber with freckles of gold stretched across their nose and cheeks. Multiple braids were held together by a piece of leather, but that didn't stop a stray few from resting against Senna's high cheekbones.

"If you know, then you know you won't win. You should leave while you have a chance," Senna said, the corner of her mouth lifted into a smile.

With their partner cradled in their arms, they stepped back into the forest and disappeared instantly as if the trees had swallowed them whole. Clearly, they knew how to hide in the forest. It made Alannah wonder how long they had been following. And why they had decided to strike when they did.

A hand entered her field of vision and she jerked back. Senna had leaned over, her hand held out for Alannah. "Face down was an interesting choice of position."

"To be fair, I was facing the arrow at first," Alannah grumbled, ignoring the hand, and pushing herself up onto her hands and knees. A difficult task with a weight on her back, but Mr. Pinkus jumped down beside her. Just because this person saved them didn't mean Alannah had to automatically trust them.

"Who are you?" Elliot asked, already kneeling, dirt smeared on his cheeks, chin, and hands. He didn't look hurt.

Thank the goddess.

Senna stepped back, hands on their hips. "My name is Senna. I've been paid to take you to the witches. And to make sure nothing happens to you."

"And how can I trust that?" Alannah asked.

Senna raised an eyebrow.

"It's all right, Alannah." Mr. Pinkus said. "Senna won't hurt us."

Senna's mouth twisted in a frown and she crouched down to get a better look at Mr. Pinkus. "Lysanthvir, is that you?"

"Who else would it be?"

"Pardon me for not expecting you to show up as a fat housecat," Senna answered. "Although, it is a good look for you."

Mr. Pinkus sat up straight. "I think so too. I've rather enjoyed my years of being pampered and loved."

Senna snorted. "You haven't changed at all, have you."

"Only by being a cat."

"You two know each other?" Elliot asked.

"We were friends for many years before I was cast out. It is nice that the friendship still remains," Mr. Pinkus answered.

Senna nodded. "And I would like to catch up, but we should move. The assassins will take a little time to lick their wounds and then try again."

Alannah gulped. "They will?"

"Of course. Assassins are not so easily stopped. And Ciradyl is especially stubborn, but Maiel being injured will keep them occupied for a while." Senna plucked the string of her bow. "Take a moment to breathe and get your bearings again. Then we're moving. I don't like to waste time, and I hear you don't have much time at all."

"Who hired you?" Alannah asked.

Senna shrugged. "Someone who's invested in your success apparently."

"That's not an answer."

Senna grinned, clearly not going to give Alannah a straight answer. Was it supposed to be a secret? Alannah didn't know anyone who wanted her to succeed that wasn't already with her. Had Mr. Pinkus paid her? Unlikely. He had been with Alannah the whole time.

A hand came down on her shoulder, startling her back to reality.

"Are you hurt?" Elliot asked.

"Hmm?" She looked down at her hands. Scrapes on her palms were red and still oozing blood. The dirt didn't sting as much. "A little."

Elliot unclipped and shrugged his backpack off while unzipping it. He pulled a bottle of water out and twisted off the top. "Here. Give me your hands."

Water washed away the dirt from her palms. He dug another bottle out of the bag and flipped the top open to pour the cool liquid on her hands. Alannah hissed and jerked her hands back as it began to burn.

"Sorry. It won't last long," he said, reaching for her hands again.

"You could've warned me."

"I forgot you probably haven't used this before." Liquid foamed around the broken skin. Elliot waited a moment before he pulled out a small kit. The letters on the front read FIRST AID. Elliot opened the kit and grabbed a small tube. "This won't hurt," he reassured her, dabbing the gel onto her palms.

"What is for?" she asked.

"Triple antibiotic. It's so you don't get an infection."

"And it's a gel?"

He nodded.

"Interesting," she said, staring down at her hands while he put everything back in his bag. She looked over at Senna and Mr. Pinkus. "What do you think?"

He followed her gaze. "I don't think we have much of a choice. We've already been attacked and it's the first day."

"You're right," she said, heaving a sigh. "But I'm worried it's a trap."

"This entire place is a trap. It looks pretty from the outside, but everything inside wants to kill you."

"Fair enough."

Elliot slung his bag back over his shoulder and refastened it around his waist while standing up. "Come on." With his hand on her elbow, he guided her up to her feet so her hands didn't touch the ground.

Alannah hurt everywhere. Between the walking, the running, and the fall, she was ready to lay down and not get up for a while. Her thighs burned and her feet ached. And if she thought she was feeling it now, she was definitely going to feel it tomorrow. "You're taking that fall much better than I did."

"It's not the first time I've fallen, especially while hiking. I'm used to it by now."

"Are you ready?" Senna called over to them.

"As ready as I'm going to be," she answered. She moved to follow Senna, but Elliot's hand was still on her elbow. "What's wrong?"

He wasn't looking at her, his brows knit together and frown etched into his face. "Do me favor?"

"What?"

He let go of her arm. "Next time someone has an arrow pointed at you, don't just lie there and take it."

***

Lysanthvir could tell something was wrong. Other than this entire foray into the forest, of course. He could feel the tension between Alannah and Elliot. They both looked upset and neither of them were looking at the other. As they continued down the path, he would watch them drift together, notice, and then put distance between themselves once more.

He wasn't the only who noticed. Senna would look over her shoulder at them and shake her head. "They don't communicate well, do they?"

"No, not really." He sighed. "But Alannah hasn't spent enough time around other people to learn, and it seems Elliot has his own issues. I'm sure they will work it out eventually."

Senna looked over her shoulder again. "How did you end up with her anyway?"

"It was shortly after the change. I wasn't taking it well, ended up on her property nearly half-dead. Her grandmother found me, realized what I was, and nurtured me back to health."

"And then you stayed?"

"She offered. I turned her down at first."

"What changed your mind?"

"Alannah," he said. "She was two at the time. The first time we met, she pulled my tail and laughed."

Senna chuckled. "And this was the deciding factor?"

"No. It was when I tried to leave. She tried to follow me into the forest and when her grandmother took her back, she cried. An awful, pitiful sound. I decided to stay longer and longer and longer. Eventually, I stopped thinking about leaving at all."

"I'm glad you found your place. Although, I wish you had told us."

"I'm sorry."

Senna shrugged. "We looked for you. I knew you weren't dead, but I thought you were angry at us."

"For what?"

"For not protecting you better." She glanced at him. "And for not helping you protect Fia."

He nearly stopped in his tracks. He had said that name over and over in his head, but it was the first time in a long time that he heard it out loud. It hung in the air between them. "I'd prefer not to talk about it," he said.

"She doesn't know, does she?" Senna said, tilting her head in Alannah's direction.

"No. And I'm not ready to talk about it."

Senna nodded.

They walked in silence for a few minutes, accompanied only by the sounds of their footsteps. He cleared his throat. "I didn't blame you, just so you know. And I was never angry. I didn't want to face it."

"And now here you are. Back here again."

"Yes."

"Will you face it now?" she asked.

"I don't know," he admitted. "I'm more worried about Alannah."

"Ah. The deck does seem stacked against her."

He snorted. "You have no idea."

The trees thinned out as they grew closer to the edge. It was a good place to stop for the night. Past the forest was an open field and that was not an ideal place to camp for the night. Not when he wanted to keep Alannah being in Underhill under wraps for as long as possible. Under normal circumstance, no one would care. But Valeria had many who were loyal to her. No telling who would see Alannah as a joke and who would see her as a threat.

"This a good place. We'll rest for the night and set out first thing in the morning," Senna said.

"Is there a place to wash up?" Elliot asked.

Senna shook her head. "Not here. I would suggest changing into dry clothes and we can dry those," –she pointed to their wet clothes— "by the fire."

Alannah looked around. "Change? Right here?"

"The trees are large enough. Use one."

"Right," Alannah muttered before walking away and disappearing behind one of the trees.

Elliot walked behind a different tree to change as well. Senna began to collect small twigs in the area and piled them together. Everyone was doing something except Lysanthvir. He remembered a time where he was useful. Helpful. While being trapped in this body had been a perk these past 26 years—food, treats, and sleeping whenever he wanted—it was a hindrance now. He couldn't do anything. Couldn't keep Alannah from being hurt.

Watching her stare down an arrow while he could do nothing was the worst feeling in the world. In his old body, assassins would have been nothing. He could've taken care of them easily. Thank goodness Senna found them when she had.

Elliot emerged from behind the tree first with wet clothes and his backpack in hand. He set his backpack on the ground beside Lysanthvir. Wet clothes landed with a plop on top of the bag.

"I'm going to get firewood," Senna announced.

"I'll help you," Elliot said.

"Thank you."

Alannah didn't come out from behind the tree until they had walked off. She had pulled her damp hair free from the braid to dry. Stray pieces clung to her face and neck. She set her bag down beside Elliot's and sat down on a root with her clothes in her hands.

"What's the matter?" Lysanthvir asked.

"Nothing."

He stood up and stretched before closing the distance between them. With a quick hop, he was in her lap. "We both know that isn't true."

She huffed and set her clothes down beside her. "Elliot is mad at me because I didn't do anything when we were about to be killed." She sighed, her hand reaching to scratch him behind the ears. "I don't know what the hell he wanted me to do. I can't use my magic. I certainly can't wield a bow or daggers."

"Perhaps he is not mad at you."

She scratched under his chin. "What do you mean?"

"I believe he is scared, maybe even mad at himself, and he took it out on you."

"That's not exactly fair, is it?"

"No, but it happens."

Alannah stared down at him. "I wish you could've spoken to me all these years."

Lysanthvir purred, butting his head against her hand. "Me too."

A rustling in the trees made them pause, but they both relaxed upon realizing it was Elliot and Senna returning with firewood. Alannah watched Elliot in silence as the helped Senna build the campfire. It was mere minutes before the quiet was broken by the sound of crackling. Elliot grabbed their clothes—Alannah tried to do her own, but he batted her hand away—and laid them out on a large rock closest to the fire.

"Have you camped before, Elliot?" Senna asked.

"All the time," he answered, his voice flat.

Lysanthvir turned around in a circle until he felt comfortable enough to lay down on Alannah's lap. Smoke from the fire smelled sweet, repelling any insects that tried to get too close. Good thing. They could keep their grubby little hands to themselves.

Elliot sat down on the root beside Alannah and Senna sat down opposite of them. "May I ask you a question, Senna?"

She looked up, her golden eyes glinting in the light. "Sure."

"How did you know where to find us?"

"I am an excellent hunter."

Elliot stiffened. "A hunter?"

Senna tilted her head, looking unsure of his tone, but understanding dawned on her. "Not like those buffoons in Valeria's court. They hunt the easiest prey and think themselves talented." She stretched her legs out and crossed her ankles. "I hunt monsters. Beasts."

Elliot perked up. "Monsters?"

She nodded. "There are many kinds all over Underhill. Perhaps you have heard of some in your realm. The ones that tend to bleed through anyway."

Elliot looked excited. "Like cryptids? Mythological monsters?"

"Perhaps. Although, I don't know what a cryptid is."

"Like bigfoot or the mothman."

Alannah raised an eyebrow. "Bigfoot? Mothman? What kind of names are those?"

"I didn't choose them," Elliot protested. "And it's because it's what they look like."

"We don't have a monster that looks like a giant foot," Senna said.

"No, it's not that he is a giant foot. He has big…why are you laughing?"

Both Alannah and Senna were laughing. Even Lysanthvir found himself chuckling. The tension between Alannah and Elliot fizzled away in the laughter. Lysanthvir was glad for it. He found himself hoping the two could be friends. Alannah needed friends. She needed relationships no matter how much she protested the idea. It would be good for her. And he wanted her to be happy.

Night came quickly as if a switch had been flicked off and plunged the forest into darkness. The fire provided the only light. Shadows danced on Alannah's face. Her eyes darted around nervously.

"We're fine here," Senna reassured her. "I'll be keeping watch."

"By yourself?" Elliot asked.

She shrugged. "It's nothing I haven't done before. And neither of you can fight."

Elliot looked sheepish.

"Would you like one of us to stay up with you?" Alannah asked.

Senna shook her head. "Get some sleep. We have a lot of ground to cover tomorrow."

Lysanthvir jumped off Alannah's lap. He padded over to Senna. The others could sleep, but he would spend some time with his old friend. Alannah and Elliot laid down next to each other, as close to the fire as they could get. They moved around, trying to get comfortable—an impossible feat—before finally settling down. Lysanthvir should've reminded them to bring something to sleep on. But the events from the day didn't take long to catch up to them both. A few minutes later, he heard Alannah's breathing even out.

He took the moment of quiet to whisper a small plea in his head.

Please let her succeed.

Chapter 16

Senna kept true to her word. She woke them at the first sign of sunlight through the trees. It took Alannah a few minutes to remember where they were and why her body ached after a night of sleep. The hard ground wasn't very forgiving. When she pushed herself up onto her elbows, her shoulders and upper back cracked. She looked over to see Elliot already sitting up, his hair sticking up on end, rubbing the sleep from his eyes.

"Morning," he mumbled to her.

Alannah grunted in response. She needed a few minutes before she could speak. The early morning chill made her shiver.

"You only have a few minutes," Senna said, already putting out the fire. "Eat and drink. Then we're on our way. I want to make it past the city today."

"A city?" Elliot asked while stretching his arms above his head.

She nodded. "Our visit will be brief. I need a few things."

"It's a shame we can't look around," he commented.

"It is. But the less people know about you, the better." Her eyes strayed to Alannah. "And we don't have the time."

lannah heaved a sigh and pushed herself up the rest of the way. "If we survive this, maybe we can go next time."

"That's the spirit," Senna said.

Elliot chuckled.

Alannah yawned into her palm. She pulled her hands away to look at the cuts. They were scabbed over, but otherwise looked fine. Elliot did a good job cleaning them. She wondered how many times he had done it before. For himself and for others. She knew of his friends but didn't know much else. Did he have siblings? What was his family like?

Why haven't I asked him before?

Something sharp dug into her elbow and she turned her head. Elliot was poking her with what he called a breakfast bar wrapped in a foil wrapper. She took it. "Thank you," she said, her voice raspy with sleep. She unwrapped the bar and took a bite. It was sweet but not overwhelmingly so. Dried cranberries gave it a tartness that she liked. The chocolate bits weren't bad either. He handed her a bottle of water that he had already opened for her. This time her mouth was too full to thank him.

The water soothed her parched throat. Alannah took a few gulps before capping the bottle. Everyone was moving so much faster than she was. Elliot already stood beside her, packing his clothes into his bag. When finished, he tossed hers into her lap. Senna kept watch at the edge of their camp, looking between the trees. Alannah shoved her clothes into her bag. She didn't care about it being neat.

Getting up was a slow and loud process. Every bone in her body protested her movement. She hoped the next place they stopped had softer ground, but she had a feeling she was going to be disappointed.

"Ready?" Senna asked.

"No," Alannah answered.

"Good. Let's go." Senna started walking away from the camp.

Alannah picked up her backpack with a sigh and pulled it on. While she walked, she pulled her hair up into a ponytail and secured with the band around her wrist. It wasn't getting any better than this.

Light between the trees grew brighter, illuminating everything around her. Blues and greens between the sparse trees made her excited and nervous to leave the confines of the forest. From her side, it was all she had ever seen of Underhill. A tiny glimpse. To find out it was so much bigger than she imagined terrified her in some ways. And it reminded her of how little she knew of the world her family came from.

The Fae obviously didn't accept her, and probably never would. But would the witches? Would they be better? Or would they consider her an outsider because she had lived in a bubble for so long? So many questions she was finally going to get an answer for. She hoped she liked the answers.

Alannah wasn't prepared for the way the world opened up the moment she stepped foot outside of the forest. Fields of wildflowers of all colors stretched until they met the sky in the distance. Clouds of pinks and purples drifted across a deep blue sky. A breeze—a real one this time—ruffled the flowers, carrying the sweet fragrance to her.

"Wow," Elliot said.

"Wow," she echoed.

They grinned at each other. If she had seen this part of Underhill first, perhaps she wouldn't have been so pensive. It was hard to believe they left a forest that purposefully tried to confuse them and trick them, when a beautiful place such as this existed right beside it.

Senna kept on going, clearly not as moved as Alannah, but then again, she probably saw this place far more often. The mystique must have worn off. Mr. Pinkus trailed right behind her, his tail sticking out of the flowers like a periscope. She tried not to crush the flowers, but there were too many to avoid them all.

No one spoke. Alannah was glad for it. She didn't want to interrupt the sound of the wind or of small animals chittering through the fields. It felt like peace. Like safety. She wanted to relish it for as long as she could.

As the sun rose higher and higher, the morning chill disappeared. Alannah wasn't sure how much time had passed. Whether minutes or hours, it felt like time didn't exist in the vast space. However, Senna kept looking up at the sun's position. Based on what she saw, she either sped up or slowed down. Alannah kept pace surprisingly well when she wasn't so sure she would be able to. Perhaps pain was waiting for the opportunity to strike.

The sun still hung low when Alannah saw shapes in the distance. At first, she thought it might be city sitting towards the north. But Senna didn't veer in that direction and as they moved closer, Alannah realized it was another forest. But this one looked…sick.

Unease settled in her gut. The closer they got to the forest, the queasier she became. Gnarled trees with blackened trunks grew close together. Large knots in the trunks revealed darkness that no animal would dare live in. Branches didn't grow up to the sky and form a canopy like the forest she was used to. These branches bore no leaves or fruit—not that she would eat anything from them—and the branches grew together, forming a wall to keep people out.

Or keep something in.

"What's in there?" Alannah asked as they walked past it. She was thankful they weren't walking in.

Senna shrugged. "I've heard rumors. But I don't know for sure."

"What rumors?" Elliot asked.

"That it's where Reluvethel sleeps."

A name Alannah had never heard of, and yet her heartbeat spiked and the sickening feeling in the pit of her stomach grew worse. "Who is that?"

Senna looked at Mr. Pinkus. "You really didn't tell her anything."

"I've only been speaking for a week. Give me a break."

Senna turned her gaze to Alannah. "Reluvethel was one of the leaders of the Fae. A king of his court. I don't know which one. I believe it was struck from the record—"

"That's the Fae for you. Pretend it doesn't exist," Mr. Pinkus muttered.

"From what I've heard, he didn't take kindly to the witches being allowed into Underhill. While many agreed with him, only a few vocally supported him. No one stopped him when he went after the witches," Senna continued.

"Why was he angry? Who let the witches in?" Elliot asked.

"No one really. There's no one person or even a group of people in charge of letting people in. Underhill...this place lives and breathes. It thinks for itself. The witches were normal humans once. But they lived near thin spots in the veil and after a few generations, began to show magical abilities. The magic just sort of..." Senna trailed off, a frown twisting her lips as she tried to find the right word.

"Seeped in," Mr. Pinkus said. "It began to change them. Some more than others."

"Humans are different in many ways, but collectively they share a fear of the unknown and the uncontrollable. The witches needed safety and Underhill provides for its people," Senna continued.

"So, he was angry because...?" Elliot asked.

"Reluvethel, and others like him, believe that the resources of Underhill will be depleted and the magic will disappear if more people partake of it. They believe it's a resource they can control and deprive others of," Mr. Pinkus answered. "But that's not how magic works. I believe it's because their society is crumbling and they scramble to maintain whatever control they can. They refuse to change."

"They will destroy themselves in the process," Senna muttered.

"Is that why there are strict rules about the Fae and the witches having relationships?" Alannah asked.

"Ridiculous rules," Senna spat.

"Yes," Mr. Pinkus answered. "Another way they believe they can keep their magic to themselves."

"I remember the first time you told me of these rules. I thought you were joking," Senna said.

Elliot gripped the straps of his backpack. "You never heard of them before?"

"There are no such rules where I'm from. Anyone that enters Underhill is treated with respect. After all, they wouldn't be here if they weren't wanted." Senna paused to stretch her arms over her head. "Not that there are no problems where I'm from, but this is definitely not one of them." She began walking again.

"Too bad I didn't get lost there," Elliot mumbled.

Alannah threw him a sideways glance. While she understood where he was coming from, the statement still stung. Why? She was supposedly fine with the way things were before he showed up. Him getting lost in a different part shouldn't hurt her feelings at all. But it did. "What happened to him?" she asked, bringing the conversation back to Reluvethel.

"It was hard for the witches to fight back on their own. They were still scattered, entering Underhill in small groups, and trying to find each other. It was only a matter of time before they realized they would be slaughtered if they didn't do something," –Mr. Pinkus yawned—"so they chose one of their own and elevated her."

"Elevated her?" Alannah asked.

"Yes. I don't know what her name was before, but she became the Morrigan—"

Alannah gasped. "The goddess?"

Mr. Pinkus chuckled. "Yes. She wasn't always a goddess. She was a leader of her people. And they gave her strength and power. Enough to keep Reluvethel at bay. It worked for a while. And it even seemed as though he would leave them alone. The Morrigan had her daughters and split the power between them because she didn't feel it was fair for one person to rule."

"What happened when Reluvethel backed off?" Elliot asked, as invested in the story as Alannah.

"He didn't like to lose. He took his time and coordinated a better attack. This time against the Morrigan herself. And the witches...they were losing again. She was afraid he would finish what he set out to do and so she did the only thing she could. She cursed them both. Locked them together in time and space to stop Reluvethel from succeeding," Mr. Pinkus finished.

Elliot looked back at the forest. "And they're supposedly in there?"

"For now."

Elliot made a choking sound. "For now?!"

"Some people believe he will find a way again. But that is speculation," Mr. Pinkus chuckled, clearly enjoying Elliot's reaction.

"How much of this story is actually true?" Senna asked.

"It's hard to say. Maybe all of it. Maybe none of it. Well, except for the Morrigan. It is true that she wasn't always a goddess, and she did have daughters, and she did oppose Reluvethel. But as to whether or not she was the reason for his disappearance, I don't know. The witches might," Mr. Pinkus said.

Elliot rolled his eyes. "You were pulling my leg?"

"Maybe a little," Mr. Pinkus admitted. "Although, it could all be true. You never know."

Alannah wondered how much of it was true herself. Her mother and grandmother had told her of the Morrigan. Their goddess. But from what they told her, the Morrigan had led the witches to Underhill, and she was already a goddess by then. Could they have been wrong?

"We're close," Senna said, pointing to a cluster of buildings in the distance. She turned and faced them, walking backwards. "Remember, this is a quick visit. Stick together and nobody wanders off. And take nothing from anyone. Got it?"

They nodded. But as they got closer and Alannah could see the sheer size of the city, she wanted nothing more than to walk around and get lost in it. The gate itself was huge. Beyond it she could see market stalls and smoke that would probably smell amazing. She could see buildings that got larger and larger until they were just towers made of crystal and an opalescent metal that shined in the sunlight. She could spend weeks exploring it and there would still be so much more to know.

Senna gestured to the gate. "Welcome to Morthilas."

Chapter 17

Alannah breathed deep, thrilled that she had been right about the heavily scented smoke that lingered in the market. Her stomach growled as the scents curled around her nose, enticing her to partake in the number of foods. Some she recognized instantly. Sausages wrapped in pastry and served with warm syrup. Tiny chocolate cakes with caramels shards and chocolate shavings covering the top. Then there were foods she had never seen before. Clear cakes in the shape of rain drops that produced a small rain cloud when eaten. A confectionary that produced fire and smoke when a person placed it on their tongue. Alannah wanted to try them. She wanted to know how they were made. Questions filled her with such ferocity she just might burst at the seams if someone were to pull a thread.

    She wasn't the only one. Elliot looked around with wide-eyed wonder. If it weren't for the stern looks Senna kept throwing over her shoulder at them, they might have forgotten they weren't supposed to wander off. And if Alannah didn't have a clock ticking down the time to her demise, she might've defied Senna anyway.

    Alannah wasn't used to seeing so many people in one place and everyone was so different. Short. Tall. Fat. Thin. Fae with extra fingers and sharp teeth. Skin like porcelain. Skin like the sun. Skin like the bark of a tree.

Eyes as black as night. Eyes that looked like glittering jewels. No eyes at all. Too many eyes. Hairstyles that defied reality and gravity. Hair that bloomed flowers. It was so strange and wonderful and so much. And not one looked at her or lamented at her purple eye as if it was strange and out of place. In fact, she felt plain and boring in their midst. Just another person walking in a crowded marketplace, not the scary witch of the woods that no one survived.

Alannah's eyes darted everywhere but right in front of her and didn't notice how close she had gotten to someone until she bumped into them. She was met with a baring of teeth and a growl. "I'm s-s-sorry," she stammered out her apology and darted away from them as fast as she could.

She was alone.

Senna, Elliot, Mr. Pinkus had vanished in the crowd. She didn't even know which way they were going. Alannah turned in a circle, careful not to bump into anyone else until she caught a glimpse of braids and gold. With her heart racing, she tried not to lose sight of Senna.

I hope that's her.

Alannah gulped. On her own, the city seemed less friendly and more like a place that would swallow her alive.

A gnarled hand gripped her wrist and tugged her in a different direction. "Oh!"

The hand shoved a jewel into her face. It filled the palm of the persons hand—although their hand wasn't very large—and was a brilliant purple with green and black veins running through it. "Would the young witch like a gem? It matches her eye," a voice cooed.

Alannah looked down into the face of an older

woman with milky white eyes. She grinned at Alannah, having far too many teeth for her mouth.

"It's beautiful, but I couldn't," Alannah said, trying to get her hand back.

"But it is perfect for the young witch. She should take it. It is a gift," the woman said, her voice climbing an octave.

"Oh no, thank you. I really have to go—"

The grip on her wrist tightened and the woman jerked Alannah closer. "Are my gifts not good enough for the half-witch?" she hissed.

"Please let me go—"

"Does the half-witch think she is better than everyone else? Does she—"

A silver blade pressed against the woman's throat, cutting her off midsentence. She and Alannah both looked at the person on the other end. Alannah expected Senna, but it was Odhran's sister who wielded the sword and glared at the old woman. "Let her go."

"Daughter of the Ruby Court, the witch insulted—"

"Let her go or you lose the arm," Selanna cut her off again.

The woman did so, albeit begrudgingly. Alannah pulled her hand back and cradled her wrist. Despite the woman's appearance, she was strong.

"I was trying to give a gift," the woman said.

Selanna looked at the jewel. "That is no gift. It's a parasite." She looked at Alannah while sheathing her sword. "It would've broken its shell as you slept and crawled in. Usually through the ear or nose, whichever is closest. And it would've—"

Alannah held up her hand. "I don't need to know anymore."

The woman sneered at her. "Children don't have manners anymore. Don't know their place."

Selanna rolled her eyes. "Piss off." She gently cupped Alannah's elbow and began to steer her away from the woman. "I know where the others are. I'll make sure you get there."

"Thank you," Alannah said, taking in a deep breath. "That was scary."

"I can imagine it is for you. You don't really know anything about this place." Selanna kept people from getting too close. Mostly because they gave her a wide berth. Alannah couldn't tell if it was fear or respect.

"Why are you helping me?" Alannah asked.

"Why wouldn't I?"

"I mean, you don't know me. And you're Valeria's daughter."

"I don't have to know everyone to help them. As for being Valeria's daughter," –Selanna frowned— "I don't exactly get along with my mother."

"Oh."

"None of us really like her. She is a mother more in name than anything. But she didn't have children because she wanted them."

"There's another reason to have children?"

Selanna laughed. "That should be the only reason. But my mother doesn't do anything unless it benefits her. We are pawns to her. Pieces she can move into place to get what she wants. She only likes us when we're useful."

"That's terrible."

"That's Valeria."

Alannah kept close to Selanna. They were moving past the markets and onto a street lined with shops.

"That's explains Odhran then," she muttered.

Selanna sighed. "My brother is...lost. And he keeps trying to win something from my mother that she won't give."

"What's that?"

"Acceptance. Respect. Love." Selanna rested her hand on her pommel. "He thinks if he acts like her, or the asses that come to her court, that she will magically turn into the mother he wants. It's not going to happen."

"He does act like an asshole," Alannah agreed.

"I wish I had been there to see his face the first time you insulted him. I would've paid a hefty price to see it."

"He deserved it. He destroyed my mother's flowers, all of them. Thought it was funny to destroy the last thing I had left of her that she truly loved," Alannah said, crossing her arms over her chest. "I could plant new ones, but they wouldn't be hers."

"I'm sorry he did that."

"Thank you. He didn't even give me the courtesy of an apology or some measure of guilt for what he had done. Every time I see him, I want to smack him." Alannah tucked a piece of stray hair behind her ear. "I've never felt that way about someone before."

"It seems you are learning many new things lately."

Alannah snorted. "Yeah, you could say that."

Selanna pointed at a shop at the end of the street with a plaque over the door with a bow and a sword seared into the wood. "They're in there. I know Senna needed arrows."

"Did you hire Senna?" Alannah asked.

"No."

"Do you know who did?"

"Yes."

"Are you going to tell me?"

"No."

Alannah huffed. "I don't understand why it's a secret."

"I doubt it will remain one for very long. I have a feeling you'll figure it out soon enough." She pushed open the door.

Relief made her uncross her arms when she saw her companions inside. And with that relief came a realization. Mr. Pinkus had been a constant in her life and she was growing used to Elliot's presence. What if she started to rely on them? What if she did and they left? What if she got used to this feeling and then she ended up alone? Fear held her heart in a vise.

Elliot strode across the room—and before she could stop him—pulled her into a hug. "Are you okay?" he asked. "I looked and you were gone. Senna said I couldn't go looking for you because she didn't want to look for two missing people."

Alannah remained stiff. Her mother didn't even hug her. The most Alannah had ever gotten from her was a gentle touch to the forehead or a smack to the elbows. And now she was enveloped in warmth and a feeling she couldn't quite identify and she didn't know what to do. Thankfully, Elliot stepped back after a few seconds.

"I would've been right," Senna said, fastening a quiver of arrows to her back. "I knew Selanna was coming, and she's almost as good of a hunter as me. Alannah wouldn't have been lost for long."

Selanna rolled her eyes but grinned at the teasing remark. "You're so humble."

"You're friends?" Elliot asked.

"Longtime friends," Mr. Pinkus said.

Selanna frowned. "It's nice to see you too, Lysanthvir. I would've greeted you yesterday had I known you had been turned into a cat."

"Life's full of surprises."

"We're done here," Senna said before Selanna could respond. "I want to get out of the city quickly."

"That's for the best. Someone already tried to get to Alannah," Selanna agreed.

"What happened?" Elliot asked.

Alannah shook her head. "I'll tell you later. Let's go first."

"Make sure you stick close to us this time," Senna said.

"I'll go with you to the gates in case anyone feels like trying anything else." Selanna tapped her pommel.

The way back was less fraught. Alannah made sure to stick close and pay attention. Elliot had the same mindset, if the way he kept bumping into her every few steps was any indication. She was surprised he didn't grab her hand again. But after the hug, she was a little thankful. She didn't know what to make of it all.

They exited the gates and Selanna stopped there. "How many days to the witches?"

"I'm hoping for no more than four," Senna said. "Maybe three if we can push."

"You're not coming with us?" Alannah asked.

Selanna shook her head. "I'd like to, but I'm keeping the hunters corralled in my mother's court so they leave you be."

"Too bad you couldn't corral the assassins," Senna teased.

"Who did she send?"

"Ciradyl and Maiel."

Selanna nodded. "Her best then. But they're no match for you." She looked at Alannah. "There are no better hands to be in."

"I've noticed."

"Safe travels, Alannah," Selanna said.

"Thank you."

Selanna stayed at the gates while Senna began to lead them past the sprawling city. "Alannah!"

Alannah turned back.

"For what it's worth, I'm rooting for you."

Chapter 18

Selanna returned to the court late into the night. To her surprise, and delight, the hunters had turned in for the night. That meant her mother would be asleep as well. Selanna walked past her room and listened at the door to be certain. When she didn't hear Valeria stir, Selanna walked on to Odhran's room. A quick peek revealed that he wasn't in his room. She frowned. There were only a few places he would be.

She checked Meralith's room, but it also sat empty. Selanna backtracked to the kitchens, but neither of them were there. The only other place he would be, the only other place he might feel safe, was down in the archives. Selanna walked through the maze of hallways downstairs until she reached the door to the archives in an abandoned study room. She oft felt like the court had been built to confuse its occupants. Some doors led to nowhere. Sometimes they were carved into the wall but didn't open at all. If she didn't live here, she might get lost herself.

The stairs down to the archives were sparsely lit by blue wall sconces. Selanna hugged the wall as she descended. Halfway down she heard the whispers. She sighed in relief at the sound of their voices. She always worried when she left them behind. That was the reason she came back all those years ago. She had wanted to break away from Valeria. Needed room to breathe. But she couldn't leave her siblings for long. Not with Valeria. Not unprotected. She paused on the bottom step, watching the two of them.

The same blue sconces lined the walls. Burning candles spilled wax all over the table Meralith and Odhran occupied. What wasn't bathed in light was plunged in shadow. If Selanna looked hard enough she would see darkness twisting into macabre shapes with disjointed hands that would reach for her. A shiver ran down her back. The archives had always creeped Selanna out, but it was a place Valeria didn't come to and so it was a safe haven. Several books sat open on the table. Even from where she was standing, she could tell they were records. It didn't take a genius to guess what they were looking for.

"Did you find anything?" she asked.

Neither of them jumped at the sound of her voice. Nor did they show any surprise when they looked up to see her standing there.

"Nothing," Odhran said.

"It's strange. Mother keeps meticulous records of her work," Meralith added.

"Perhaps it wasn't recorded then," Selanna said, stepping fully into the room. "Or it was struck from the record."

"She wouldn't do that, unless..." Meralith pursed her lips, the movement tugged at the scars on her cheek and Selanna dropped her gaze.

"Unless it was embarrassing for her," Odhran said.

Selanna leaned over the table and stared down at the records. "Or she didn't want an official record that way Alannah's family would have no way to challenge her for removal."

"If that were the case, then why would she give Alannah a quest?" Meralith asked.

"We didn't give her much of a choice. The court was full and she couldn't deal with it quietly. Hard to sweep something under the rug when everyone is watching."

Meralith sighed. "I still don't understand why she would do this. What did Alannah's family do?"

Selanna shrugged. "There's no way to know unless Alannah tells us or Valeria does."

"Like that will happen," Odhran sneered.

"The best way to find out is to ensure Alannah succeeds," Selanna said.

Odhran cleared his throat and leaned back. "Did you see her?"

Selanna raised an eyebrow. "I did."

"And?" he demanded.

"And?"

He tipped his head back and heaved a sigh. "Selanna—"

"She's fine," she chuckled. "She's with Senna. They've already escaped one assassination attempt—"

"Who?"

"Ciradyl and Maiel."

"Mother really doesn't want her to succeed," Meralith said.

Odhran closed the books. "It isn't just that. Finding a person with Fae and witch blood in the time she has is enough to ensure that she would not succeed. Mother wants her dead."

"So, what you are going to do about Alannah?" Selanna asked.

"I don't believe there is anything I can do."

"Well...you could start with an apology—"

"Why would I apologize?" Odhran asked, crossing his arms over his chest.

Selanna mirrored him. "I don't know, maybe it's because your cruel pranks really hurt her."

He scoffed and rolled his eyes.

"The flowers you destroyed were her mother's—"

"They're flowers—"

"Her mother is dead, Odhran. You destroyed a living memory." Selanna shook her head. "If you don't feel bad about that, then I truly wonder about you, brother."

"Guilt won't work on me," he deadpanned, but his eyes shifted to the side.

She smirked. "If you say so."

Meralith touched his arm. "Don't apologize because Selanna might beat you up if you don't. Apologize because you mean it."

"You two are ridiculous," he grumbled.

"She'll be reaching Witches End in a few days. Perhaps you should go see her. You are paying for her safe passage after all," Selanna suggested.

"She does not want to see me."

"Of course, she doesn't. But I don't think you'll be able to stay away."

Odhran stood up from the table. "Whatever you're thinking, you're sorely mistaken. I have no need nor desire to see her. I paid Senna to escort her and keep her safe and I don't need to do anything more. Now if you'll excuse me, I'm going to bed."

Selanna and Meralith shared a look of disbelief and then a grin. Now that the idea was in his head, he was definitely going to go. It was like he couldn't help it. And she hoped it would be good for him. He needed to be around more people, be empathetic, make friends. Selanna was afraid if he didn't, he would turn into their mother and she didn't want that for him. They all deserved better.

She lingered behind with Meralith to clean up the books in case anyone was watching them. The last thing she needed was her mother to know they were snooping. A short while later she bid Meralith good night, but before Selanna went to her own room she stopped outside Odhran's room. She knocked, and when he didn't answer, she poked her head inside. Empty.

Please let this work.

***

The fire warmed her feet. Alannah sat with her legs crossed under her. Elliot laid beside her, his snoring soft and barely heard over the crackling of the fire. Mr. Pinkus had curled up beside Elliot, his back touching Elliot's side. Alannah wished she could sleep, but despite complete and utter exhaustion, it remained out of her reach. The journal sat open on her lap. She stared down at the words until they swam together in a jumbled mess.

"Anything new?" Senna asked.

Alannah looked up and shook her head. "No, it's all the same vague explanations." She sighed. "I don't know why I keep expecting there to be more."

"Because you're lost, confused, and searching for clarity."

Alannah closed the journal and wrapped it back in the shirt. "You're not wrong. I honestly have no idea what I'm doing." She placed the journal into her bag and zipped it closed.

"Very few people do."

"I find it hard to believe that you don't know what you're doing."

Senna chuckled. "Confidence does most of the work. And I have an advantage most people don't."

"What's that?"

"A clairvoyant wife."

Alannah snorted and leaned back onto her elbows. "That is quite an advantage."

"Lysanthvir tells me your grandmother was something of a clairvoyant."

"I never knew, really," Alannah admitted, lying down the rest of the way and putting one arm behind her head as a cushion. "Or maybe it's that I didn't notice. She was my nina. She taught me healing and growing herbs and baking bread, but I don't remember her ever telling me that she possessed a second sight."

Senna shifted to the side, a little closer to Alannah, and leaned against a tree trunk. "Nina?"

Alannah shrugged. "Apparently, I had a little trouble saying nana as a child. Nina stuck."

"It's cute," Senna said, crossing her ankles. "It's clear she had a plan for you. Perhaps that's why she kept it from you."

"If the journal is any indication, she did. I wish I knew what it was." Alannah drew in a deep breath. "The letter she left me was cryptic and that the journal would reveal more secrets to me when it was time. Mr. Pinkus said it was to help me break the curse, but I can't help the feeling that there is so much more they kept from me."

"What are you doing to do if that's the truth?"

Alannah shook her head. "I honestly don't know. I already feel lied to. I'm not sure how much more I can take of that."

"Understandable."

They lapsed into silence. Alannah stared at the starry sky above her. It was the same sky she saw every night in the fringe, but it still felt different. Bigger. Everything felt bigger after leaving the fringe. Except for her. She felt small. Infinitesimal. Like a tiny speck in the universe. And if she died, she would die as a tiny, lonely, speck of dust against a vast world.

It scared her.

Elliot's snore climbed an octave and she choked down a laugh. She didn't know how he could sleep so well in the dirt. Admittedly, she was a little jealous. If only she could sleep so well. Alannah found herself staring at Elliot. The gentle rise and fall of his chest. His cheek smooshed against his arm. A speck of drool at the corner of his mouth. It still surprised her that he was here at all. She marveled at his courage. But it also made her feel guilty. If she failed—and that was incredibly likely—then she doomed the three of them. It didn't seem fair. Why should he suffer for her choice? Her curse?

Why would he take such a risk?

"You should get some rest," Senna said, pulling Alannah from her thoughts.

"I will certainly try." Alannah cleared her throat. "Do you think I can succeed?"

"I think it will be difficult, but over the years I have learned to believe in the impossible."

"Too bad it can't be easy."

"I suppose this is where I say something about it being about the journey not the destination, but in this case, it should be easier. It shouldn't be difficult to find such a person. The Fae will never grow if they don't stop trying to cut themselves off from everyone else." Senna cross her arms over her chest. "They will learn it too late if they aren't careful."

"I don't understand their hatred. I know the reason, but I don't understand it."

Senna sighed. "It is difficult for people to shed their prejudices. Especially when it's passed from one generation to the next and they risk losing the connections they've always had. Some are brave enough to break the cycle and some are not."

"Do you think they're weak when they don't break the cycle?" Alannah asked.

"I wouldn't say that they're weak, especially since the Fae are often needlessly cruel. I've met many who are controlling and abusive and I can understand why some would have difficulty fighting that. Especially since many think they're alone in the fight." Senna uncrossed her ankles.

"Aren't they?"

"Not as much as they think."

"I wonder if there is something that can be done to help," Alannah said.

"There is always something that can be done, Alannah. Even if it's helping one person." Senna leaned her head back against the tree. "Now, let's get some sleep. Morning will be here sooner than we like."

Chapter 19

Three days.

Three days of walking, and sleeping on the ground, and of not bathing. Alannah's sweaty shirt stuck to her back. Dirt had ground itself into her elbows no matter how much she tried to wipe it away. It clung to her neck and hair and sometimes she found a wayward streak on her cheek. Alannah would give everything she had —which wasn't much—for one shower. Cold. Hot. She didn't care. Wiping herself down with a wet washcloth at the end of the day wasn't cutting it.

Elliot and Senna were faring much better than she was. Of course, they would be, considering Senna was a hunter and Elliot was an outdoorsman. Alannah hoped she would be able to clean herself properly before meeting the witches. Smelling like three days of sweat and dirt wasn't a good first impression.

At least there had been so signs of assassins or people trying to shove a parasite in her hand as a "gift." It was almost strange how little resistance they had on this journey. Not that Alannah dared to question it out loud. She learned her lesson with the rain. But the lack of attention left her on edge. As if it was bound to change at any moment.

The fields came to an end after the first day. While they weren't making their way through a densely packed forest, there were more trees. And according to Senna, there were smaller villages and holdings they were passing. They skirted the edge of these places, sometimes Alannah could even see lights and smoke through the trees, but Senna wouldn't let them get any closer. A shame. She had finally gathered the courage to walk into Underhill and she could barely see any of it.

Now they were coming upon another forest. This one was darker than the one that edged her property. Many of the trees were stripped bare of their bark and leaves. The ones that had their bark still intact were covered in a bark that was as black as night. Brown grass that smelled of ash grew sparsely around the roots of the trees.

"What's this place?" Elliot asked, wrinkling his nose.

"Black spider forest," Senna answered.

Alannah and Elliot both balked, stopping right at the edge. Was the forest true to its name? Alannah wasn't sure she wanted to find out.

Senna grinned at them. "What's the matter?"

"Are there really spiders in there?" Alannah asked.

"There are spiders everywhere, Alannah."

"Right, but are they like small spiders that do normal spider stuff, or are they like humongous spiders that will make me shit my pants?" Elliot got out before she could. Although, she didn't think she would've phrased it quite like that.

Senna snorted. "It's fine, Elliot. I actually live here."

He looked incredulous. "With the big ass spiders?"

"There are no giant spiders here. It's only a name." She smirked "Perhaps even one I made up."

"Why would you do that?"

She shrugged. "I thought it was funny. And I don't like its true name."

"What's that?" Alannah asked.

"Witches End."

Alannah swallowed. "Why would they name it that?" She had a feeling the answer would be exactly what she expected, and she didn't like that at all.

"The forest borders their land...and many died here during the attacks by Reluvethel. Some say the blood and magic spilled here still lingers in the soil."

"Why do you live here?" Elliot asked.

"It's quiet. Very few venture here," Senna answered. "Now are you coming?"

Elliot looked at Alannah, trying to gauge her reaction. "Do we have to?"

"If you want to make it to the witches."

Alannah's mouth twisted in a frown. "Let's go then," she muttered. She followed Senna in silence, unnerved by stepping into such a place. All the years of hearing stories about Underhill and they never told her about this. Her mother told her the witches didn't quite fit in, but Alannah never knew it was to this degree. That they were killed in such numbers that a forest had grown from their defeat. *Witches End.* She hoped it wasn't hers.

"You okay?" Elliot's whispered, sticking close to her left.

Her eyes traveled over the sparse trees. "I'm starting to wonder what exactly my family missed about this place."

"Not every place is perfect, Alannah. There will always be bad. That's why it's so important to find the good and help it grow," he said.

"Has anyone every told you that you're fairly wise,

Elliot."

He snorted. "No, not really. I have...experiences that have dictated how I look at things. No big deal."

"I realize I've never asked before...what is your world like? Your family?" she asked.

In the short time they had known each other she had seen many emotions from Elliot. Anger. Fear. Grief. But she had never seen nothing before. The wrinkles in his forehead smoothed. His eyes went blank, glazed over, and nothing could be gleaned from them. He shrugged. "Same as everyone else's."

It was a lie. And a well-practiced one from the sound of it. Why? "Really?"

His eyes darted to Senna. "We should catch up. Don't want to fall behind." Without another word, he jogged away from Alannah, effectively ending any follow-up questions she had. And she had many.

What was so bad about his life that he lied about it? How could it be worse than anything that had happened to him here? A small part of her was upset that he lied. She didn't completely understand why. Perhaps she thought that they had grown closer only to find out she was wrong. Or perhaps it was because he had learned so much of her own life but was unwilling to share any of his own.

Senna stopped in a small clearing. "We'll camp here for the night."

Elliot looked around. No animals scampered about in the underbrush. Bugs didn't chitter under the dead leaves. Even the air was still. "Are you sure?"

"It will be dark soon." Senna kicked a few rocks with her boots. "And it is unlikely anyone will come here because we're close to the witches. In fact, you'll be in the closest village by early afternoon."

Finally. Excitement and relief intermingled in her chest, making her heart pound, but she felt the lightest she had ever been since stepping foot into Underhill. She hoped they liked her. She hoped she liked them. And imagine what she could learn—

Quest first.

She heaved a sigh. Right. She couldn't waste any time if she wanted to succeed. If she even could. Her excitement dampened. Damn it. She was finally going to meet people like her. She was going to see the home her family had missed for so many generations. And she couldn't even enjoy it. Savor it. Celebrate it. *Unfair.*

"I'll go get wood," Elliot said, dropping his pack to the ground.

Mr. Pinkus stretched his back legs. "I'll come with you."

"Why? You can't even carry anything—"

Mr. Pinkus' tail twitched. "I can carry *something*."

The two continued bickering—their voices echoing back to clearing—as they walked into the trees. Alannah couldn't help but smile and shake her head. Who knew that she would enjoy traveling with them? It was pleasant surprise to no one more than her. She almost didn't want it to end. But she knew it would. Soon. And probably not well. The smile dropped from her face.

Guilt hit her full force, dragging the air from her lungs. Alannah sank down onto the damp ground. If she failed then they failed. She wasn't going to go down alone. They would be yanked down with her. It didn't matter that they volunteered, it didn't feel right. They had more faith in her than she probably deserved.

"You okay?" Senna was the one to ask her this time.

"Everyone keeps asking me that."

"Because you don't look okay. You look like you believe you're doomed already," Senna said.

"Aren't I?"

"Some people believe in you, so no, I don't think so. Not yet at least." Senna crossed her arms over her chest. "You're raw, uneasy, that much is clear but I don't think that means you will fail. I'm actually thinking you're going to surprise us all."

Alannah shrugged off her pack. It hit the ground with a thud. "Everyone is much more confident in me than I am in myself. I don't understand it."

"That's because you can't see yourself the way everyone else does. And sometimes, other people notice things that you don't." Senna patted Alannah's shoulder. "Don't give up yet. You're barely to the midway point of this journey."

"Thank you."

"You're wel—"

"You can only carry one stick, how is that helpful?" Elliot's voice grew louder. They were coming back to camp.

Mr. Pinkus' voice was muffled, and when he stepped back in the clearing, Alannah knew why. She muffled a laugh with her palm. He was carrying a stick nearly twice as long as he was in his mouth. And when he moved his head, he hit Elliot in the shins.

I hope I don't fail.

Elliot muttered a curse every time the stick hit him. Mr. Pinkus' eyes twinkled, clearly pleased with what he was doing.

I think I would miss them.

Of all the thoughts to have, she wasn't expecting

that one. She expected guilt. And she expected wanting to succeed so she could be free. But she hadn't really considered what that meant. What it would look like. Feel like. And what about them? Would they leave? Stay? Would she be alone again? She had told Elliot she would be fine alone. She wasn't sure about that anymore. Answers would come with more questions. Uncertainty. The stable, normal—boring—life she was used to would be gone. What would take its place?

The fire crackled to life, pulling her back to reality. Elliot and Senna were setting up a spit. They had done the same thing several nights ago to roast rabbits Senna had caught. Alannah wondered if tonight would be the same.

"I'll be back. I'm going to catch dinner," Senna said, pulling her bow from her back.

"Do you need any help?" Elliot asked.

She shook her head. "I won't be gone long."

Alannah held her hands out to the fire. She didn't know how seasons worked in Underhill, some places felt like spring and summer, but Witches End felt like the cusp between autumn and winter. A damp chill made her shiver.

Elliot sat down opposite of her. She found herself staring at him. *Will he evade if I ask him about his life again?* She wasn't used to seeing him closed off and it made her even more curious than usual, but she also didn't want to upset him. *I'll wait.* She crossed her legs and rested her elbows on her knees. The crackling of the fire coupled with exhaustion from walking made her eyelids grow heavy.

Finally. I might get some sleep.

The loud crack of a stick breaking made her jump.

Senna walked back into the clearing carrying a basket that she hadn't left with.

"That's a strange catch," Elliot said, eyeing the basket.

"Yes, well, someone was thinking ahead," Senna said. She pulled back a cloth that covered the basket and pulled out sausage links. She draped them over the spit to cook over the fire.

"Where did that come from?" Alannah asked. Leaning over, she spied bread and cheese peeking out from underneath the cloth.

"I did tell you that I lived close by," Senna answered.

Elliot shook his head. "That close? Why are we here then?"

"No offense to either of you, but I would prefer not to involve my wife." Senna sat down and placed the basket in her lap.

"You have a wife?" Elliot asked.

Senna pulled out a loaf of bread and began tearing it into pieces. "Why do you sound so surprised?"

He shrugged, accepting the piece that she handed him. "You seemed like the lone wolf type."

Senna handed Alannah a piece. "I was...briefly. But she showed me that I was not meant to."

"How is Eletha?" Mr. Pinkus asked.

"She is well. I thought I would have to convince her to stay at home, but she agreed easily. Which makes me suspicious," Senna said, grabbing a piece of cheese and popping it in her mouth.

Mr. Pinkus moved closer to the basket. "Do you think she knows something?"

"She always knows something."

Mr. Pinkus snatched a piece of cheese from the basket and sauntered back over to the fire with it still in his mouth. Shaking her head, Senna grabbed the basket and held it out to Alannah.

"How did you two meet?" Alannah asked, grabbing a couple of pieces to eat with her bread.

Senna's expression softened. Her lips curved into a smile and her eyes twinkled. She held the basket out to Elliot. "If I am blessed by the sun, then she is blessed by the moon. We are opposites and equals in many ways. Our meetings over the years felt like fate. I first met her in my teenage years." She pulled the basket back into her lap once Elliot had grabbed what he wanted. "I was hotheaded and reckless. A cocky young warrior. She was... is calm and possesses a clarity and understanding that I don't think I ever will."

"What happened?" Alannah asked.

"We lost touch. She traveled with her family while I was more rooted." Senna's sobered, the smile dropping from her face. "She met me again when I was lost—unmoored—and angry. I ran. She followed. I didn't understand why she did at the time. I was sharp. Unaccepting. She was still so kind. Loving. She knew what could be between us and in time, so did I." Senna sighed. "I realized I didn't have to go through life alone, so I married her."

"Wow," Elliot said, his mouth full. "She sounds wonderful."

"She is."

"It's a shame you won't get to meet her," Mr. Pinkus said. "Eletha is a lovely woman. And very insightful."

"Maybe next time," Senna said.

Next time. Alannah hoped there would be a next time.

Chapter 20

Alannah didn't know what woke her. Perhaps an imperceptible noise. Or the feeling in her gut that something wasn't right. She had fallen asleep on her back and now she was facing Elliot with her cheek resting on his outstretched arm. When did that happen? Despite her surprise, she doubted it as the reason for the bad feeling in the bit of her stomach. Alannah raised her head to look around.

The fire had burned down to the embers, making the darkness that bled into the clearing so much more ominous. Alannah couldn't see anything. She opened her mouth to speak, but a hand clamped over her mouth. Her heart rate jumped. Was it an assassin? But a look to her right told her it was Senna with a finger held to her lips.

Senna leaned down. "Wake up Elliot. Quietly. And be prepared to run," she whispered in Alannah's ear before removing her hand.

Alannah nodded and rolled back towards Elliot, putting her lips to his ear. "Elliot," she whispered, shaking his shoulder. "Wake up."

He grumbled in his sleep and she covered his mouth her hand. She shook his shoulder again, more violently this time, until his eyes began to open. "What—"

"Quiet," she hissed. "Senna said be prepared to run."

His eyes widened and he pushed himself up onto his elbows. They both quietly sat up and grabbed their packs. Now she understood why they traveled so light. She pulled her pack onto her back.

Senna crouched beside them, her bow in her hand and an arrow already nocked. Mr. Pinkus stood poised beside her as if he intended to launch himself at anyone that came too close. Given how many times he had swiped at her with those claws, they were indeed suitable weapons. Alannah began to stand up. A familiar whistling filled the dead air.

Everything moved so quickly.

"Get down!" Senna shouted, raising her bow.

Elliot launched himself at Alannah, knocking her back down. The weight of him landing on top of her knocked the air from her lungs. She wheezed. And then he didn't move. "Elliot," she muttered, trying to pull air back into her lungs. "We have to go."

He grunted.

"What's wro—"

She saw the fletching first, and then her eyes traveled down the wood to where it had buried itself in his back. Alannah pushed herself back onto her knees. She didn't give a damn if it made her a larger target. The pounding in her ears drowned out the sounds of arrows flying around her. *He's hurt again.* Alannah reached for the utility tool she knew he kept in his pocket. She carefully cut the shirt so she didn't jostle the arrow. Fabric peeled away to reveal the wound. The arrow had struck deep. Removing it would hurt and be dangerous if she wasn't careful. But that wasn't the worst part. Black veins branched out from the wound, a poison snaking its way under his skin.

It's my fault.
"How bad?" he asked.
She swallowed. "It's fine. Just fine."
"You're lying."
Alannah swiped her eyes. She was crying. Why was she crying? "I can heal you."
"No!"
"Elliot—"
"You can't use your magic, Alannah. You know that" he argued. "Wait for Senna. She'll know what to do."
Alannah searched around for Senna. She saw her at the edge of the clearing fighting one of the assassins —Ciradyl, if memory served her correctly—their bows discarded to the side as they grappled with each other. Mr. Pinkus clung to Ciradyl's leg. But that was only one assassin. Where was the other?
A glint of silver in the darkness gave away Maiel's position. Alannah had nothing to defend her or Elliot. She was damned if they were going to hurt Elliot again. When asked later, she would say she had a hard time describing the feeling. But her heart called out for a way to defend him and Underhill answered. Beckoning to her. Calling her. Reaching out from underneath the soil. *I can't.* Magic had never felt so overwhelming before. It thrummed through her, singing a song she had never heard before, but she still knew it. Alannah closed her eyes and allowed it in.
She realized what it was her family had missed.
The sheer power that coursed through was unlike any magic she had used in the fringe. She was like an empty cup and it filled her until she felt like it spill over. The daggers grew closer as Maiel readied herself to

strike. "NO!" Alannah's voice reverberated through the trees and into the soil. The ground rumbled underneath her, awakened from its slumber by the witch's cry.

With the ground unsteady beneath her feet, Maiel stumbled backward. The ground split around her. Vines grew from the cracks with frightening speed. Her black eyes bulged with fear. They wrapped around Maiel's legs, tightening as she tried to move away. Her daggers slashed at the vines. She'd cut one and two would take its place.

"Alannah!"

The cry went unnoticed. Alannah was not going to let someone else hurt Elliot. She was not going to let his death be her fault. And the power...she didn't want to stop. This is what had been kept from her. This is what she was going to reclaim. The vines wrapped around Maiel's throat.

It wasn't without cost.

The power that had filled her until she was brimming, was running out. It no longer thrummed through her like a long-lost song. The edges of the world began to grow dark. Glass shards felt like they were being dragged through her veins. Something warm and wet dripped down her lips. The coppery taste seeped into her mouth. Blood.

I have to stop.
I don't think I can.

Soft hands touched her shoulders. Warm. Firm. "You have to stop, Alannah." A voice she knew but couldn't place. Deep. Calming. Like a pool of undisturbed water.

Her shoulders dropped. The energy left her as quickly as it came. Her eyes fluttered. *I can't sleep now.*

Maiel ripped the vines away, stumbling away from Alannah. The rest remained dormant across the forest floor. The only green in the entirety of Witches End. She did that.

"You have lost. Go home and lick your wounds, Maiel," the voice commanded.

Maiel bared her teeth but didn't move towards Alannah again. "Fuck you, Odhran," she hissed as she backed away into the trees.

Odhran? Here? Alannah tilted her head back. He stared down at her, his silver eyes alight in the darkness. Why would he be here? She doubted he was a hallucination. He felt real enough. And his hands were the only thing keeping her upright. Should she say thank you? She wasn't sure if she could get the words out.

The darkness crept closer.

Odhran leaned down, his eyes searching hers. For what, she didn't know. "You're full of surprises, aren't you?"

The darkness dragged her down.

***

Odhran carried Alannah and Senna carried Elliot. Mr. Pinkus ran in front of them towards Senna's cabin. A warm light drew them closer until Odhran saw Eletha standing on the porch steps. Cerulean blue fabric clung to the round shape of her belly and skimmed the tops of her bare feet. A silver scarf pulled tight black curls away from her face. Bright silver eyes focused on Odhran and then drifted to Alannah. Eletha didn't look surprised to see them.

"Hello, Lysanthvir," Eletha greeted the cat first as he bounded up the steps.

Ah. That's why the cat had seemed familiar. Funny.

He didn't remember Lysanthvir being a cat. But then again, they weren't close and Odhran wouldn't pretend to know anything about the man other than seeing Lysanthvir around the court when he worked for Valeria.

Eletha held the door open for them. Senna stepped in first, carrying Elliot to their kitchen table. She laid him down on his stomach. The arrow still protruded from his back. Black veins of poison were spreading across his shoulder and down his back. If it reached his brain, he wouldn't survive. Eletha and Senna worked in tandem. Senna cut away the rest of Elliot's shirt while Eletha grabbed a bowl from the counter along with cloth she had set out.

Clairvoyance was truly a blessing in this situation.

Odhran carried Alannah to their couch and gently set her down on the cushions. She looked pale. Dark circles under her eyes were pronounced. Blood under her nose had crusted to a muddy brown. Lysanthvir jumped up onto the couch and climbed on her chest. He eyed Odhran balefully.

"I can take it from here, thank you," Lysanthvir sniffed and laid down on her chest.

"If you say so." Odhran stepped away.

"I don't trust you."

"I didn't ask for your trust."

"What—"

"A hand please, Odhran," Eletha interrupted. "We don't have time for arguing."

Odhran turned and walked to the table, ignoring the feeling of eyes boring into his back. "What do you need?"

Eletha held out her hand, her bright silver eyes holding him still. "Your blood."

He felt a sharp prick in the pad of his finger and he gasped. Eletha gathered the blood with her fingertip and smeared it down the arrow. "It's your mother's silverite arrows. I need blood of her blood to neutralize it so I can remove it. Otherwise, it would've burrowed deeper."

"You could have warned me," he grumbled.

"Time is of the essence," she said, carefully pulling the arrow free and tossing it to the side.

Senna held the bowl out for her. The pastel green paste inside smelled disgusting, like rotten cabbage that had been left sitting in the sun. Odhran wrinkled his nose. Eletha grabbed a glob and pressed it into Elliot's wound. A groan fell from his lips, but she didn't stop. Eletha packed as much as she could into the wound. Odhran wondered what the point of it was until he saw the black veins retreating. Whatever it was, it was absorbing the poison.

"Cloth, please," Eletha murmured.

Senna set the bowl on the counter and grabbed a cloth from the pile. With the cloth in her hand, Eletha began to squeeze the paste back out of the wound. It somehow smelled worse. Odhran gagged. He held his hand to his nose. Black ichor mixed with the green paste oozed from the wound. Eletha cleaned it away with the cloth. Once one was dirty, Senna exchanged it for a clean one.

"Done," Eletha said, handing over the last cloth. "Now I have to clean and dress the wound. He will be fine."

"What about her?" Odhran asked, tilting his head in Alannah's direction.

Eletha's eyes flicked over to Alannah for a brief moment. "There's nothing I can do for her. She needs rest."

"You told me she was a healer. A garden witch," Senna said to Odhran. "You didn't tell me she could do that."

Odhran shook his head. "I am as surprised as you are. I didn't realize she had that kind of power."

Eletha smirked.

"What?" Senna asked.

"She is no mere garden witch, that much is certain." Eletha walked away from the table to grab a bowl filled with water and a wet cloth. She wrung the cloth and dabbed at Elliot's wound.

Odhran crossed his arms over his chest. "What is she then?"

Eletha's smile grew. "It is far too early to know."

"So, you're not going to tell us." Senna rested her hands on her hips.

"I am not."

Senna snorted. "One day I will tire of you dangling information in front of my nose and then snatching it away."

"No, you won't."

"You're right," Senna said, kissing Eletha on the cheek. "I will not."

"I will tell you this, son of the Ruby Court," –Eletha paused and looked up at him— "your mother will never forgive you."

Odhran stiffened. What was that supposed to mean? His mother didn't like him much anyway. But why would bringing Alannah here, and helping her, make his mother never forgive him? What was it about Alannah that bothered his mother so much? He had spent the last few days poking around and trying to find out. Centuries of meticulous records, but nothing on Alannah or her family. Odhran had even tried to bribe a few of Valeria's confidants, but their fear of her outweighed their greed.

Senna sighed. "I could use a drink. Join me," she said, gesturing for Odhran to follow her outside.

She left the front door cracked open and walked to the right side of the porch. A bottle of amber liquid and two glasses sat on a table between two rocking chairs. Senna sat down to uncork the bottle and pour both glasses two-fingers full. She handed one to Odhran. He accepted the drink and leaned against the porch railing.

She took a sip. "You know, I still don't understand your motive."

"My motive?"

"For helping her. If Selanna had been the one to hire me, I would've understood. But you...I don't know what your angle is yet."

"Do I have to have one?" he asked.

She chuckled. "You are an incredibly selfish and self-centered person Odhran. More like your mother than you would like. So yes, I believe you need one. Do you even know what it is?"

"He doesn't," Eletha answered for him, stepping into the cool night air. She brushed a wayward curl away from her face. "But one day he will."

Odhran sighed. "You are always so cryptic."

"It keeps you on your toes."

Senna laughed, reaching for her wife's hand. Their fingers intertwined. "Have I told you I loved you today?" she asked, raising Eletha's knuckles to her lips.

"Three times. But I will not deprive you of telling me a fourth," Eletha teased.

Odhran dropped his gaze. It was...different watching two people interact while being completely in love with each other. It wasn't something he saw often, if ever. The Fae weren't well known for being affectionate. At least, not in these parts. Marriages were business transactions. As were murder plots. Being free and open with one's feelings was a foreign concept. Odhran had never seen it with his own parents. They despised each other. And shortly after Odhran was born, his father left, leaving Odhran with a woman who hated him.

Meralith's and Selanna's fathers also left in the same fashion. None could stand to stay with Valeria. Hatred was the only emotion she openly showed. She didn't care who saw it. No one in her court corrected her. No one cared. He didn't expect them to. Children were expected to live obediently and quietly.

Your mother will never forgive you for this.

For what? Momentarily inconveniencing her with a witch unlikely to succeed in the first place. Odhran stared at Eletha as if it would somehow give him an answer, but the woman did like her secrets.

"She's awake," Eletha murmured.

Alannah stepped onto the porch. She looked terrible. Pale. Dried blood still sat under her nose. Her eyes darted around. First to Senna and Eletha and then to Odhran. They narrowed. "What are you doing here?" she asked, her voice scratchy.

"Leaving," Odhran said. There was no doubt she wouldn't want him here. He had only wanted to check on her progress, and having done so, he could leave. He placed the glass down on the railing and swept past Alannah, intent on departing before an argument ensued.

"Not so fast." She followed him down the steps, leaning heavily on the railing.

He paused.

"You hired Senna. Why? Why are you helping me?"

"Is that so strange?"

She took a step forward, leaving the security of the railing. "You wanted me dead not to so long ago. You made a mockery of my existence and my choice to save someone who needed help. Of course, it's strange."

Odhran waved his hand. "Bygones—"

"That is not how that works!" Alannah's hands balled into fists. If he was closer, she might've actually swung at him. "You are so arrogant and self-centered—"

"You don't know anything about me."

"I know enough!"

They glared at each other. "I don't know what it is you hope to gain from this, Odhran," she spat his name. "But you will get nothing from me when this is over."

Odhran drew a breath in through his nose. "Rest well, Alannah. You will need it." He walked away before she could say another word. No matter what it was, it would add to the argument. And she looked like she wasn't going to be upright for much longer based on how she looked. It was better for him to leave.

He retraced his steps back to their camp. The fire still smoldered. Odhran's eyes moved to the crack in the earth. The vines hadn't retreated or withered away. They climbed up the nearest tree, entwining around the trunk and up to the branches. As he neared it, he noticed small buds had sprouted from the vines. He tapped one with his finger. The bud opened, unfurling to reveal rich purple petals. The flower was as big as his palm.

Incredible.

Alannah was so much more than he had expected. Was she truly only a half-witch? She must be something else, something more, to create life where only death existed. It made him even more curious. Something that felt impossible. He was always thinking of her. Wondering. Trying to understand her, her motives, and why he cared. But there was one thought at the forefront of his mind. It drowned out everything else.

She finally said my name.

Chapter 21

"I am pleased to see you still live."

Elliot's eyes opened. He was pleasantly warm. The hardness of the earth under his back replaced with something much softer. A real bed. With pillows. And a blanket that he had kicked off his legs at some point. His head turned in the direction the voice had come from.

Mr. Pinkus perched on a bedside table beside a cup filled with a blue liquid. A levitating crystal provided a warm amber light that illuminated the bedside table. The cat blinked at him before standing up and stretching. He hopped to the edge of the bed and clambered onto Elliot's chest. "How are you feeling?"

Tired. He winced at the twinge in his upper back, but it was nothing compared to the searing pain from earlier. He thought for sure he was done for. It was the second time this place had tried to kill him. He really hoped there wasn't a third waiting for him. "Fine," he muttered, wincing as Mr. Pinkus back claws dug into his ribs.

The cat laid down, his paws stretching out to tap Elliot's chin. "You are very resilient, you know. Then again, I've noticed most humans are."

"What do you know about humans?"

"More than you think."

Elliot shifted, trying to get comfortable under the

cat's weight. "How?"

Mr. Pinkus withdrew his paw and licked it. "If you survive this journey, I will tell you."

"Pretty slim chance."

"I'm not so sure."

Elliot sighed. "Where is Alannah? Is she okay?"

Mr. Pinkus turned his head and Elliot followed his gaze. She was breathing so quietly—or perhaps he was still out of it—that he hadn't noticed her curled on her side with a pillow separating them. Even in the sparse light, Elliot could see the dark circles under her eyes. They were more prominent than usual. Wet hair clung to her face. The clothes she wore—white linen pants and a grey tank top—didn't look familiar to him. Borrowed then. She drew in a deep breath and her eyes opened.

"Elliot," she mumbled, her voice thick.

There was a world of difference between her now and what he saw at camp. She...*glowed*. She came to life with an energy he had never seen from her before. He had seen her heal him and help nurture plants. But this was different. He saw a glimpse of the kind of power she could have.

It scared him a little.

She's still Alannah.

"How do you feel?" she asked while pushed herself up onto her elbow.

"I should be asking you the same thing."

"I'm not the one who was shot."

"Touché."

She cleared her throat. "Did you push me out of the way knowing you would be hit?"

"I was pretty sure, yeah."

"Why would you do that?"

He frowned. "Why wouldn't I?"

"Because I got you into this mess? Because I almost left you to die when you asked for my help and it doesn't make sense that you would take an arrow for someone like me." She shook her head. "I don't understand you."

Elliot pushed himself up onto his elbows which caused Mr. Pinkus to slide down. The cat grumbled his displeasure and jumped down onto the pillow in between them. "What is there to understand? I'm not the kind of person that thinks an eye for an eye is a good way to live my life. And sure, I was pretty angry at you at first."

Alannah sat up the rest of the way and rested her hands in her lap. "But you're not anymore?"

"Considering what I've seen here, I'm not surprised that you didn't want them to notice you. And you know what, in the end you still chose to save me and heal me and even keep me safe in your home." Elliot winced as he sat up. His back throbbed.

"The cup on the table should help with the pain," Mr. Pinkus said before curling up into a ball.

Elliot turned his head and eyed it warily. He was hesitant to drink anything here that wasn't water, but he also didn't distrust the cat. So far, Mr. Pinkus hadn't led them astray. He reached for the cup. His hands shook slightly. The liquid in the cup sloshed about, threatening to spill over the sides. Alannah's hand cupped the bottom to keep it still. Her other hand rested on his shoulder.

With her help, he brought the cup to his lips and took a few swallows. His eyes flitted back and forth from the cup to her. The warm light softened her features. But her lips were still set in a frown. Maybe she didn't believe him. Or she still didn't understand. The only way she would is if he told her the truth. Reveal the part of himself he never let anyone see.

When he finished, she leaned over him to set the cup back down on the table. She coaxed him into laying back down by gently pushing him down with the hand on his shoulder. "It's going to make you sleep more, but you won't be hurting." As soon as he was settled back against the pillows, she laid back down beside him. Mr. Pinkus stayed in-between them, curled up on the pillow.

"I know what it's like to want to be unseen," he whispered.

She stared at him, but she said nothing, as if she knew he needed a moment to gather his thoughts—his courage—to open himself up.

"You asked about my family earlier and I didn't answer you."

"I remember."

Elliot took a deep breath. "My mother died when I was twelve. It was sudden. An accident. Someone fell asleep at the wheel and she was…unlucky, I guess. She died instantly." He swallowed.

"I'm sorry, Elliot."

He nodded. "It was…I couldn't fathom losing her. Sometimes I even believed that she would still come home. My dad took it the hardest in the beginning. I watched him struggle to do everything she could did." Elliot stared up at the dark ceiling. "Not even six months later he was seeing someone. A few months after that he married her."

Alannah eyes were glued to the side of his face. He didn't meet her gaze. He couldn't. No. It was easier to tell the ceiling than to turn his head and tell her.

"She was nice to me when he was around, but when he wasn't, she was…cruel. Every trace of my mother vanished. Pictures were packed away." His eyes began to burn. "The touches she had added over the years were replaced with something else. When I would tell my dad, he would say that my stepmom needed to feel like this was her home and I needed to make her feel welcome." He swiped away the few tears that had begun to gather.

Alannah's finger curled around his pinky. His breath hitched.

"She was always saying horrible things about me and my mother and my father never believed me because he never heard them for himself. It wore me down over the years. When I was fourteen, she had a baby. She got worse and he was focused on his new son. It was like I didn't exist to him."

"Elliot—"

"Our house was small. They needed a room and one day my dad came home with a tent and told me that he was finally going to teach me how to camp. I was excited. I thought," –he choked back a sob— "I thought things were finally going to change. I thought he was my dad again."

She's going to pity me. I don't want her to pity me.

"I lived in that tent in the backyard. Cold or hot. Rain or snow. Sometimes my stepmom would lock the doors so I couldn't sneak in. But sometimes when I was quiet, when she forgot I existed, she would forget to lock the door. So, I would be good, quiet, obedient. I didn't complain. If she didn't notice me then I was safe."

Alannah's fingers intertwined with his and she gave

him a gentle squeeze.

"I hated her. Him. My brother. Myself. When I was sixteen I...left. I took my tent and whatever I could pack in a bag and I left." Tears dripped onto the pillow. "He didn't come looking for me, but Sean and Bev...it only took them two days to find me."

"Your friends."

He nodded. "I've known them for a long time. They've been my family. If they're really gone—dead—then I'm...lost. I won't have anyone."

"Is that why?" she asked.

"What do you mean?"

"The only way you'll know if they're alive, is if I succeed. Is that why you took the arrow?"

He shook his head. "No. Although, now that you mention it, it is a good reason," he joked, but it fell flat. He cleared this throat. "No, I...it would've been so easy grow up hateful like my stepmother. I was hurt and I could've hurt others and lashed out and been an asshole. I've worked hard so I wouldn't be like them. Sometimes it's a good thing and sometimes I care so much about others so I don't have to think about myself..." He trailed off, sighing. He still wasn't explaining himself well enough. And she wasn't going to get it if she didn't.

Elliot turned over onto his side to face her fully. "The thing is, Alannah, I saw that arrow and didn't hesitate for a moment. I wasn't going to do nothing. All I could think about was making sure you weren't hurt."

It could've been his imagination, but her eyes looked glassy in the light. She dropped her gaze. "Thank you, Elliot."

"Can I," –he yawned— "ask you a question?"

Her teeth flashed in the dark. "I see a grievous injury changes nothing. What's the question?"

"What were you thinking when back then? Back when you almost didn't save me."

It was her turn to look up at the ceiling to avoid his gaze. "I...at first, I told myself that I had to walk away. That I couldn't interfere because they would see me and mother always told me to make sure they never noticed me. That the Fae were cruel and unkind to those they considered interlopers."

"But you changed your mind."

"Yes." She sighed. "I couldn't walk away. I knew that if I did you would die and while I always knew what happened to people that never returned, I never had to reckon with it before. It never happened in a situation I could interfere in before. But you were there and I could save you—*someone*—so, I did."

He squeezed her hand. "Thanks."

She snorted. "You're welcome."

They fell silent. Elliot fought the sleep that tugged at him.

"May I ask you something, Elliot?"

"Sure thing," he mumbled.

"After what you went through, I would think you would hate camping and being outdoors. But it seems that you like it. How?"

"My friends," –a yawn interrupted him once more— "wanted to turn bad memories into something good."

"They are good friends."

His eyes closed. "Yeah."

"Goodnight, Elliot."

"Goodnight—"

***

After leaving Senna's, Odhran wandered

through Witches End. He needed time to think. Clear his head. And he didn't want to go home. He expected this stretch of woods to be silent since it stood as a dormant barrier between the witches and everyone else, but the crunching of leaves and snapping of sticks told him otherwise.

He wasn't alone.

Dark shapes drifted through the trees behind him, beside him, in front of him. He wasn't sure if he was being herded or watched. Probably a bit of both. Odhran kept a steady pace. He wasn't here to cause harm. Although not everyone would believe that. The tension between the Fae and witches had existed long before he was born. Odhran didn't particularly dislike the witches. If he had to describe how he felt about them, he would've used the word apathetic before anything else.

But that was until Alannah.

Never before had he spent so much time dwelling on one person. She lived in his head. Most of the time she sneered at him in disgust. Sometimes he pictured her laughing as she had when her boundary protection had knocked him on his ass, and he wondered if he could see it again under different circumstances.

Why?

Even now, as the shapes pursued him, he thought of her. She was plain compared to the Fae. Powerless in comparison to those she stood up to. He wanted to peer inside of her and see what made her the way she was.

A pulsing under his feet made him stop. Feeling eerily similar to Alannah's boundary protection, his body tensed in preparation. Nothing happened. Odhran the toe of his boot into the dirt. One pulse turned into multiple. Two beats. A pause. Two more beats. A heartbeat. Odhran looked up and noticed he stood in a perfect circle of trees. The trees varied from saplings to elder trees. The two largest trees sat side by side with their branches entwined. Flowering vines further tied the trees together forming intricate knots. He had never seen two trees bonded before.

Odhran turned in a circle to look at all of the trees. He stopped at the smallest sapling and took a step towards it.

"Give me one good reason why you're here," a voice boomed from outside the ring of trees. The shapes pressed close to the edge with ghastly yellow lights focusing on him. *No. Not lights.* Eyes. Sets of glowing eyes glared at him.

"I am not here to cause trouble," Odhran answered.

"That remains to be seen," the voice growled. A wolf—twice the size of a normal wolf—emerged from the trees. Black fur turned blue in the moonlight. Bright blue eyes tracked Odhran's movements. "This place is not for you." The wolf's mouth didn't move as it spoke and Odhran realized it wasn't a wolf at all.

A shapeshifter. *Interesting.* He had never heard of a witch mastering the arcane art of shapeshifting. As it stood, only the oldest of the Fae could do such a thing. "What is this place?" Odhran asked.

"Can you not feel what is here?"

"Whatever it is, it feels alive."

The wolf tilted his head.

Odhran took another step towards the young sapling. He reached out, ignoring the warning growl from the wolf, and grazed his fingertips against one of the branches. *Save my daughter. Save my daughter. Save my—*

Odhran withdrew his hand. "Who is buried here?"

"And why should I tell you? Hasn't your family done enough?"

My family? "What has my family done?"

The wolf huffed. "They are the cause of this." The wolf sank back into the trees. "You should leave, Prince of the Ruby Court, you have no business here."

The eyes blinked out one by one, leaving him with only the light of the moon, but he still felt them prowling around the clearing. Waiting.

They are the cause of the this. What could his family —

Oh.

Clarity hit him like a burst of lightning. The heartbeat. The familiar feeling magic. This had to be the resting place of Alannah's family. Nothing else made sense. But why? They had been exiled to the fringe, why would they be returned to Underhill after their death? What was the purpose of it? Was it part of the curse? And why was the shapeshifter guarding this place?

"I have questions," he said out loud. "I want to understand."

His request was met with silence.

Fine.

If the shapeshifter wouldn't speak to him, Odhran would find someone who would. This was the first time in many years that he felt invested in something other than himself and his survival.

He needed answers.

Chapter 22

Alannah held the warm mug in her hands and took a deep breath. The steam filled her nose. The taste of orange blossoms lingered on her tongue. Eggs, sausage glazed with maple syrup, toast that had been dipped in custard and fried, hot cakes drizzled with butter and honey, and strawberries. A far better breakfast than Elliot's bland breakfast bars. Where did it come from when they lived in the middle of a barren forest? Then again, she had access to all kinds of food and she couldn't even go to a market.

Eletha sat across from her, sipping her own mug of tea while waiting for Elliot and Senna. Elliot showered in the other room, feeling better after Eletha's antidote, and Senna had left early that morning. Alannah asked where, but Eletha's vague answer gave nothing away. Mr. Pinkus didn't stir when Alannah first woke up and he was still slept now. Alannah would feed him when he woke.

"How long have you lived here?" Alannah asked, trying anything to break the silence.

"Forty years give or take."

Alannah stared at the crow's feet and laugh lines carved into Eletha's face. She could believe forty years, but Eletha didn't look older than that. Granted, no one in Underhill looked their true age. Alannah knew they all lived elongated lives. "Oh."

"Is that really what you want to ask me, Alannah?" Eletha put down her cup and turned her full attention to Alannah.

Alannah set down her own cup. "You're clairvoyant?"

"Yes."

"Would you know of a person who has both Fae and witch blood then?"

Eletha sighed. "If that knowledge was meant to be known, I would know it. But as it stands now, I don't. I suspect when it is revealed then I will know."

"I don't follow," Alannah said, shaking her head.

"A person like that would be kept hidden, protected. If they could be seen by a clairvoyant then that's all anyone would ever need to do to find one. Sometimes knowledge is locked away until the time for it to be revealed, and until then, it cannot be seen by anyone that is not meant to know."

"Magic is so much more than my mother told me," Alannah murmured.

Eletha nodded. "Sometimes magic is simple. Other times it is complex." Eletha took a sip of her tea. "I'm surprised you didn't ask me whether or not you would succeed."

"Will I?"

"It is a possibility. As a clairvoyant I rarely see things in absolutes. I see possibilities. Choices. That's what life, the future, is. As you make choices a future becomes more certain, but that doesn't mean it won't change."

Alannah nodded. "Do you enjoy talking in riddles?"

Eletha grinned. "Most clairvoyants do."

Alannah chuckled. "I hope I succeed. Not just for my sake—"

"But for Elliot's."

She nodded. "I hope his friends are alive and he can return to his home with them."

"Hope is good, Alannah. It will take you far," Eletha said.

A door opened and Elliot stepped out, rubbing his hair dry with a towel. He paused when he saw the table. "Damn that looks great," he said, making a beeline for them.

"I'm glad you have an appetite," Eletha said.

Elliot pulled out a chair and sat down. "Why?"

"If you didn't, then I'd be worried I didn't get all of the poison out."

Elliot swallowed. "Well...I guess it's a good thing I'm famished." He flung the towel over his shoulder. "Alannah told me you're the one who fixed me. Thank you."

"You're welcome."

The front door opened and Senna walked in. She kicked her boots off at the door. "Morning," she said, crossing the room to kiss Eletha on the cheek. "Sorry if you were waiting long."

"We weren't," Eletha reassured her. "Is the way clear?"

Senna nodded. "If we leave after breakfast, we can make it to the witches by early evening."

"We will?" Alannah asked. Her stomach sank. It was nerve-wracking to think they were so close. The fear that they wouldn't like her bubbled up. Or what if they didn't know? She would have spent nearly half her time trying to get to them only to have nothing to show for it. And there was the fact that she used her powers and she no longer knew how much time she had left.

"It will be fine, Alannah. Don't fret," Eletha said.

"I hope they know something to help me. I'm running out of time." It was one thing to think it, but once she said it out loud it really hit her how little time she had to left to complete her quest. She needed time to get there and then time to return, and she didn't think she had enough.

"We'll make it," Elliot said. "I'm sure of it."

"A lot of people are rooting for you, Alannah." Senna picked up a fork. "Now let's eat."

Why? Why me?

As soon as they dished food on their plates, Mr. Pinkus came out of the bedroom yawning. He strutted across the room and jumped in a chair beside Alannah. She put a little bit of everything on his plate.

She was so used to quiet breakfasts, but she found that she liked the liveliness of a loud breakfast. Elliot and Mr. Pinkus traded jabs; Senna sometimes joined in to tease one or the other. Eletha remained observant and quieter than the others, but her witty insight inspired a few laughs. Alannah found herself watching Eletha and Senna together. They were constantly trading small affections. Words and small touches. Senna would often lean into Eletha as she spoke. And sometimes they would stare at each other as if they were having a conversation no one else could understand.

Was this was romantic relationships were like? Was this something she would want? How would she know? Her eyes strayed to Elliot, who was currently shoving hotcakes in his mouth. A bead of syrup dripped down his chin. Alannah snorted.

He looked up at her. "What?" he mumbled, his mouth full.

She tapped her chin. "You have a little something there."

Elliot wiped his chin with his hand, stared down at the bead of syrup, and shrugged. "They're good."

He won't stay. Don't even think about it.

That's right. If she succeeded, he would leave. There would be no reason for him to stay if he could safely do so. And if his friends were alive, then there was no way he would let them leave without him. They wouldn't even be able to remain friends.

Why does that make me sad?

She finished her breakfast in silence. Knowing that even if she succeeded, she would more than likely be alone again didn't sit well with her. She wasn't sure if she would have the courage to venture back into Underhill again let alone the human realm. Would she go back to her life? Would she be happy that way? She doubted it. But would she have the courage to change it?

Elliot helped Senna clear the table after breakfast. That meant they would be leaving soon. Alannah's insides twisted itself into knots. She appreciated everyone's reassurance, but it wasn't helping as much as she would like. Her mind raced to the worst possible outcomes causing her hands to shake as she packed her bag again.

Crisp morning air made her shiver and she shoved her hands into the pockets of her sweater. With a wave goodbye to Eletha, they embarked through the wood once more. The last stretch before they entered the witch's territory. Alannah wondered what the witches would be like and what she could learn in the short amount of time she had. Was she expected? Or an unwelcome surprise?

As her nervousness mounted, so did her excitement. They twined together and made her jittery. She found herself even outpacing Elliot and Mr. Pinkus. And when they stopped for lunch—sandwiches with smoked ham and cheese, and apples—Alannah was the first one to finish.

Conversation was sparse in those hours. Alannah didn't have the fortitude to follow along. Not when her mind was so loud.

The end of the forest came faster than Alannah expected. Evening sun filtered through the gaps, and as she grew closer, she saw homes and smoke and fire. The witches. Her heart jumped and then sank down into her belly. She froze right at the edge.

Senna stopped beside her. "Are you ready?"

"No," Alannah whispered, turning to look at Senna.

"I would be surprised if you were, but it will be okay. The village is right there."

"Aren't you coming with us?" Elliot asked.

Senna shook her head. "My job was to bring you to the witches, and you're here. There's nothing more for me to do."

"What do I do? Do I just go there and tell them?" Alannah asked.

"There's no need." Senna pointed. "You're expected."

Alannah followed Senna's hand. A group of people gathered at the edge of the village. Old. Young. Children. They crowded around each other. None of them looked surprised to see her. They looked welcoming.

A middle-aged woman with bouncy coppery curls

broke away from the crowd, coming closer, but also stopping a few hundred feet from the edge of the woods. She stood close enough for Alannah to see the diadem made of braided twigs and violets that encircling her head and disappearing into the curls. Eyes as green as emeralds drew Alannah in. Her dress matched her eyes. She raised her hand—the flared sleeve falling back—and held it out to Alannah.

"Alannah Tiernan. Daughter of Aoife, daughter of Maeve." She smiled. "Welcome home."

The words washed over Alannah, making her feel warm despite the Autumn chill. Never before had someone welcomed her home. Tears gathered at the corner of her eyes and she blinked rapidly to keep them at bay. She did not want cry and made a fool of herself right now.

"You know who I am?" Alannah asked, wincing at the crack in her voice.

The woman nodded. "We heard the rumors when you first entered. And then we felt you."

"Felt me?"

"The magic in Witches End. We knew it could be no one else."

"But how did you know my mother's name and my grandmother's?"

The woman held up her hand. "You have many questions and I will answer all I can while you're with us." She gestured for Alannah to follow. "Come with me."

Alannah stepped out from the edge and then stopped. "My friends—"

"Will not be harmed here. They are safe. As are you."

Senna clapped Alannah on the shoulder and gave

her a small nudge. "Safe travels, Alannah."

"Thank you," Alannah mumbled, watching her walk back into the forest. It was a shame Senna would not be joining them. But perhaps they would meet again on the way back. She turned her gaze to Elliot. He nodded and gestured for her to follow the woman into the village. They came this far. No use in getting cold feet now.

"I am Riona Carnahan," the woman introduced herself as they began walking. "I am the priestess here."

"Does that make you the leader?" Elliot asked.

"In some respects. I lead our rituals and host our celebrations. I am often an ear to listen, a hand to guide, and a shoulder to lean on. I settle small matters. For serious matters, I hold council with our elders."

The crowd grew closer and closer. So many people. Alannah swallowed, urging her stomach to settle. Her steps slowed. "How many people live here?" she asked.

"Thirteen families. Very large ones," Riona said. Noticing Alannah's discomfort, she waved the crowd away. "You will all get to meet her, but we have preparations to finish." The crowd began to disperse, albeit begrudgingly, until only two remained.

"Preparations?" Elliot asked.

"Samhain is tomorrow. There is much to prepare. Mostly food." Riona eyes flitted to her. "Perhaps you will stay for the day and celebrate with us."

Alannah should say no. She had a time limit. A job to complete as quickly as she could. But who knew if she would get a chance like this again? She had only ever celebrated with her mother and grandmother. To celebrate with many people was a dream.

"Sounds like fun," Elliot said.

"Indeed. It is only a night," Mr. Pinkus added.

Her heart nearly burst in her chest. "I'd love to."

Riona smiled. "I'm glad." She stopped in front of the two women that had stayed. "These are my daughters. This is Niamh," –she gestured to the shortest of the two, a woman with pale skin and freckles that covered her face and neck until they disappeared into her dark brown blouse. Her eyes were the same color as Riona's and her coppery hair was pulled back into a braid— "and my youngest, Makenna."

Alannah nearly started when she saw Makenna. Hair a vibrant red—like fire—piled on top of her head in a bun and secured with a leather cord. That didn't keep hair from falling and hanging around her face and neck. Her hair wasn't as curly as her mother's. More wavy than curly. And her eyes... Alannah could scarcely believe it. One green eye, brighter than her mother's, and one purple eye, just like Alannah.

Makenna stared at Alannah with as much scrutiny. If Alannah had doubted this was her family's birthplace, she didn't now. Was it only the two of them? Were there others? Based on Makenna's surprise, she wasn't sure if there were.

"Makenna, stop staring," Riona hissed.

Makenna pulled back a little and frowned. "Well met, Alannah," she greeted, tilting her head in Alannah's direction.

"Thank you," Alannah murmured.

"Will you be staying with us?" Niamh asked.

"Of course," Riona answered. "Follow me. We'll show you where you'll be staying."

From far away, Alannah could only see the backs of the houses. Most of them were the same. Stone and wood. Gray and brown. Moss growing up some portions of the houses. Vines on others. Windows of all shapes, round, square, even a few crescents. Sloping wooden roofs and chimneys with smoke billowing from the top. Some houses were single story, but most were multiple stories.

Riona led them between two houses. Alannah wasn't sure what she expected. Something quaint and small. But the moment they emerged from between the two houses, she saw how big the village was. The houses sat in a loose circle, some close and some far, but they all faced the center of the village. A giant fire—the one she had seen from the forest—burned in the center, surrounded by long tables and benches. She guessed the setup was for the celebration tomorrow.

Despite its seemingly small size, the village was vibrant. Delicious smells came from every home. Doors and windows were flung open wide and welcoming to everyone. People moved in and out of houses, talking and carrying things, and when they saw her, they acknowledged her, smiling at her with such open expressions. It scared her a little. Made her wonder if it was genuine.

Stop that.

They turned to the left and Riona stopped at a dark wooden door with the moon phases carved into the wood. "Niamh, Makenna, please show our guests their rooms. I would like to walk with Alannah. Alone."

Chapter 23

Why did Riona want to talk to her alone? Was this a trap? Alannah couldn't help feeling nervous. Despite the warm welcome, this was Underhill and she wasn't sure if she could trust the witches either. She would have to keep her guard up until she was certain, but she nodded at Riona.

Elliot touched her shoulder. "Will you be okay?"

Alannah patted his arm. "I'll be fine."

"We won't be long," Riona reassured them. "And we'll have supper when I return and then you can rest."

Alannah waited outside with Riona while the others walked into the house. The smell of baking bread hit her the moment the door opened and her stomach growled. She hoped they would be eating that when she returned. Riona walked away from the house, away from everyone, and Alannah followed.

"When I first heard you were coming here, I was at a loss," Riona said.

Alannah's furrowed her eyebrows. "Why?"

"A person of both Fae and witch blood. I've never known such a person to exist. I didn't know how I would be able to help you and I know you have so little time before your curse kills you." Riona clasped her hands together.

Alannah's heart plummeted. "You don't know."

"I'm afraid I don't. However, that doesn't mean I can't help you."

"I don't follow."

"Do you know much about our court? Badb and Macha?" Riona asked.

"The daughters of the Morrigan. Two of the three daughters she split her powers with," Alannah answered. She didn't know much, but she knew that much. Her grandmother had told her of them.

Riona nodded. "Yes and no. She did split her powers with them. But the Morrigan only had one flesh and blood daughter."

"Neiman."

Riona smiled. "Yes. I'm glad you were told at least some of the stories." They were walking away from the main square and towards a house that sat far away from the rest. "Neiman returned her powers to the Morrigan to help seal away Reluvethel—"

"He exists?"

"Very much so. But he is gone and nothing to worry about now." Riona shook her head. "Badb and Macha remained, they are our goddesses, and have led us ever since. Well, they have tried at least. We are very fractured..." she trailed off. "I'm getting off track. They heard of your journey and sent word ahead of your arrival. I am to send you to them."

Sounds ominous.

Alannah swallowed. "Send me?"

Riona nodded. "They have the answers you seek. It's a little over a day's trek. You'll have to stop for a night, but it won't take you long to get there."

"I hope the answer is they have someone in mind," Alannah muttered.

Riona patted her shoulder. "I'm sure they'll be able to help you." They stopped in front of a two-story home. Moss had overtaken most of the stone foundation. Rotted wood warped and pulled away from the frame of the house. "Well, this is it."

"What is it?"

"This was Moirne's home. After Moirne was exiled, her mother shut herself away from us. She exiled herself." Riona sighed. "But as your only living relative, I thought you'd like to meet her. Maybe seeing you would convince her to rejoin the world."

Alannah gaped at her. "She's still alive?"

"Quite."

"How? I mean Moirne was exiled hundreds of years ago according to the journals."

"A perk of living in Underhill is elongated life. Sure, the Fae have quite the upper hand in that some of them live into the thousands, but we are catching up," Riona said.

Hundreds? Thousands? Alannah couldn't fathom so many years. What did they do with all of it? Would her mother and grandmother still be alive if they didn't live in the fringe? Why did the fringe cut their lives so short?

Riona turned the knob. Door hinges screamed from years of not being oiled or opened. She stepped through first. Alannah wasn't sure about this, but she followed. *My only living relative.* Alannah wondered what she would be like. How old would she look? Would she be as youthful as Alannah? Or would she be older? She followed Riona past a set of broken stairs and into a sitting room. Fire smoldered in the fireplace but did nothing to combat the chill in the room.

A rocking chair creaked. Alannah followed the noise to an old woman sitting in the chair. Grey hair fell around her face in a mess of stringy curls. Her fingers were curled inward, clutching something, but Alannah couldn't see what she held.

Riona knelt by the chair. "Eleanor, I've brought someone to see you."

Eleanor stared down at her lap and then her eyes darted to the window beside her. Alannah had left behind a sunny evening, but the window held the image of an ominous storm brewing in the distance.

"Go away," Eleanor wheezed.

"Her name is Alannah. She's a descendant of Moirne—"

The creaking stopped and Eleanor looked up. Her eyes were covered in a light blue film. "Come here, girl," Eleanor croaked, her voice rusty from years of disuse, beckoning Alannah forward. "Let me look at you."

Alannah slowly approached the woman. As she grew closer, Eleanor lifted her hand. She unfurled her fingers and necklace dangled from her hand. A silver chain with pendant in the shape of wolf's face. Alannah only had a second to look at it before Eleanor grabbed Alannah's chin and pulled her close.

"My poor Moirne," Eleanor murmured, her thumbs stroking Alannah's cheekbones. Her breath smelled overwhelmingly of roses. "My poor, sweet daughter—"

Alannah tried to pull away. "I'm sorry—"

"I knew she was cursed the moment I had her."

Alannah froze. "What?"

Eleanor's fingers dug into her skin. "It's those damn eyes," she muttered. "I can fix it, Moirne. Mother can fix it." Her thumbs moved up towards Alannah's eyes.

"Eleanor!" Riona shouted. "Stop—"

"She can't claim you, Moirne, I won't allow it!"

Riona's hands landed on Alannah's shoulders and she jerked Alannah out of Eleanor's reach. Alannah fell back, her fingers scrabbling against the dusty floor, coughing at the cloud that wafted into her mouth and nose. Eleanor's fingers were still outstretched. Still poised to gouge Alannah's eyes out. "What on earth is wrong with you?" Riona yelled.

Eleanor looked at Alannah. Even though she was blind, Alannah felt as if Eleanor could still see her. Not just her appearance, but *her*.

Eleanor sat back in her chair. "My Moirne didn't belong to me. And you never belonged to your mother either. I'm sure she knew that."

"What are you talking about?" Alannah asked, accepting Riona's outstretched hand so she could stand. "My mother bore me."

"Of course she did. But that doesn't mean you were ever hers." Eleanor curled her fingers around the pendant. "If Valeria's curse doesn't kill you, the other will."

Riona shook her head. "Eleanor—"

"My girl, my beautiful girl," Eleanor's sob turned into a bitter laugh. "She threw off the balance, and you —" she looked at Alannah, "you will pay for it."

"What balance?" Alannah asked.

Before Eleanor could answer, Riona intervened. "You're scaring her, Eleanor."

The woman huffed and leaned back in her rocking chair. "Leave me to die in peace, Riona. I've been trying for many years." A tear dripped down her cheek. "I want to see my Moirne again."

Riona sighed.

Eleanor looked down at the pendant before thrusting her hand in Alannah's direction. "Here, girl. An heirloom. It's all that is left of my daughter."

Alannah stared warily at the woman before taking the pendant. The tarnished silver wolf head rested in her palm. Two purples gemstones for eyes glittered in the firelight. "Thank you." *I think.*

Eleanor waved her away. "It is no gift. Now go."

Riona gently steered Alannah back outside. The door slammed shut behind them making Alannah jump.

Riona rubbed her temples. "I'm so sorry, Alannah. I didn't know she would react that way. Are you alright?"

Alannah looked down at the pendant. Her thumb smoothed over the wolf's face. "Why did she say my eyes were cursed?"

Riona looked away. "I don't know, Alannah."

I'm not sure I believe you.

***

Elliot walked into the room to find Alannah already in her pajamas and sitting on top of the brown quilted bedspread. His bed sat a few feet away from hers—separated by a bedside table—covered by the same bedspread. A mirror sat in the corner by a dresser. Sparse accommodations. He didn't mind. They wouldn't be staying long and he really only needed a place to sleep. He was happy it was in the same room as Alannah. Made him feel safer. Less lonely.

Alannah stared at the pendant in her hands. Ever since she had returned from her walk with Riona she had been quiet. More so than usual. He had expected her to bombard Riona with questions while they were here, but she ate her dinner in silence.

He sat down beside her. "So...you got to meet a relative today. That's pretty cool."

"She tried to gouge my eyes out."

What the fuck? "Well, nobody's perfect, I guess," he said.

Alannah sighed.

"I know I ask you this a lot, but are you okay?"

She set the pendant down on the bedside table. "I feel so small here, Elliot."

"What do you mean?"

Alannah tucked a piece of hair behind her ear. "At home, I knew what to do. What to expect. I had learned to not worry or think about what I couldn't control and to focus on what I could. And it was stifling, but here..." she trailed off, shaking her head. "I feel small. I have no control over anything. And I feel like there is so much going on, so many things that I wouldn't even know where to begin and every time I try to start, I'm reminded of how I don't know anything."

Elliot turned towards her, leaving one foot on the floor. "That's okay, Alannah. You're not going to know everything. That's impossible. But knowing nothing is a good place to start learning something."

Her lips parted—why was he looking at her mouth—and she let out a small laugh. "You're right again. You're pretty good at this."

He shrugged. "I did say I was better at caring for others than I am at caring for myself."

"And I've only ever really cared about myself," she said.

"Maybe we can learn something from each other then."

"It's a nice thought." Her eyebrows drew together

and she dropped her gaze. "But when this is over, you'll leave."

"Why would I—"

Oh.

That's right. If his friends were alive, and he was no longer fair game, then they would leave. There wouldn't be a reason to stay. Would there? He should want to run away when given the chance. But he found himself searching for a reason to do the opposite.

"Well, maybe I could visit. Or you could. I could show you the human realm," he suggested. "I mean think of all the food you haven't eaten. Pizza. Nachos. Potato chips. And places. There's mountains, beaches, a diner at two in the morning."

She raised an eyebrow, one corner of her mouth lifting. "Would we have time to see it all?"

His eyes drifted down to her mouth again. "I'd make time, Alannah."

He didn't know who leaned in first, but they were inches apart. A little more and he could—

"I'm exhausted, I...oh..." Mr. Pinkus paused right inside the door. "Am I interrupting?"

"No," they both answered at the same time looking everywhere but at each other.

"Uh-huh."

Elliot pushed himself up. "I'm tired too. Let's get some sleep." He walked around the bottom of Alannah's bed to his own. *I almost kissed her.* With his back to her—to hide his burning cheeks—he pulled down the blankets. He hummed under his breath, believing her capable of hearing his thudding heart in silence.

She pulled her sheets up to her chin and stared up at the ceiling. Mr. Pinkus jumped up and found a comfortable spot by Alannah's feet. Elliot briefly faced her as he reached over to the lamp on the bedside table to turn it off. He noticed her ears had turned pink. *Does she like me too?* He pulled the blankets up and stared up at the ceiling.

He cleared his throat. "Goodnight, Alannah."

"Goodnight, Elliot," she whispered.

Elliot felt eyes on him. Very large yellow eyes. He turned his head to glare at Mr. Pinkus. *Damn cat.*

Chapter 24

Dough squished between her fingers. Alannah worked the dough—kneading it against the wooden countertop—until her upper arms ached. The entirety of the trip, the fear and the hurt and the confusion, was beaten into dough.

She shaped the dough before placing it in a bowl and covering it with a towel. "Done."

"That's two in the last half hour. You're pretty good at this," Makenna said, stirring a giant bowl of batter.

Alannah shrugged. "I've always enjoyed making bread."

"Good thing you came then. Samhain always calls for a lot of bread," –Makenna turned her head to look at the kitchen table that was already covered with several baked loaves and platters of tiny cakes— "and cake." She set the bowl down on the counter to grab baking pans.

Alannah started measuring her ingredients for another batch of bread. They had been at this for about an hour. At first, Makenna refused her help but Alannah eventually stopped asking and jumped in anyway. She didn't want to stand around and do nothing, and she craved the normalcy.

Alannah had woken up before dawn and left Elliot and Mr. Pinkus to sleep past the still hours of the early morning. She hoped to catch Riona, but Riona and

Niamh had already left to finish last minute preparations for the celebration. Which meant Makenna had been left to do all of the baking herself until Alannah intervened.

She tried not to stare at Makenna every time she had a chance. It wasn't polite. But she couldn't help wondering if there was something similar about them. Why else would they share an uncommon trait?

"You're staring again," Makenna said. The teasing lilt of her voice sounded false. Something lurked underneath her tone. Guarded. Wary.

"Are you the only one?"

"The only one what?"

"With eyes like mine?"

"I could ask you the same question."

"I am the only one in my family, that I know of." Alannah paused. "Although from what Eleanor said, I'm guessing Moirne did too."

Makenna filled the molds with the batter. "Did she say what it meant? The purple eye, I mean."

Alannah shook her head. "Not really. Just that it was a curse. That Moirne didn't belong to her and I didn't belong to my mother. It didn't really make sense."

"Mother always said Eleanor wasn't the same after her daughter was exiled. Perhaps it was just…ramblings of an angry and brokenhearted woman."

"Maybe," Alannah murmured while mixing the dough. "I thought things would make sense when I came here and now…"

"It doesn't quite live up to expectations?" Makenna laughed. "I live here and sometimes I don't understand a damn thing."

"Maybe as we get older—"

"Oh, no," Makenna groaned. "Please don't open your mouth and sound like my mother."

Alannah chuckled. "Sorry."

Makenna tapped the pans against the counter before she began to move them into the hot oven. "May I ask you something?"

"Sure."

"What's it like, I mean...living in the fringe? Not being able to live in Underhill and not being able to live in the human realm."

"Lonely," Alannah blurted. Although, that probably wasn't the answer Makenna was looking for. Something more insightful perhaps. Alannah winced. "I didn't mean—"

"It's okay. I can't even imagine. None of us can," Makenna whispered, her voice soft. "Even when someone loses many of their family members, the rest of the villages is there to help. No one is ever alone, really. Although...I do understand loneliness..."

"You have your mother and your sister."

Bitter laughter burst from Makenna's mouth. "I do. I love them, I do. But I still don't...fit in. It's like everyone else is a puzzle piece and I'm the only piece that doesn't fit."

Alannah frowned. "What do you mean?"

"Everyone here is a healer or a kitchen witch or herb witch. And then there's me." Makenna closed the oven door. She held up her hand for Alannah to see. A flame flickered to life in Makenna's palm, growing into the size of an orange before Makenna closed her hand. "I am none of those things."

"Oh." Alannah had never seen magic that wasn't like hers before. Fire was hard to control. Unpredictable.

Destructive. Something she couldn't fathom using.

"I've gotten blamed for a lot of fire-related accidents over the years."

"I'm sorry."

Makenna shrugged. "I was only responsible for less than half of them. Not that it mattered, really." She sighed.

Alannah didn't know what to say. She dumped the dough onto the counter and rubbed her hands with flour. The ceiling creaked and footsteps thumped overhead which meant Elliot was awake. Which meant she would see him soon. Alannah's cheeks grew hot.

Kissing was something she had only ever read in the romance novels left behind by guests. The ones with hand painted covers of men holding women in a tender embrace. Alannah had never kissed anyone. Nor had she ever thought about it before. At least, not until Elliot had leaned close last night while staring at her mouth. That she definitely thought about. And then dreamed about it. Now she was thinking of it again. Whether or not he really was going to. Whether or not she wanted him to.

I wouldn't hate it.

Elliot came down the stairs, hair still mussed from sleep. A yawn escaped his mouth. When he reached the bottom of the stairs, his eyes darted to meet hers. His cheeks turned pink and he looked at Makenna instead. Mr. Pinkus trotted down the stairs behind him.

"Morning," Elliot said, walking into the main room. His eyes traveled over the kitchen table. "You've been busy."

"Are you hungry?" Makenna asked. "Mother left breakfast on the stove."

"What is it?"

"Oatmeal."

Elliot walked into the kitchen, his arm brushing against her back as he moved past her. Her heartbeat stuttered and then picked up pace. If he was affected as she was, he didn't show it.

"Morning, Alannah," he murmured.

"Good morning, Elliot," she said, trying to keep her voice as even as possible. "How did you sleep?"

"Pretty good."

She nodded.

Elliot grabbed the towel and lifted the lid from the cast iron pot on the stove. He took a deep breath through his nose. "Brown sugar and cinnamon?"

"Good nose." Makenna pointed to a stack of bowls beside the counter. "Help yourself."

Elliot filled his bowl almost to the top. "My mother used to make it like this. She would also put raisins or cranberries in it when we had them."

"Do you like it the same way?" Makenna asked.

"I prefer bananas over raisins, and cranberries are okay." Mr. Pinkus walked up behind him and stretched up Elliot's leg. "What?"

"Would you put some in a bowl for me?" the cat asked.

"Why can't you?" Elliot teased.

Mr. Pinkus sniffed. "Because while I got all the brains, you got all the thumbs."

Elliot chuckled and grabbed another bowl. He filled it halfway and set it on the floor. "There."

"Thank you."

Elliot blew on a spoonful to cool it before taking a bite. "Can I help with anything?" he asked, still chewing.

"You could swallow before asking," Alannah said, pressing her knuckles into the dough.

"Ha ha."

"Have you two been together long?" Makenna asked, grabbing a jar of honey from a shelf.

"A month? Maybe a little longer," Alannah answered while trying to calculate the time in her head.

"Oh? You seem well suited. Do you think you'll get married?"

Elliot choked on a spoonful of oatmeal. "Married?"

Makenna looked between, her wide-eyed expression matching theirs. "Yes. Do humans not have marriage customs anymore?"

Elliot coughed. "We do, but Alannah and I aren't *together* together, we travel together. Well, we sort of live together but only because she saved my life from some asshole and he said I couldn't leave or he'd kill me so obviously I stayed—"

"We're not together in that way," Alannah added.

Makenna nodded along, not looking altogether convinced. "Oh," she sounded disappointed. "I thought for sure you were courting. My mistake."

Elliot turned his back to them, eating his oatmeal in silence, but she could see the red tinge of his ears. He said a lot to make sure Makenna knew they weren't together. And he seemed embarrassed now. Was he embarrassed of her? Of the thought of courting her? Or did it bother him? Alannah had never asked him if he had someone in the human realm. Perhaps he did and he was upset at the notion of betraying them.

Alannah smacked the dough against the counter, making everyone jump. "Sorry," she grumbled. Why was this even bothering her? It's not like she had feelings for him, with the exception of tentative friendship. Right?

Elliot set his bowl in the sink. "Do you need my help?" he asked.

"There's plenty of apples to peel and chop. We'll need them for the hand pies," Makenna answered pointing to a wooden barrel sitting under the kitchen window that was filled to the brim with red and green apples. "Save some the prettier ones for bobbing."

Alannah chuckled. "Pies too?"

Makenna began to collect the dirty dishes to wash. They were running low. "Did I forget to mention that?"

"Maybe a little."

"Oops." Makenna shrugged. "There's much to remember. It's hard to keep track."

"What still needs done?" Alannah asked, setting the last bread dough in a bowl to rise.

"The cakes need icing, need to make the pie dough, and we need to start baking the bread. Thank goodness we have more than one stove," Makenna sighed and swiped her forehead with her arm.

"I can start the pie dough. By the time I'm done it'll be time for the bread to go in," Alannah said.

"I know I refused your help at first but thank you for doing it anyway. I would've been here forever trying to get it all done."

"I'm glad to. I love baking for the holidays. It was one of the few activities my mother and I did together."

"Mine too," Elliot chimed in. "My mom loved cookies though. She wasn't great at making pies. The crust was either raw or burnt."

"You two are lucky. For the last few years, I've been doing most of the baking myself. I do a lot of things around here myself," she said with a bitter tone.

"Your sister doesn't help?" Elliot asked.

"Not anymore. Eventually, as the firstborn daughter, she will take my mother's place as priestess. And she's "too busy training" to help now," Makenna spat, rolling her eyes. "I love her, but I swear she loves to use it as an excuse so she doesn't have to do the busy work."

Alannah shook her head. "I used to wish for a sister."

"Would you like mine?" Makenna deadpanned.

Alannah snorted. "Not if she doesn't like busy work. That's all there is back at home."

"I want to go on an adventure," Makenna sighed wistfully. "It would be nice to not have to bake bread and pull weeds every day. I'm a little envious of you, Alannah."

"Why?"

"You left your home and embarked on an adventure. I wish I had that kind of courage."

"I don't know if I'd call it that," Alannah mumbled.

"It is. It's not easy leaving behind what's familiar for what's unknown," Makenna argued. "Maybe one day I will as well."

***

"Don't move, I don't want to burn you," Makenna muttered, her teeth digging into her bottom lip while she concentrated.

Alannah stayed very still. Heat emanated from the porcelain rod Makenna held. The rod that hovered precariously close to her face. Makenna wrapped a strand of Alannah's hair around the rod, let it sit for a few seconds, and then undid it. The warm curl bounced against Alannah's cheek before settling around her face.

"This is not something I would imagine using one's power for," Alannah commented.

Makenna grinned. "Might as well make some use of it and have the best hair in the village."

Alannah snorted.

Makenna curled the last strand and stepped back, setting the rod down in a bowl of water to cool. "Let's see," she said, her eyes looking Alannah up and down. "Not bad. But I think we should go softer." She grabbed a brush.

Alannah never had a reason to dress up at home. She dressed for comfort and whatever job she had at hand. Even on holidays she was usually too tired from preparations that dressing up wasn't important. Especially when it was only her and her mother. But Makenna had insisted.

When all the baking had been finished, shortly after lunch, Makenna had pulled Alannah upstairs to get ready. Alannah scrubbed her skin pink and then soaked in warm water and lavender petals until she almost fell asleep. She was so tired. All the time. Especially after using her powers in Witches End.

Makenna had laid out a dress for Alannah to wear. Part of Alannah knew she should refuse. They were already so hospitable, it felt like taking advantage. But the rich royal blue fabric felt so soft against her fingers and before she had another thought, she slipped it on. The bodice hugged her perfectly without feeling too tight. She pulled the thin straps over her shoulder to secure it. The straight neckline ended right below her collarbone. Alannah found herself doing a spin to feel the skirt skim her ankles. The dress glittered in the light even though she couldn't find any jewels. Another perk of magic.

"Are you sure it's alright that I wear the dress?" Alannah asked, while Makenna brushed her hair.

"I wouldn't have left it out for you if it wasn't." Makenna set the brush down. "Besides, I thought you might like to dress up while you're here. It doesn't seem like you do often."

"Try never."

"Well," –Makenna held out her hands— "you might now."

Alannah placed her hands in Makenna's and let herself be led out of the chair and to a mirror. She gasped. "Wow. I love it." Her hair fell in soft waves down her back. A tendril brushed her cheek and she tucked it behind her ear.

Makenna sat on the bed and met Alannah's gaze in the mirror. "I was going to do makeup too, but it tends to run when you sweat. And we do a lot dancing."

"Samhain was always more of a somber celebration with my mother. Said it was to honor the dead."

"Well, it is, but it's a celebration of them too. And of life. Celebrations should be fun." Makenna adjusted her black dress—the style was the same but she had a sweetheart neckline and far more cleavage—before standing up. "Are you ready?"

Alannah smiled, marveling at the way her eyes lit up. "I am."

Chapter 25

Music filled the cool night air. The bonfire roared in the middle of the village. Bodies danced around it, barefoot, with hands flung skyward. Alannah saw Makenna in the thick of them. She danced with a man that was around her age with dark hair and dark eyes. Even though Makenna looked as if she was having fun, he looked like he was having even more. Alannah's eyes moved past them to search the others out. Riona and Niamh sat at one of the tables with a small group of more mature people. Possibly the council she had spoken about. Niamh alternated between listening with rapt attention and looking at the man dancing with Makenna. The longer she stared the more her lips pressed into a thin line and her eyes narrowed.

Jealousy, maybe.

Alannah sipped her mead. The taste of crisp apples and honey made the mead go down smoothly. The alcohol helped her relax—she had started the celebration tense—but she had done little more than sit on a bench and eat and drink. Her eyes searched for Elliot and found him dancing not far from Makenna, surrounded by quite a few of the younger women. They were taking turns dancing with him.

That should be me.

"What are you doing?" Mr. Pinkus asked, jumping

onto the bench beside her.

"Drinking."

He sighed. "I mean why aren't you over there with everyone else?"

"Because I'm drinking here."

"You should be having fun, like Elliot."

Alannah looked over at him again and made eye contact. Her face flushed and she looked away. "I'm glad they're treating him well here."

"You're deflecting," Mr. Pinkus accused.

"I don't want to make a fool of myself." She downed the rest of her mead. It was her third or maybe fourth cup, she wasn't quite sure. But it left her feeling pleasantly warm. "And besides, what if no one wants to dance with me?"

"I know of at least one person who does," Mr. Pinkus muttered.

The song changed. A woman's voice joined in. This was the kind of celebration she had always imagined. Dreamed of. Now she had a chance to apart of a dream and she couldn't even bring herself to join in. *I'm wasting my chance.* Alannah poured more mead into her cup and took a gulp. A little more and she might find some courage.

"Alannah!" Makenna pushed through the bodies, making her way to Alannah. Her hand reached for Alannah. "Come on!"

"I don't—"

Makenna didn't hearing any of the excuses Alannah tried to give. Her hand snatched the cup from Alannah's hand and set it on the table before grabbing both of Alannah's hands and pulling her up from the bench. "Come dance." It wasn't a suggestion.

"I don't know the steps!"

"There are no steps, Alannah," Makenna laughed and tugged her close. "We feel the music and move."

To call Alannah clumsy was an understatement. She tried to follow and mimic the others, but the movements felt strange and unnatural. Her feet didn't go where she wanted them and she found herself stumbling more than dancing.

"You're trying to feel what everyone else is!" Makenna shouted over the music.

"What am I supposed to feel?"

Makenna snagged a scarf from the man she had been dancing with before. Before Alannah could protest, she covered Alannah's eyes and tied the scarf. "Just listen, Alannah, and dance."

"I'm going to fall into the fire like this," Alannah complained.

Makenna giggled. "No one will let that happen." Makenna—at least, she hoped it was Makenna—grabbed her hands once more and pulled her into a spin. "Now, let's try again."

With nothing but the feeling of Makenna's hands, the earth underneath her feet, and the music in her ears, Alannah began to sway. The song was in a language that she didn't know but still felt familiar. She felt the drumbeats under her feet and in her chest. Her heart thumped in time to the song. Her feet followed, clumsily at first, but as she kept moving, she became more confident.

Until Makenna let go of her hands.

Alannah reeled at the loss of contact and stability. She spun in a circle, unmoored in a sea she didn't know. Hands grabbed hers again and she breathed a sigh of relief.

"Makenna?"

"Rowan."

"Oh, nice to meet you."

"Likewise."

His hands left her and another took his place. They would dance with her for a minute and then hand her off to someone else. Her heart jumped every time. She couldn't see them and she worried that someone might take advantage. But all offered their names.

"Caoimhe."

"Rian."

"Siobhan."

"Donnchad."

Names she could connect to faces later.

Another person—Grainne—let her go and hands she had come to know well, took their place. Fingers interlaced without a second thought. Elliot pulled her closer, one hand moving to her waist. They danced like in sync as if it was second nature to them. The steps came easily. He didn't pass her to anyone else.

"I see you're finally having fun," he teased.

"Just when I can't see anything."

The hand left her waist and she felt the knot loosen on the scarf before it drifted down. "Better?"

Strange to be surrounded by people, but only see one person. Elliot held her close—the fire reflected in his eyes—and it struck her how much she would miss him. He had shown an understanding and wisdom that she never would have expected. And he was comforting. Kind. Caring. She didn't want him to leave.

"What if you stayed?" she blurted out, unable to catch the words and swallow them back down in time.

The music stopped, and so did he. "What?"

Red creeped up her neck. "What if you stayed...with me...and Mr. Pinkus. I..." she trailed off, not knowing what to offer to convince him. It's not as if she had much.

Another song started, but Elliot didn't move. He gawked at her. *Say something.* His eyebrows furrowed. *Anything.* He opened his mouth, but then he closed it again.

Oh no.

Alannah dropped his hand and stepped back out of his grasp. "Sorry, I must've had too much to drink."

"Alannah—"

"It's fine. It was a bad idea anyway."

She turned on her heels before he could say anything—or nothing—and marched away from the crowd as quickly as she could. She walked past the tables and past Mr. Pinkus. The air grew colder the further away she moved from the fire. She didn't stop until she found a place the fire didn't reach in-between Riona's house and another's. *What am I thinking?* Alannah slumped against the wood exterior and covered her face with her hands. Hot cheeks burned against her palms.

"Is something the matter?"

The irritatingly familiar voice made her jump. He shouldn't be here. This place wasn't for the Fae. And yet here he was. *Odhran.* Alannah dropped her hands to glare at him. "What do you want?"

He stood only a foot in front of her, his hands clasped behind his back. "To check your progress."

"My progress is none of your concern."

"Do you think it wise to linger here?"

Alannah huffed. "What do you want, Odhran?"

"Clarity."

"Of what?" Alannah shook her head, not understanding.

"You."

"What about me?"

Odhran sighed and ran his fingers through his hair. If she didn't know any better, she'd say he was nervous. "You asked me why I'm helping you and the truth is, I don't know. My sisters pushed me at first and I hired Senna. I was going to wash my hands of it afterwards."

"But you didn't."

"You are oddly compelling to me."

"Is that supposed to be a compliment?"

Odhran looked away from her. "Being Valeria's son, I have always been treated with a certain amount of... respect, my sisters are an exception to this of course. But even if someone doesn't like me personally, they do me the courtesy of talking behind my back."

Alannah rolled her eyes. "And?"

"And there it is." He turned his gaze to her again. "You are defiant. Stubborn. Strong-willed. You make me feel uncertain," –he took a step closer— "unsteady. I don't know what to make of it. Of you."

Alannah had her back against the wall and Odhran stalked closer. Too close. She swallowed. "You don't need to make anything of me. It would be better if you didn't think of me at all."

He placed his hands on either side of her head. "I've tried. To no avail. Trust me, I do not want to think of you, Alannah. I've never had much use for those kinds of thoughts."

She swallowed. "Those kinds?"

"Perhaps if I give in, sate my curiosity, then I won't

think of you at all."

"I don't think—"

"Would you allow me to bed you, Alannah? It could benefit us both."

The request took a moment to register. Why would...and why would he think...what the fuck? "You—"

"I could rid myself of you in my thoughts and you would be rid of me in turn."

She gaped at him, still processing what he said. Did this make sense to him? Truly? Her blood grew hot—boiling even—and her heart pounded in her ears. "Just when I think you couldn't possibly be more vile...more disgusting, you—"

He kissed her. A hand cupped her face, thumb grazing her cheekbones. The other pushed her hair over her shoulder. Despite his quick action, the kiss was surprisingly gentle as if he was unsure of what he was doing. She wouldn't have expected that from him, but it still pissed her off.

The smack echoed in between the houses. She had never hit someone before. And she didn't like how it felt.

Odhran stepped back. His cheek pink. The outline of her hand faint against his pale skin. The look on his face...she didn't think she had ever seen him look devastated before. Or vulnerable. And it didn't last. As quickly as it had slipped, the mask was back and he looked at her with cool indifference.

"I'm sorry—"

"Why? You said you found me vile, I should've believed you."

"Do you really expect me to think anything else of

you? After what you've done, how could I?"

He frowned. "I hardly think a few pranks could warrant—"

Her laugh was abrupt. Sharp. Short-lived. "Pranks! Destroying my mother's flowers was in no way a prank."

"They were just flowers."

She felt the fire under her skin again. "They were all that remained of her. But of course, I shouldn't expect someone like you to understand."

"What does that mean?"

"Someone as cruel and as heartless as his own mother. Someone who has no idea what it's like to lose everything." She took a step forward and he took a step back. "Do you have any idea what it was like to wake up in the morning and try to find a reason to go on only to find nothing? To be alone. Unseen. Unknown."

"Alannah—"

She took another step and this time she trapped him. His back against the wooden siding. "Have you any idea what it was like to watch my mother waste away. To watch her draw a breath and never exhale again. To strip her and clean her and use all of my strength to carry her to edge and to wake up to her gone because I wasn't even allowed to bury her. I smelled her on my clothes and heard her voice in my head and the only comfort I had were those damn flowers."

"I'm sorry, I—"

She laughed. "You're sorry? Those words mean nothing coming from you." She shook her head. "Your mother punished the entirety of my family because she was hurt. She made sure we would always be alone. She laid down her curse—her justice—and I'm sure she laughed as she laughed at me in her court. You are cut from the same cloth and I'm supposed to believe you're sorry?"

"I didn't know—"

"I was being punished enough. And because I dared to save a person from death you thought I deserved more punishment and pain," she whispered. "Not knowing doesn't excuse you, Odhran. It doesn't mean you can be horrible and cruel and you were. You are."

He stood silent. Frozen. The mask slowly slipping away once more, but she had no interest in seeing what lived underneath. She had seen enough. Alannah stepped back. This was not the night she had envisioned. Ruined by her blunder and then by him. She should not have stayed. *It was a mistake. This was a mistake.* Alannah turned her back to him.

He drew in a shaky breath. "Alannah—"

She paused and looked over her shoulder. "Selanna was wrong. There is nothing redeemable about you."

The sharp intake of breath almost made her pause. Perhaps it her words had surprised him. Or maybe she had even finally said something that hurt him. Although she doubted mere words would be able to reach him.

Alannah didn't want to go back to the celebration. She wanted to sleep. To hasten the morning so she could leave. She turned to the right to enter Riona's house and stopped at the sight of someone sitting in a rocking chair beside the door. It wasn't Elliot, much to her relief. Makenna was sitting there with a bottle of spiced wine in her lap and a cloth bundle.

"Some people can be real asses," Makenna said, standing up.

"Were you waiting for me?" Alannah asked.

Makenna shrugged. "Perhaps." She gestured for Alannah to follow her inside.

The door closed behind them, muffling the sounds of the celebration. Makenna walked up the stairs and led Alannah into her room. The house was so quiet in comparison. Makenna set the bundle down on her bed and the wine on the bedside table.

"You don't have to keep me company," Alannah said.

"I have had thirty-five Samhains and I will have many more." Makenna patted a spot on the deep purple bedspread. "Besides, you wanted to know what sisters are like. Sisters sneak away from parties to drink. When they're not arguing, of course."

Alannah sat down. "Would you like to argue first?"

"I imagine you don't have much arguing left in you after that."

Alannah pressed her lips into a thin line. "You heard?"

Makenna grabbed the bottle and uncorked it. "Heard. Saw. Was going to interfere, but you seemed to have handle on it." She took a sip and handed it to Alannah.

"He is arrogant," Alannah sneered, taking a drink.

"It would seem so."

"And rude and awful. And he really thought I would go to bed with him!" She took another sip and gave the bottle back.

"What a jerk." Makenna glanced at her. "He certainly riles you up."

"In a way no one else ever has. I don't like it," Alannah admitted. "I'm not the most positive person, but that doesn't mean I like being so…angry."

Makenna hummed in agreement. Her fingers tapped at the bottle before she shifted closer to Alannah. "Was the kiss nice at least?"

"What!"

Makenna leaned back. "That bad, huh."

"No. I mean, yes. I don't know. Are you supposed to rate them?"

"If he wasn't an asshole, would you have liked it?" Makenna asked instead.

Maybe? It wasn't terrible. She didn't think. It's not she had another experience to compare it to. The longer it took for her to answer the more Makenna grinned. She should've said no right away. It was better than thinking about it. Why was she even thinking about it?

She shook her head and reached for the bottle. "Let's talk about something else."

She didn't want to spend another second thinking about Odhran and the not-awful, ill-timed kiss.

***

Odhran slumped against the side of the house. He exhaled slowly and pinched the bridge of his nose. *What was I thinking?* He shook his head. He didn't even come here to see her and yet when he did, he floundered like a bumbling fool. And the way she had looked at him? He shuddered. He wasn't well liked, but never before had someone looked at him like he was pond scum. *And I kissed her.* Odhran touched his fingertips to his lips.

If only she liked it as he had.

But he was vile. Disgusting. Irredeemable. There was possibly no coming back from this. If there was a chance to show her he wasn't terrible, he blew it.

"Well, this is a surprise."

Odhran met Riona's gaze. She didn't look displeased

to see him, but the tension in her shoulders told him she was guarded. Despite what he told Alannah, Riona was the reason he came. She was a gifted witch. Even many of the Fae knew. There were whispers that she would help anyone who came to her. Odhran hoped that extended to him.

He drew himself up to his full height and tilted his head at her. "I hope this is not a bad time."

"That depends on why you're here."

Odhran reached into his pocket and her fingers flexed as if to prepare herself for an attack, but he pulled a clump of dead flowers from his pocket. The same clump Alannah had thrown at him. He held it out to the priestess and she furrowed her eyebrows in confusion. Taking the clump in her hands, she frowned down at it. She tapped the excess dirt from the roots and inspected them.

"I was hoping you could revive it," he said.

"May I ask why?"

"I...made an error. Many errors. I would like to correct it if I can."

Riona looked back up at him. "Strange."

"What is?"

"Your request. Especially from a child of Valeria. I never would have expected her children to know when they've done wrong and try to apologize for it. Especially for someone your mother's cursed."

"How did you know?"

She smiled. "All magic has a signature. I know her family's magic and it is woven into the roots. Although, you did a damn near perfect job of destroying it."

His shoulders dropped. "You can't save it?"

"I might. I cannot guarantee anything, but since

you are sincere in your request, I will give it a try."

"I…thank you. Name your price and—"

She held up her hand. "All I ask is that you keep on this path, Odhran. There is no reason for us to remain enemies and I am hoping that bonds can be created between us."

Ah, yes, because I'm good at that. He nodded. "I will… certainly try."

Perhaps I can start with Alannah.

Chapter 26

Her head pulsated behind her eyes. She didn't even want to open them. Quiet snores filled the room, but they weren't Elliot's or Mr. Pinkus'. Alannah cracked one eye open. The room was dark, but she could see Makenna's silhouette clearly. They must've fallen asleep after finishing the bottles and the cakes that Makenna had snuck away from the party. Must be why the inside of her mouth felt coated in a film. She swallowed, tried to, but her throat felt dry and cracked.

Headache. Dry throat. She rolled over, careful not to disturb Makenna, and her stomach protested. Nauseous.

Is this what a hangover felt like?

Alannah pushed the covers off. Sweaty clothes clung to her skin, from sleeping right next to Makenna or fever, but a cool breeze made her sigh in relief. She should get up and find medicine. There was bound to be something in a healer's house, but Alannah couldn't make herself get up.

Her eyes closed.

Bright sun warmed the room to an unbearable temperature. Or maybe it was just her. Alannah drew in a breath. Sweat dripped from her forehead, but she shivered. A blessedly cool cloth covered her forehead. A hand moved across her upper back. *Elliot.* Alannah blinked up at him. He gently pulled her upright. Another hand—Makenna's—brought a warm cup to Alannah's chapped lips. She didn't want to drink something warm it would only make her hotter, and she was already burning up.

"It will make you feel better," Makenna reassured.

Elliot took the cup from Makenna's hands. "Please drink, Alannah."

They weren't going to let her go back to sleep if she didn't. Her protests didn't make it out of her mouth. She took a tentative sip. The mint overwhelmed whatever else swirled in the cup, and the sharp aftertaste wasn't pleasant either. She grimaced.

Elliot laid her back down against the pillows and Alannah's eyes immediately closed.

"She was feeling fine last night. What happened?" Elliot asked.

"Has she been feeling tired?" Riona's voice came from far away.

"Yeah, but we both have."

"I'm afraid this means her time it's..." Riona hesitated. "It's running short."

"We're not even halfway. How can this be happening now?"

"She used her powers. It's hard to say how much time that took. But it will only get worse from here."

"The medicine will get her up on her feet," Makenna chimed in. "The goddesses might have something for her when you make it to the court."

"Let her rest now. We'll make sure you're prepared to the leave the moment she's ready," Riona said.

Alannah felt sleep calling at her. If they were right then she couldn't afford to sleep, but she couldn't make herself get up either. She shivered again. Weight gently settled onto her chest. Cloth tickled her chin. A low purr filled her ears. Fingers brushed hair from her forehead.

"Don't worry, Alannah. I will get you there."

Oh, Elliot.

The third time she woke, she woke alone. Damp sheets clung to her skin. She felt gross. Alannah pushed the blankets off and sat up. Her arms shook under her weight. This was bad. Very bad. How would she reach the court like this? The door opened and she looked up.

"You're awake," Makenna said, stepping into the room with a pitcher and cup in her hand. "How are you feeling?"

"Awful." Alannah's voice cracked.

Makenna poured a cup of water and handed it to Alannah. "This should help."

The water soothed her aching throat. She held the cup in her hands while Makenna poured more water into the cup. "How long was I out?" Alannah asked.

"It's almost noon so a few hours."

Alannah groaned. "So much time wasted."

Makenna rested her hand on Alannah's forearm. "There was no way you were leaving in that state."

"It's going to get worse. How am I going to make it?" Alannah whispered.

"I packed more medicine for you. You dissolve it in water. It will help you get there." Makenna sighed. "I am hoping the goddesses will have something more for you."

"Me too."

"I've left a change of clothes in the washroom for you. The water will be cold, but that might make you feel better."

"Thank you, Makenna."

Makenna set the pitcher down on the bedside table and turned to leave the room. She paused in the open doorway with her head angled in Alannah's direction. "I believe you will succeed, Alannah," she said before leaving the room.

You and everyone else.

Alannah sighed and downed the rest of her water. With shaky hands, she pushed herself to the edge of the bed and swung her legs to the floor. Moving felt like dragging around dead weight. It seemed impossible to move forward from here. That was probably the point. And if she were alone, she might have given up now. Accepted that she made a terrible decision. But Elliot's life, and the truth of what happened to his friends, hinged on her success. She would get to the court if she had to crawl there.

The cold water invigorated her and washed away the layer of sweat. She stood under the spray after she had finished washing—a monumental task given how much it hurt to raise her arms—and took a moment to steel herself for the next leg of the journey.

With shaky hands, she managed to button every button and pull her hair back into a ponytail. Alannah stared at the dress she had hung on the back of the door. A shame she wouldn't get to wear it again. She pulled it down and folded it over her arm. Did she have time to wash it? Probably not, but she didn't want to leave it like this. Alannah walked back into Makenna's room to strip the bed only to find it already done.

Alannah leaned heavily on the wall as she walked down the stairs. Everyone waited in the kitchen. Elliot and Mr. Pinkus sat at the table, the plates in front of them untouched much to her surprise. Were they waiting for her? Riona stood at the stove while Makenna and Niamh packed food into satchels.

"Feeling better?" Riona asked.

"A little," Alannah lied not wanting them to feel bad. Or feel sorry. But none of them looked like they believed her. She walked into the kitchen and held out the dress to Makenna. "Thank you for letting me wear it."

Makenna smiled and took it from her hands. "It was perfect on you."

"Make sure to eat plenty, Alannah. You'll need your strength," Riona said, gesturing to the chair beside Elliot.

Alannah sat down. The food looked delicious—eggs, bacon, and toast with raspberry jam—but it also made her stomach flip. She swallowed hard. A mug of steaming tea sat to the left of the plate. It smelled similar to the same tea from earlier.

"Drink the tea first," Makenna instructed.

She reached for it and took a tentative sip. With no bitter aftertaste, Alannah downed the tea in less than a minute. Her stomach settled almost instantly making the food a little more appetizing. Everyone had their eyes on her. It unsettled her. Made her uncomfortable. She picked up her fork and speared a piece of egg.

"You can have mine too if you need it," Elliot said.

"I'm okay, Elliot," she reassured. "I'm fine. Eat."

The somber atmosphere left no room for conversation. Only the sound of utensils scraping against porcelain. Alannah cleared her plate, knowing she would never hear the end of it from Elliot and Mr. Pinkus if she didn't. They were worried. Hell, she was worried too.

Riona wouldn't hear of her helping to clean up.

They had to leave. Alannah didn't want to. And if she didn't have to worry about a damn quest, she would've stayed. She sat on the stairs and pulled on her boots. Her fingers shook as she tried to lace them. Elliot knelt in front of her to do it.

"Thank you," she murmured.

"You're welcome."

When Alannah stood up, Makenna pulled her into a hug. "Come back and see us."

"I would like that," Alannah said into Makenna's hair.

Niamh's goodbye was more formal and reserved. After all, they hardly spent any time together.

With their backpacks on their backs and a satchel of food in hand, Alannah and Elliot followed Riona outside. Mr. Pinkus trailed behind them. Riona led them outside of the village.

"You will need to rest for the night, but you don't have to worry about being bothered," Riona said, stopping past Eleanor's house. She pointed to the northwest. "It is a straight shot from here. If you make good time, you will be there by tomorrow evening."

"Thank you for everything, Riona," Alannah said.

Riona put her hands on Alannah's shoulders. "You're welcome back anytime. All of you are. For a visit or even to stay if you like." She squeezed Alannah's shoulders. "This can be your home."

Something worth considering if Alannah succeeded. She wouldn't be alone anymore if she came back. She nodded and Riona let her go. With that, Alannah turned her back on the village and began to walk. There was a sense of relief in knowing they wouldn't be bothered. The assassins wouldn't stray here. Getting back to Valeria would be another story.

Alannah started off strong, but after lunch, her energy begin to wane. She should've taken some medicine at lunch, but she thought it could wait until they stopped for the night. She had miscalculated. Every step became harder than the last. She stumbled over roots and small rocks. Her head spun. No one said anything, but Elliot slowed his pace. She was holding everyone back, costing them time, all because she had to use her powers. All because she stayed in the village a day longer than she should've. How selfish of her.

They walked for another hour before Elliot stopped. "Maybe we should stop for the night."

"Really? It's still so early," she said.

"I'm not sure you're going to make it farther without stopping."

"I can make it."

"You're unwell," Mr. Pinkus chimed in. "If you push too hard you won't make it at all."

She sighed. "Maybe for a short. I can drink some medicine and then we can go a little further."

Elliot and Mr. Pinkus shared a look. Apparently, they reached an unspoken agreement because they both nodded. "We'll take a break, but if it still looks like you need rest then we're camping here for the night."

She nodded, knowing she wasn't going to get a better deal. She shrugged her backpack from her shoulders before sitting down on a tree stump.

Elliot sat down across from her and watched her unscrew her water bottle and pour in some of the powder Makenna had made for her. Alannah closed the bottle and shook it to dissolve the powder. With the water being cold some of it stayed clumped together. She swallowed it down quickly, grimacing at the texture.

"What do you think it will be like?" Elliot asked.

"Hm?" She closed the bottle.

"Meeting the goddesses. It must be exciting for you."

"It's a little scary actually. I don't know what to expect," Alannah admitted, placing the bottle back into her bag.

"I'm sure it will be fine," Mr. Pinkus piped up.

They sat in silence. Not once had he mentioned what she had said the night before. Perhaps he was trying to forget it. She was. Mostly because she doubted she would like the answer and she didn't want to ruin anything between them. He could be her first friend besides Mr. Pinkus. She would like that.

Minutes ticked by and Alannah felt a tiny bit better. She stood up. "Let's go. I'd like to cover a little more ground before we stop."

They trailed behind her, watching her for the first sign of exhaustion. The medicine helped her for an hour then her energy began to wane again. Alannah yawned but pushed on. Despite her exhaustion, they walked until the sun began to sink below the horizon.

Elliot wouldn't let her help make camp. She sat off to the side, her fingers in Mr. Pinkus' fur while Elliot made the fire. Flames blazed to life. Warmth spread to her toes and first and then up to her chest. She sighed. Elliot sat down next to her, opening the satchel of food. Makenna and Niamh had packed leftover bread and hand pies, as well as meats, cheeses, dried fruits, and nuts. *Simple. Perfect.* Anything heavier and Alannah didn't think her stomach would handle it.

She picked at the food and drank more tea. While

the silence saved them from having any awkward conversations, she found herself missing the ease at which they conversed before she had suggested something so awful.

Elliot tied the satchels closed and stored them in his backpack. "Feeling okay?"

A yawn caught her by surprise and she did her best to muffle it in her hand while she nodded. She wasn't excited to sleep on the ground again. Still, she laid back and stared up at the twinkling lights overhead. Were they the same lights Elliot saw in his home? Or were they different? What else was different? It would be exciting to find out.

Elliot laid down beside her. Mr. Pinkus moved in-between them and sat down near her shoulder. There were no ominous sounds in the distance or shadows that scared her. The only sounds were the crackling fire and their combined breathing.

"I am proud of you, Alannah," Mr. Pinkus said abruptly.

"Why?"

"For coming this far. For being brave and taking a chance. I know your grandmother would be proud too."

She turned her head to look at him. "I couldn't have done it without you. Both of you."

He sighed. "I wasn't that much help. Not in this form."

She scratched behind his ears. "Nonsense."

"I think...I think I'd like to tell you why I am in this form," he said.

Her interest piqued, but he sounded unsure. "You don't have to if you don't want to."

"I do, Alannah. I promise." He cocked his head to the

side. "I know a fair deal about humans because...I fell in love with a human."

"Really?" Elliot asked, rolling onto his side and propping his chin up with his hand.

"Really. Her name was Fia and she was wonderful. Kind. Caring. Open. We met in the forest often. I showed her what I could of our world and she showed me what she could of hers. I truly believed that we would be together against all odds, and there were many."

Alannah tucked a piece of hair behind her ear. "Like what?"

"Well, it wasn't allowed for one thing. Living in her world would've been difficult for me. Too long in the human realm would be difficult for any of the Fair Folk. And there is the fact that she would grow old and die and I wouldn't for a long time."

"That sucks," Elliot said.

"That's the price of loving someone from Underhill. You have to accept that they will greatly outlive you. And they have to accept that they will lose you." Mr. Pinkus' tailed twitched. "It doesn't mean the love wouldn't be worth it. I certainly believed it was."

"What happened to her?" Alannah asked.

He took a moment. She didn't think he would answer at first, but he sighed. "She came into the forest to meet me, but I was late. She was captured. I was a part of Valeria's court, mostly because of my friendship with Selanna, and I was able to set Fia free. But I was found out. Fia escaped, and this was my punishment."

Tears gathered in the corner of her eye. Valeria wasn't only horrible to her. It wasn't a surprise, but it still upset her. "Did you ever see Fia again?"

"No. I made it to the fringe but that's as far as I got.

That's when your grandmother found me and nursed me back to health."

The tears spilled over and she sniffed. Mr. Pinkus rubbed his cheek on hers. "You don't have to cry for me, Alannah. I have treasured my years as your companion and friend. And I will see my Fia again."

She reached for him and tugged him close, much like she used to when she was a child. He purred as she did so and he curled up against her chest. How could she ever have doubted him? He was her best friend when he couldn't speak, and he was still her best friend now. Alannah kissed him on top of his head.

***

Elliot watched her sleep, looking for any sign that her fever was returning, but so far, she seemed alright. Her chest moved up and down with deep breaths. The fire still blazed, mostly because he kept sitting up to put another log on. He didn't want her to get cold. *What if you stayed?* She had asked him that and he it had floored him. Left him struggling to find an answer he didn't have. What if he stayed? One of the reasons he came here with her was to find a way to go back home. To leave with Bev and Sean if they were still alive. But what if he didn't?

Mr. Pinkus was curled up to her side. His yellow eyes tracked Elliot's movements. "Are you going to tell her?" he asked.

"Tell her what?"

"That you care for her?"

Elliot sighed. "I don't know. I don't think she would want me to."

"Truly?"

"She's confused. Experiencing things for the first

time. Hell, I'm confused." Elliot ran his fingers through his hair. "And do I only care for her because we've been forced together? If I had met her under any other circumstances, would I still have these feelings?"

"Does it matter?"

"I mean...I think so."

"The important thing is Elliot, you didn't. You met her. You care for her. Is that not enough for you? To have met her under different circumstances means you would not have met the Alannah you care for."

He sucked in a breath. Damn. The cat had a point. "But what if it doesn't work out? We're different in the end, and what if she realizes she doesn't like me at all?"

"I told the story about Fia, not only because I wanted to unburden myself, but also for your benefit. There are challenges in any relationship and one with Alannah would be no different. But you have to decide that it's worth the risk. That the possible love will be worth it."

"Do you think it is?" Elliot asked.

"Always."

Chapter 27

When Elliot first woke her, she noticed the dark circles under his eyes. She had a bad feeling it was because of her. That he abandoned sleep to watch over her instead. Guilt burrowed in her chest, clawed at her ribs, even more than it already did. Especially when he had her breakfast ready for her to eat and her tea ready to drink—the powder fully dissolved in the warm water—and he had already doused the fire. She felt useless. *Like baggage.*

Mr. Pinkus stayed by her side. She fed him shredded pieces of ham and cheese while she finished her breakfast. The fever had her feeling hot the day before, but now she felt chilly. A breeze drifted across the grass and she shivered. When they got up to leave, Elliot shoved a sweater in her hands before she could put her bag on.

The warm knit fabric smelled like him and smoke and spiced apples. She pulled it tightly around herself, pretending for a brief moment, that he was hugging her, his warmth combating her chill. And this time when they began to walk, Elliot reached for her hand. Their fingers interlaced together. He wasn't really speaking, but it said enough.

Gentle rays of light reflected against the morning dew, making the grass sparkle. A beautiful morning. She hoped that it was a sign that meeting with the goddesses would go well. But it wasn't the meeting that worried her.

Yesterday the medicine had held her over past lunchtime. Now they had barely walked for two hours and she was already dragging. She shivered even while bundled up in the warm sweater. Her feet grew heavy as if weights were tied to her ankles. Her stomach rolled, threatening to get rid of breakfast. Wisps of hair clung to her sweaty face and neck.

Fuck Valeria.

Using her powers to save Elliot shouldn't have cost this much. Saving someone shouldn't cost anything. Certainly not this kind of punishment. Yet here she was, so close to making it those who had offered help and feeling like she wouldn't make it at all.

Alannah kept going. Kept pushing. She held it together until lunchtime and took another dose. The medicine barely made her feel any better, but she didn't stop, if only to spite Valeria. Alannah would relish the look on the woman's face when she succeeded. All of this pain and suffering she had caused and it was only fair to have it blow up in her face.

The sun sat high in the sky, but its warmth barely touched her. Her teeth chattered. A root caught her boot and she stumbled, reaching out for a tree to steady her. Rough bark scraped against her fingers. She doubled over, her breathing labored, her hand on her knee. *I don't think I can do it.*

"Alannah," Elliot called her name, crouching down in front of her. "Do we need to take a break?"

She shook her head. "It will cost too much time."

"Sitting down for a few minutes won't cost much. Come on." He tried to coax her to sit down with him.

"Elliot, I..." she trailed off. She wanted to make it. Goddess, she wanted to succeed so badly. But she had to face the reality that she might not. That her odds were slim. She drew in a breath. "I need you to promise me something."

"What is it?"

"If I don't make it, I need you to leave me here—"

"What!"

"You have to make it back to the fringe, to the house. It will protect you and Mr. Pinkus. I know it will," she continued, knowing that if she didn't, he would talk her out of saying it at all. "It's the only way that you'll be safe."

Elliot cupped her face between his hands and tilted her face up. "Listen to me carefully, Alannah. I'm not leaving you here."

She sighed. "Elliot—"

"No!" His voice was loud and forceful and slightly panicked. "I will not leave you behind. We walked into this damn place together and we are going to walk out of it together or not at all. I'm not leaving anyone behind again. Is that clear?"

Alannah looked away, ashamed of what she was asking of him. She just wanted him to be safe, but after what happened to his friends, there was no way he would leave her behind no matter how much she begged. "Why are you so damn stubborn?" she grumbled.

"Part of my charm." He let go of her face and unclipped his backpack, letting it hit the dirt. "Besides there's no way I'm spending the rest of my life with Mr. Pinkus as my only companion."

"Ditto," Mr. Pinkus replied. "Please don't suggest

something like that again, Alannah. We will not leave you."

She sighed. "Fine." Regardless of their protests, she hoped when the time came that they would reconsider. Her life wasn't worth theirs.

Elliot turned around and crouched down in front of her again. "Get on," he instructed.

"What?"

"On my back."

"Why?"

He chuckled. "So I can carry you."

"You can't carry me all the way there, Elliot," she argued.

"I can and I will. Now get on, we don't have all day."

He wasn't going to let it go. With a sigh, she placed her hands on his shoulders and climbed on his back. He waited until she was steady before he stood up. His hands clutched her thighs to keep her from sliding down and she clasped her arms over his chest. When she was secure, he grabbed the backpack and carried it in his hand.

"Are you sure?" she asked.

"I don't think we have much further to go. It will be fine."

Relieved she didn't have to walk, Alannah leaned into him, pressing her cheek to his back. Where it used to be awkward to be this close, she now found herself liking it more and more. Elliot kept her steady against his back. That was him. Steady. An anchor in a storm. Not once did he complain about how difficult carrying her was.

While she didn't mind the thought of him carrying her back across Underhill to Valeria, she hoped the goddesses would have something for her. The answer to get guest. A way back to Valeria that wouldn't cost her time. Alannah wanted to walk across the threshold of the Ruby Court on her own two feet.

She noticed the court first. Or at least, she thought it was the court. Valeria's court had been huge. Opulent. The forest had merged with it and created a harmony together, but this wasn't that. Columns that were probably once large had crumbled to stumps. Chunks of marble littered the ground around them. Weeds and vines choked out flowers—she could see some of the petals peeking out from underneath the green—and twisted around each other. Her eyes followed them up a wall that looked as if the vines were the only thing that kept it standing. Windows were broken, their sills peeling and cracking.

Elliot stopped in front of the stone steps so she could stand on her own. She kept her hands on his shoulders to keep herself upright. A large, gaping opening in the stone façade looked as if it held doors once. "This can't be right…can it?"

"This place is falling apart," Elliot murmured.

"It has been this way for quite some time," a voice came from inside.

Alannah jumped and Elliot stepped in front of her. Two people emerged from the opening. They were both tall, at least a foot and a half taller than Alannah. One had stark white hair that fell to her waist and pitch-black eyes. A black long-sleeved dress covered her from neck to ankles, the skirt brushed the top of her black boots. Her nails were black and sharp. The other had dark brown hair that was pulled back into a braid. Her face was softer, chubbier, and her eyes a deep green.

A sage green dress accentuated the plump curves of her body. Billowy sleeves fell back to reveal green ink-stained fingers.

"Welcome Alannah, I am Macha," the woman in the green dress spoke.

The woman in black inclined her head. "And I am Badb."

Alannah nodded. "Hello. I'm here—"

"We know why you're here," Badb interrupted. "We have what you seek if you are ready."

"I am," Alannah said, taking a step forward. "I don't have much time left."

"We know." Macha frowned. "Using your power was not a wise choice, but it would be hard not to in Witches End."

Alannah shook her head. "Why?"

"Many of our people died there and their spirits linger. You called to them when you needed help and they answered." Badb clasped her hands in front of her. "Unfortunately, it cost you, but we will do our best to make sure you succeed."

"Why?" Elliot piped up.

Both of them turned to him with a piercing gaze. He swallowed and shrugged. "Sorry. I'm a bit skeptical after some of the things that have happened lately."

"We help our own, and Alannah is one of us," Macha answered.

"This is our duty," Badb added.

"You have a person of Fae and witch blood here?" Alannah asked.

The sisters shared a look before they gestured for her to follow them inside. Their silence made her uneasy or maybe it was her nerves that made her stomach do flips. She reached for Elliot's hand. She needed an anchor right now. Meeting actual goddesses was surreal enough, but if they had what she needed then she might actually succeed. She would be free. She could go anywhere in either world. That thought was wonderful and terrifying at the same time.

She carefully walked up the crumbling stone steps. Nothing about this place seemed stable. If she breathed too hard, she might send the whole structure tumbling down. "What happened to this place?" Alannah asked while stepping through the doorway.

The inside was no better. Walls were barely standing. Sunlight came in through holes in the walls and illuminated the inside. Vines had slithered in through the openings and were growing across the floor. A grand staircase in the middle of the room no longer had a banister. Alannah could tell there one had existed at some point in time because a handful of the posts remained. A few of the steps were missing. Two archways stood on either side of the staircase.

"It started when the Morrigan left," Badb said.

"When she trapped herself with Reluvethel?" Elliot asked.

Badb paused and turned to face them. "That's right. How did you know that?"

"I told them what I remembered of the stories," Mr. Pinkus said, his tail standing straight up.

"I see." Badb turned back around and led them through the archway on the left. "Yes, the Morrigan trapped herself with Reluvethel to keep him contained. But the witches were still fractured. It became worse when none could agree on how to move forward with so many scattered."

"This place was built by our people and with their displacement, it began to fall apart," Macha added. "We've have held it together as much as we could, but without unity it will not stand for much longer."

"That's sad," Alannah whispered. "Valeria gets a beautiful court and we get this."

Macha sniffed. "Valeria's court is built on blood, bones, and lies. I would much rather have this."

The sisters led Alannah down a long corridor. They passed doorways, some with actual doors and some with nothing. She saw a library, a few bedrooms, a dining hall, and a kitchen. The other doors were closed. They stopped in front of a door that marked the end of the hallway. Badb opened it to reveal a set of stairs that led down into darkness. Alannah gulped. They had to go down there?

"What you seek is down below. Are you ready, Alannah?" Badb asked.

"I...I'm..."

Elliot squeezed her hand. "It's okay. We're right here."

"Alannah must do this alone," Macha said. "But you can wait here for her."

"Alone?" Alannah shook her head. "I don't think I can."

Elliot put his hands on her shoulders and turned her to face him. "You've come this far. And we'll be waiting for you no matter what. You don't have to be scared."

"Easier said than done," she muttered.

"If you truly feel that you cannot then we can return you home and deal with the fallout with Valeria," Macha said.

"It would not be the first time we've done so," Badb

added. "But be warned, you will not be able to attempt this journey again. You will never be able to enter Underhill again without dying."

I don't want that to happen.

"So, this is my only chance?" Alannah asked.

Badb nodded. "Correct."

"Unless Valeria has a change of heart," Macha grumbled.

"That would require Valeria to have a heart," Badb sneered.

Elliot's fingers tightened before he pulled her into a hug. "You're really brave you know that, right?" His lips moved against her ear. "You could've given up at any point and you kept going. Whatever decision you make...I'll understand."

He would give up his friends? Give up finding the truth? Why would he do that? For her? What was she worth? *No.* This wasn't right. She couldn't give up now. She made it here. Sure, it was a crumbling shadow of a court. Nothing like she imagined, but she was here. With her friends. They loved her. Believed in her.

She needed to believe in herself.

She only had one shot. If she didn't take it then she could kiss visiting the village again goodbye. There would be no seeing the human realm and diners at two in the morning with Elliot. She would be trapped again. And she didn't want that. Even if she went home and decided to stay, she at least wanted it to be by her own choice.

"I'm ready," she said.

Elliot squeezed her shoulders and let her go. The sisters pointed down the stairs and Alannah drew in a deep breath. *I can do this.* Alannah braced her hand on the wall and took the first step, leaning against the cool and damp stone wall. With nothing to grab onto if she were to trip, Alannah descended carefully.

The sisters followed; the door slammed shut behind them. Darkness swallowed Alannah. She froze on the steps, afraid to move and possibly fall. As her eyes adjusted, she noticed a faint light coming from below.

"You will not fall, Alannah," Macha said. "Keep going."

Alannah took another shaky step down. And then another. The light grew a little brighter and she breathed a little easier, but she didn't truly relax until she stood on solid ground. The stairs came to a stop in a circular room with only a mirror sitting in the center. The rectangular mirror loomed a foot taller than her. Purpleheart framed the glass, much like the mirror in her grandmother's room. Faint blue light came from within the mirror.

"What you seek is in the mirror," Badb said.

Had they really managed to fit a whole person in a mirror? Alannah pointed to it. "In there?"

Badb nodded with a bemused expression. With a shrug, Alannah stepped in front of the mirror. She waited for a second then two then three, but nothing changed. She stared at herself in bewilderment. She didn't understand. Wasn't something supposed to happen?

"Nothing happened. It's me," she muttered, turning back to face the goddesses. "I thought you knew, I thought you were supposed to help me! Did you just bring me down here to stare at myself in a mirror! I could've done that at home and saved myself this…this bullshit!" she exploded and turned, pointing at herself in the mirror. "There's nothing special here, no answer, it's just me!"

"Yes, that's right," Macha said, stepping forward to rest her hands on Alannah's shoulders. "It *is* you, Alannah. You're the answer."

No…they couldn't mean…could they?

It's me.

Chapter 28

"That's not possible. I'm half human and half witch. I'm not—"

"We stepped in and begged Valeria for exile because Moirne was pregnant. The only way to give her and the child a fighting chance was to get them out of Underhill," Macha interrupted. "The child was half Fae and half witch and would not have survived here if the Fae knew."

Badb touched Alannah's shoulder. "You have both Fae and witch blood, Alannah. You are a marvel to us, but a threat to them."

Me? No...no...

She sucked in a breath. "How could I not know? Did my family? Did they keep it from me?"

"Moirne took a human lover shortly after her exile. It is possible that she withheld the truth, but it is hard to know for sure," Badb said.

"Why would she do that? I don't understand...I did all this...and it was me." Alannah's hands shook as she brushed a piece of hair behind her ear. "I wasted so much time—"

"Was it truly a waste?" Macha asked.

If she had known beforehand, she could've ended her curse before her journey began. Elliot would know the truth about his friends and he could've gone home instead of throwing himself into danger. But it wouldn't have been the same traversing this place without him. None of this would've been the same. "No, no it wasn't," she corrected herself. "But I don't think I'll make it back in time."

"You will have to leave immediately," Badb said.

"And you can't dawdle," Macha added.

"You can't help me, can you?" Alannah asked.

Macha looked down and shook her head. "Not in a way that you're hoping, no."

Alannah's shoulders dropped. "Even if I do make it back, how will I prove it. Valeria will call me a liar and kill me."

"Did you bring the journal with you?" Badb asked.

"How did you—"

Badb smiled. "I know many things."

Alannah took off her backpack. The journal had remained safe and sound at the bottom, wrapped in a shirt. She pulled it out and handed it to Badb. The woman flipped through the pages until she reached the blank ones. Her fingers traced the blank pages, a frown etched into her face. It was like she was looking for something but there was nothing there. Alannah had scoured it enough to know.

Badb turned to a page and paused. "Here," she said, reaching for Alannah's hand. Her thumbnail dug into Alannah's forefinger. A hiss escaped Alannah's lips as blood welled up from the cut. Badb dragged Alannah's forefinger across the page. The blood moved down the page forming names and lines. Connections. A family tree. And at the bottom, her. The product of all that came before. Proof.

Badb handed the journal back. "Valeria will not call

you a liar."

Alannah stared down at the writing. It was right here in front of her and still so hard to believe. Did her grandmother figure it out? She had to. Why else was the page there, hidden and waiting for her blood? Then why didn't she try to break it? Why had it been so important for Alannah to do it? So many more questions now and none she would have the answers to. It hardly seemed fair. She closed the journal and held it to her chest. "What do I do now?" she asked. *I won't make it.*

Macha clasped her hands in front of her. "We have nothing to delay the effects of the curse—"

"But we can provide aide," Badb finished.

"Aide? What kind of aide?"

"The kind that will get you back to the Ruby Court as quickly as possible. If you are ready to leave?" Badb asked.

If the situation weren't so dire, she wouldn't mind staying a bit longer. Give herself more time for the truth to sink in. For her to believe it. And to pick the goddesses' brain for their knowledge. Not just of her family, but for everything she could stand to learn. *I can always come back.* Alannah wrapped the journal again and put it back in her bag. "I'm ready." She followed Macha back up the stairs with Badb at her back.

Elliot bounced between the walls, his footsteps echoing amongst the stone, and came to a stop when the door open. His eyes went to Alannah first and then looked behind her for another person. "Well?"

"It's me," she said, hooking her thumbs in her backpack straps.

"Of course," Mr. Pinkus murmured.

"This entire time it was you?" Elliot nearly shouted.

"How did…" his eyes darted back and forth. "How did we miss the most obvious choice?"

"Moirne was pregnant before her exile then," Mr. Pinkus said. "It makes the most sense and yet I didn't even think of it."

"Some things aren't meant to be known until the right time," Badb said. "Such is the way of things sometimes."

Mr. Pinkus huffed in annoyance. "Naturally. Now we must leave. And quickly."

"Will we even make it back in time?" Elliot asked the question she had been asking herself on repeat.

"That is the plan," Macha said.

"Follow us." Badb walked back down the hallway towards the foyer.

Shame this was all they would see of the court. Who cared that it was a crumbling shell of a building? Alannah wanted to discover it secret nooks and crannies. Something to be explored at a later date. Elliot fell in step beside her, his hand grazing hers. "So…it's you…"

"Yeah."

"Hell of a surprise, huh?"

"I'll say."

"How do you feel?"

She shrugged. "It hasn't quite sunk in all the way."

He nodded.

"I'm sorry."

"For what?"

"For dragging you through all this and it was me all along." She shot him a sideways glance. "That isn't to say I'm not happy to have met you and traveled with you, I just…I could've saved us both a lot of trouble."

He grabbed her hand. "I don't regret it, Alannah."

The tips of her ears felt hot. "Me neither, Elliot."

The goddesses led them back outside into the warm sun. They had been vague about the kind of aide they were offering, but she didn't expect three familiar faces—one she didn't want to see at all—sitting astride three horses.

"Horses," Elliot mumbled. "Why couldn't we use horses before?"

"We needed to be quiet then. Now we need to be swift," Senna answered.

"How did you know?" Alannah asked.

"We were called to help," Selanna said.

Thankfully, Odhran stayed quiet. He didn't even look at Alannah. She wasn't sure why he came at all. Perhaps, Selanna had strong-armed into doing so. She seemed the type. Alannah couldn't think of any other reason than coercion. *It's fine. I can deal with it.* She could ignore him the entire trip back.

"This is all we can do, Alannah. The rest is up to you," Macha said.

"Thank you." They gave her the answer she needed. A way to beat Valeria and end her curse. She couldn't help her disappointment over how little power they held here. But after everything she'd learned so far, it wasn't a surprise. Underhill wasn't anything like she expected and this was another thing to add to that list.

Senna held her hand out for Elliot and pulled him up behind her. Alannah picked up Mr. Pinkus and handed him to Selanna before letting Selanna help her up. Mr. Pinkus sat in front of Selanna while Alannah leaned against Selanna's back. Nobody wanted to ride with Odhran, least of all, Alannah. If it bothered him, he kept it to himself. The horse shifted and Alannah wrapped her arms around Selanna's waist to keep herself steady.

Mr. Pinkus sighed. "Thank goodness. I don't know how much more walking I could take. When we return home, I will not be going anywhere for a while."

Senna snorted. "So eager to return to the life of a fat housecat."

"You got that right."

Alannah watched the court get smaller and smaller behind them. It still felt like she was missing something. Like there was something else there for her. She had a piece now, but a bigger picture loomed in the distance. What if she needed the bigger picture to confront Valeria? What if not knowing got her and Elliot killed? What if all of this was for nothing after all?

Selanna patted the top of Alannah's hand. "You're squeezing me a little tight, are you nervous?" she asked, keeping her voice low.

"Terrified."

"It's going to be okay. You won't walk in there alone."

Alannah looked to her right to see Odhran staring at her. His gaze shifted away the moment their eyes met. "Yeah...thanks."

***

Alannah looked terrible. The circles under her eyes were dark purple bruises and made her eyes look sunken. An hour into their journey and he began to shiver in the warm air as if it were freezing. He knew the signs of a fever when saw them. She had seemed fine the night they argued—the night she hit him—and now she looked as if she had one foot in the grave already.

Odhran had doubts that they would make it at all.

Not without better help than horses.

Her eyes flitted in his direction and he averted his own. If she kept catching him staring it might start another argument. And he didn't want to argue with her. The opposite, in fact. He wondered what it would be like to talk to her without saying something asinine. *Like asking to have sex with her when she hates me.* He had to fight the urge to roll his eyes at himself. It wasn't his brightest moment, but he didn't know what else he could possibly offer her in exchange for learning more about her. Nor did he know what else would sate his curiosity so thoroughly that he wouldn't spare her a second thought when this was over.

But he wasn't sure that would be enough at all.

What do I want?

Odhran looked over at her again at the risk of being caught. But she wasn't looking at anyone. Her forehead rested on Selanna's shoulder. Was she even awake? He pulled the reins of his horse to move closer. Had she passed out? He inched closer, his hand inches from her upper arm, when she began to slide to the side.

The reins fell out of his hands as he caught her by the shoulders. Her head lolled back. Bright red blood dripped from her nose. If it weren't for the movement of her eyes behind her eyelids, he might've thought they were far too late.

"Alannah!" Elliot cried out as if it would stir her awake.

Everything came to a stop. "What do we do, we're not even in Witches End," Selanna hissed.

"I have medicine for her," Elliot said, unclipping his bag. "She has to drink it."

"I'm not sure she's in a state to drink anything,"

Senna commented.

"What about Eletha?" Selanna asked.

Senna shook her head. "I've asked. There isn't anything that can be done. We can keep going and hope she holds on long enough."

Odhran's grip on Alannah tightened. False hope would get them nowhere. His mother had mastered creating punishing curses. Alannah's survival would've been a miracle. *It still can be.* "I have an idea. Let me take her."

"Over my dead body," Elliot argued.

"Not the wisest choice of words," Odhran snapped back.

"Don't!" Selanna held her finger up at him. "Alannah is the concern now, so knock it off."

"You can't seriously be considering letting him take her," Elliot said.

Selanna stared at Odhran. Her eyes searched his as if it would tell her what he was planning. And if he had planned something nefarious. She seemed satisfied with whatever she found because she leaned back and nodded. "We'll keep going. Catch up with us when you can."

Elliot sputtered. "Wait—"

Senna patted his arm. "It'll be fine. Alannah will be safe. Right?" she levied the question at Odhran.

"She will be safe," he promised, gently maneuvering Alannah off of Selanna's horse and onto his own. He pulled her in front of him, adjusting her so her head rested on his shoulder and his arm braced against her back. "We'll catch up as soon as we can."

Before anyone could change their mind—mostly Elliot—Odhran pulled the reins and his horse took off. His idea might not work, it was a longshot, but he couldn't think of anything else. And that was only if this place was what he thought it was.

He was taking her to the place he found a few nights ago. At the time, stumbling upon that place had seemed like an accident, but he didn't think so now. He didn't waste time finding it again. In the daylight he could see how alive these trees were compared to the dead ones of Witches End. Wisteria wrapped around the branches and the flowers dripped down to the forest floor. Petals scattered in the wind.

Odhran stopped the horse right on the edge. A moan escaped her lips and the trees seemed to breathe in response, the wood expanding and then deflating like lungs. The petals raced across the forest floor towards her. Odhran carefully dismounted before pulling her into his arms. This has to be her family's resting place and they had to help her. He cradled her against his chest and walked towards the central trees.

"She's your descendant. Please help her," he announced to the trees.

Nothing happened and for a moment he wondered if he had been wrong. Again. That there was nothing he could do for her. But the roots between the two largest trees creaked and cracked and untangled. They parted in the middle, revealing a space for her. Odhran carefully set her down. The roots cradled her like a child. Petals dripped down onto her cheeks. He breathed a sigh of relief. *I was right.*

The magic under his feet flared to life, beginning at each of the outer trees and moving inward towards her. All of those that came before her, all of those that had lived and died by the curse, were helping her. The color slowly returned to her cheeks.

Odhran didn't know how long this would take. He paced back and forth, snapping twigs under his feet, and wearing a path into the dirt, with his hands clasped behind his back and his eyes on her. She was pretty. Not in the way he was used to. The Fae were beautiful in an otherworldly way. They were bright. Elegant. But Alannah was homey. Warm. Stable ground and earthy, until she was angry, and then she shattered the ground under one's feet like an earthquake.

She made a small noise in her throat, and he froze. Her eyes were shut tight. Was she asleep? Was this helping? Waiting made his fingers twitch. Odhran sat down beside her, one leg tucked under the other. He brushed a petal from her cheek. "What are you, Alannah?"

Naturally, she didn't answer.

He rested his elbows on his knees and leaned forward. "The more I search for answers, the less I seem to learn. I searched the records, I've spoken to my mother's advisors even though she doesn't trust any of them, and even Eletha seems to know something but she won't say a word." He sighed. "I thought I wouldn't learn anything and then I stumble upon a place like this."

Odhran leaned back and looked around at the trees in their varying stages of maturity. "I'm sure you wondered—agonized even—over where your family ended up after they were reclaimed. You don't have to wonder anymore."

Why does that bring me some measure of relief? Why am I talking to her like this? She can't even hear me.

She sighed. Was she dreaming? Odhran reached down and curled a stray lock of her hair around his finger. "You know, with the exception of my mother, you're the first person that's ever hit me. Perhaps you're surprised that more people haven't." He chuckled humorlessly. "She hits me more than enough to make up for it."

Still nothing.

Odhran sighed. "I hope this works, Alannah. I would like to see my mother lose for once."

Chapter 29

Wood creaked underneath her thighs. Rope rubbed her palms raw. Alannah swung back and forth, her feet grazing the grass. Dew clung to her toes. Funny. She could've sworn the swing had broken years ago and she had never fixed it. Alannah focused on her feet. The grass moved and blurred like watercolor on canvas. The edges of her body were sharp against the shifting grass. Alannah didn't want to look up. She was afraid the rest of the world would look as unstable as the grass.

I think I'm dreaming.

A voice echoed around her. Odhran. The words were muffled, garbled, and yet she understood them anyway. At least, the feeling of them. The sadness that hid beneath the humor. The derision that dripped from their mouth. And a tinge desperation that she had never heard before.

Why did she hear him but didn't see him? Where was she? She remembered the warmth of Selanna's back through leather armor and then nothing.

The swing came to an abrupt stop and the whispers ceased. Alannah winced at the sudden, sharp ringing in her ears. The grass stilled. She looked up and froze as another version of herself smiled back at her.

No. Not me.

The woman standing before her was taller. She had

wrinkles and crow's feet and laugh lines and auburn hair streaked with grey. The same eyes as Alannah. *Moirne.* Alannah stood up, her fingers clutching the rope to anchor herself to something. Moirne's mouth moved but nothing came out. Perhaps Alannah couldn't dream her voice because she had never heard it before. The corner of Moirne's mouth twitched, her smile more melancholy than happy, and she reached out to run her fingers through Alannah's hair.

"Did you know?" Alannah asked.

Moirne nodded.

"Did we forget along the way? Or did you not tell us?"

Moirne shook her head and pressed a finger to her lips. Alannah understood what she meant. The secret had died with Moirne but Alannah didn't understand why. Why keep it a secret at all? If Alannah had known from the start, she could've ended the curse quickly.

"I don't understand why you wouldn't tell us," Alannah said.

Moirne held out a trembling hand, reaching across the distance, and Alannah grasped her hand as if it were a lifeline. If Moirne had something to tell show her, Alannah wanted to know. Needed to know. Alannah held a new puzzle piece about herself and now she needed to understand how it fit.

With a firm grip, Moirne led Alannah away from the swing and towards the family home. The house looked exactly how she left it and Alannah briefly wondered if she had somehow returned home. The door swung open. Shapes blinked in and out, their lines blurring and sometimes disappearing altogether, as Moirne tugged her through the dream. They walked up the stairs together. Alannah knew where they were going without having to ask. Did the secret room have something she needed to find? Alannah hoped it wasn't another cryptic journal. Although, she doubted she would find anything that offered straightforward answers.

Alannah turned to Moirne but the woman had disappeared and left Alannah standing alone on the landing without so much as a goodbye. Perhaps it was too much to hope for in the dreaming world. Alannah curled her fingers and cradled her hand against her chest.

Raised voices burst from her grandmother's room and Alannah jumped. Something brushed against her legs and she spun around. A younger version of her darted past Alannah without seeing her and came to a stop outside of her grandmother's door. *Is this a memory?* Alannah crept up behind herself and pressed her ear to the wood.

"Stop filling her head with ideas, mother!"

The sound of her mother's voice—clear and untainted by sickness—caused tears to gather in Alannah's eyes. In the final years, her mother fought to gather words on her tongue. The sickness siphoned everything from her and didn't even the decency to leave her words intact. Alannah leaned into the wood, hoping her mother would speak again with the clarity she had lacked in the end.

"I'm not filling her head. There are things she has to know," her grandmother said, sounding exasperated. "You are overreacting."

"I am not! This is the third time this month that I've caught her trying to cross the boundary!"

Did I do that? How do I not remember that?

"Good. She is eager."

"Mother, please."

"She will be the one to break our curse. I know it. I will not hide it from her."

"I'll never allow it!"

Her grandmother sighed. "You think you're protecting her, but it won't work."

"She is safe here. If she stays here then she will never hear the call—"

"The Morrigan will still call for her, Aoife. There is nothing we can do to change that."

"I can! I will! I will not let my child be a sacrifice."

A sacrifice? The Morrigan?

"Even if it means teaching her to fear everything?"

"Yes."

More pieces fell into her hand that she didn't know what to do with. How many secrets had they kept from her? Why?

Alannah blinked.

She stood in the dark, dank room, staring at her wall of herbs. *No. I don't want to be here.* A rattling breath wheezed behind her. A sound committed to memory. She heard it so many times. In her sleep. In the silence. Alannah held a bottle in her hand, the glass cool against her palm, and her thumb rubbed over the label.

"You remember how much?" her mother asked, her voice warbled and unclear.

Alannah nodded, her fingers tightening around the bottle. She looked down at the cup of tea sitting on top of the hutch. Steam curled from the surface. *I don't want to do this.* She uncorked the bottle. Her fingers shook, threatening to spill the liquid in the bottle anywhere but into the tea. For a moment, she considered doing it on purpose, but Mother would have her make more.

"You remember what to do?" her mother asked.

"Yes," Alannah whispered, pouring the contents of the bottle into the cup.

"You don't sound certain."

"I remember, mother. We've gone over it many times."

Silence.

"You remember the rules?" her mother asked, changing the subject.

Alannah sighed. "Yes."

"Don't sigh, Alannah. I need to know you remember. That you will heed my warnings."

"Mother—"

"Never go into Underhill, Alannah. And never give the inhabitants of that forest a reason to see you."

"I know."

"Promise me, Alannah."

Alannah set the empty bottle down. "I promise." Her fingers curled around the handle of the mug, but she couldn't pick it up. She didn't want to. She didn't want to be alone. Tears spilled down her cheeks. She hastily wiped them away.

"I'm sorry, Alannah…if I had my way, I would… nevermind," her mother murmured. "Dying takes too long. I know my choice hurts you."

Alannah grabbed the cup with both hands and turned to face her mother. She didn't want to see her mother's sunken cheeks and eyes, the yellowing skin that hung loose around her face, the bleeding cracks in her lips. Her mother reached for the cup, but she was too weak to grip it. Alannah held it steady for her. Of all things to relive…

Why this?

Her mother drained the contents of the cup. *It won't be long now.* Alannah turned to set the cup down on the hutch, but her mother gripped her wrist with a strength she shouldn't have. *This isn't how it happened.* Her mother yanked Alannah back around to face...not her mother.

Eleanor's face hovered inches from Alannah's. Yellowing teeth and dull blue eyes stared into hers. Eleanor grinned with more teeth than she should have. *Why?*

"Two of you now, only one to go," Eleanor said, cackling. "Find the third. Find the crone."

Alannah jerked back, trying to shake the woman off but Eleanor's vise grip only tightened. "What are you talking about?" Alannah shouted.

"The Morrigan needs her daughters."

"I don't know what that means! What does the Morrigan need?"

"Your life." Eleanor let her go and Alannah reeled back.

The floor disappeared from underneath her. She felt herself falling down...down...down...

***

Alannah's eyes flew open and she drew in a gasping breath. Tears lingered on her cheeks. She raised her hand to brush them away, dragging small purple petals across her skin. Wisteria hung over her head. *Where am I?* She looked around until she saw a familiar face.

"You were crying," Odhran said.

"I was dreaming," she responded, her voice hoarse.

"Oh."

Alannah glanced at the trees looming above her.

"Where am I?"

"I brought you to your family."

"My family?"

Odhran held out his hand to help her up. She stared at the elongated fingers for a moment. *She hits me more than enough to make up for it.* His eyebrows shot up when she grasped his hand. He probably didn't think she would. Not after the last time they spoke, well, argued was more accurate. Sharp pain shot up her back as he helped her sit up. How long had she been lying there? Alannah stumbled on her feet, but Odhran moved his other hand to her back to keep her steady.

She stayed still to give herself a moment. While she still felt tired and weak, she had a new energy that kept her upright. *Will it get me to Valeria?* If it did, then it was good enough. Alannah turned in a slow circle, her eyes darting between the differently sized trees, and stopped when her gaze reached what looked like a cradle in between two of the larger trees.

"What is this place?" *Why did you bring me here?*

"The place where your family rests," he explained, his tone gentle. "I believed it would help, and it seems I was right."

She shook her head. "Why would they be here? Who brought them here?"

"I don't know."

"When did you find this?"

"After we…spoke…at Senna's. I was wandering and I found this place."

"Wandering," she repeated. "Makes it seem like a coincidence."

"I don't think it was."

It took her moment to find the tree younger than

the others. Still a sapling. "Neither do I," she murmured, walking past him towards the tree. A lone plant sprouted from the ashen soil near the trunk of the sapling. Alannah leaned down, rubbing her thumb over the bud until it opened. Petals unfurled, grazing her fingers, to reveal golden petals edged in crimson. A Gerber daisy.

Mother.

The tears came unbidden, dripping from her chin and soaking into her shirt. "She didn't want me to come here. She wanted me to be too afraid of this place to ever consider it."

"Yet here you are."

Her laugh was flat. "I broke her rules so easily after promising her I wouldn't."

"Would she understand?"

Alannah shook her head. "She was afraid of something. I'm not sure what it was. I get pieces here and there, but nothing is snapping into place yet." The flower broke off from the stem and fell into her palm. "I killed her you know."

The confession sat in the silence, growing stagnant with each passing second. *Why did I say that?* She doubted he cared. Or that it would shock him. Murder was commonplace in Underhill. At least it was in his part of it.

His hand touched her shoulder and she jumped. "I doubt you are a cold-blooded killer, Alannah."

"You don't know anything about me."

He shrugged. "Perhaps I know enough."

Her eyes narrowed. He wasn't being rude or condescending, but she didn't miss that those were her words he threw back at her. "I doubt it."

"Why did you kill your mother then?"

"She asked me to."

"Why?"

"Because she was already dying and she was in pain." Alannah choked back a sob.

He squeezed her shoulder. "Then it was mercy, Alannah."

"Mercy," she spat that word as if burned her mouth. "Doesn't make it right."

"You are trying to make a gray situation into something that is black and white. It's not so simple. Your mother asked for death because she tired of suffering. Which would've been better? Letting her go on her terms or letting her suffer until she inevitably died?"

Alannah didn't want to answer. She knew what the right answer was; why she had yielded to her mother's request in the first place. But a part of her wanted to be punished for it. Isolation. Loneliness. Even death. Appropriate for what she had done. Now she didn't want any of those things and she didn't know what to do.

Odhran curled his fingers under chin and tipped her face up to meet his gaze. *When did he get so close?* Not as close as they had been before—he had kissed her after all—but she could still see the flecks of blue in his silver eyes. *I never noticed those before.* "She asked you to do something because she knew you loved her enough to do so. You don't have to suffer for it, Alannah."

"What do you know?" she grumbled.

He sighed. "More than you might think, if you cared to ask."

"Whose fault is that? You can't decide if you want to kill me or kiss me. How am I supposed to ask you anything?"

"I've decided."

Her cheeks grew hot. "Well, whichever it is, you can forget about it."

He dropped his hand from her chin, his mouth curving into a smile. "That's better."

Alannah gnashed her teeth together. He was goading her. Why? Was it to make her feel better? Was it because he liked teasing her? Or was he being serious? She didn't know. *Do I want to know?* She watched him stride over to the horse and gesture for her to follow. He confused her. Whether it was on accident or on purpose, she couldn't say. But she did know that she wasn't sure how to feel about him. It should be clear, but it wasn't.

Odhran held the horse steady. "You first."

"Why?"

"We won't be stopping. It will be easier for you to rest if I can hold onto you," he said.

Alannah wanted to argue, but he wasn't wrong. If she rode behind him, she might fall off. She stepped into the stirrup and swung her leg over. Mounting a horse wasn't as easy as the novels made it seem. She might not have made it over the first time if it weren't for the thought that if she fell, Odhran would catch her. He would take too much joy in that. And she didn't want to give him the satisfaction.

His chest pressed solidly against her back. With an arm on either side of her, he held the reins in his hands. "Are you ready?"

"As ready as I'm going to be."

My mantra now, I guess.

"Then let's go. You have a curse to break."

Chapter 30

Cold rain splashed against her cheeks. Startled awake, Alannah almost fell off the horse but Odhran's arms tightened around her. He kept silent as if to allow her to gather her bearings. If someone had told her about this predicament days ago, she would've called them a liar. Being comfortable in Odhran's embrace would've been unfathomable before now. *Absolutely not.* Alannah straightened, pulling away to put a little space between them. Rain came down in a steady drizzle. The dark clouds threatened even more. Alannah shivered as it began to soak into her sweater.

"Where are we?" she asked.

"Almost to Morthilas. We'll be stopping there for the night."

"Shouldn't we keep going? We have to catch up with the others."

"If I let you get sick, I'll never hear the end of it. We're stopping."

She huffed. "I wonder how far they got."

"Perhaps they'll be there. If not, they will find a dry place to stop."

I hope Elliot's okay.

"Are you worried about the human?" Odhran asked as if he could hear her thoughts.

"His name is Elliot."

"Are you?" he asked again.

"Why do you care?"

"I don't."

"Then why ask?"

He sighed, his chest rising and falling against her back. Cool breath ghosted her ear lobe and she shivered. If asked, she would chalk it up to the rain. They fell back into silence. A better solution than the possible argument they might have. Alannah didn't see a conversation with him going any other way. Despite his help now, she still couldn't forget their first meetings. His actions now didn't overwrite those. Especially since she knew he was only helping her to get back at his mother. While she didn't blame him, she didn't like being used.

The city came into view. Light reflected off the glass towers in the middle and that light bathed most of the city in the light. They rode a little past the gates and towards a stable. Alannah peered in through the gates to see the market sat empty and sparsely lit by silver streetlamps. The vendors must've been chased off by the rain. She didn't mind. If she never ran into that creepy woman again it would be too soon.

Odhran stopped at the stables and dismounted. She heard other horses—she was pretty sure they were horses—nickering in the stables. Keeping one hand on the reins, Odhran offered his other hand to her. His palm was cool against hers. She used his shoulder to steady herself as she got off the horse.

"Wait," he said before she moved away. Odhran undid his cloak and quickly draped it over her shoulders. He pulled the hood over her head. "Keep your head down. I don't want anyone realizing who you are."

"Am I that well known?" she joked.

"Among the worst kind of people, you are," he said.

She gulped. "Who are the worst kind of people?"

"My mother's supporters."

"Oh."

She waited under the eaves while he took the horse inside the stable. Every time she considered looking around, she remembered his warning. Morthilas was Fae territory. She was no longer safe. And if Valeria were to find out that Alannah was close to success, she would try to have Alannah killed again.

When Odhran came back out, he grabbed her by the arm, and gently steered her towards the gates. "Let's go."

"Where are we going?"

"There's a small tavern. A hole in the wall. A bit unsavory, but it'll be safe enough for the night."

They walked through the dark and quiet market. "Safe enough," she repeated.

He nodded. "There are nicer ones, but we risk garnering attention. It's not worth it."

She would have to trust him, an idea that left a sour taste in her mouth. Of all people, she never expected she would have to place her trust and well-being with him. If he didn't despise his mother so strongly, she might worry that he would betray her. But she knew he would, at the very least, get her back to the Ruby Court in one piece.

The streets were mostly empty. Some people lingered under awnings and eaves. She felt their eyes tracking her. Light and sound spilled out onto the streets from open doorways; snippets of conversations reached her ears. Nothing about her. She breathed a small sigh of relief.

Odhran stopped at one of the open doors. A tall

woman with piercing rust-colored eyes stood beside the opening. A cigarette dangled from her wine-stained mouth. Long, spindly fingers reached up to pull the cigarette away. She blew the clove-scented smoke at Alannah. "This place is not fit for a prince," she rasped, taking another drag. "Who's the poor soul with you?"

"A friend," he answered, his hand tightening around Alannah's elbow. "Just need a room for the night, Amare."

"A friend," Amare said, tilting her head towards Alannah. "You've brought friends before Odhran, but this is the first time you've brought a witch. Experimenting, are we?"

Alannah stiffened. Experimenting? Did the woman think Odhran brought Alannah here for sex? How often did he do that for Amare to think that? Alannah opened her mouth to say something, but Odhran squeezed her arm and she pressed her lips together. Saying something would expose her.

"Amare," he sighed.

The woman chuckled. "Don't worry, Odhran. I'm only teasing. You know where the keys are. Take your usual room. I'll expect my payment before you leave."

He inclined his head. "Of course."

The overwhelming scent of cloves and smoke permeated the room. People sat around small tables scattered throughout the room. Others sat at a bar. Odhran left her by a set of stairs near the front door to go behind the bar and grab a key from a set of hooks on the wall. No one paid attention to her. He was right about that at least.

Odhran grabbed her hand to lead her upstairs. His hand lacked Elliot's warmth. Their fingers didn't intertwine naturally. He probably doesn't hold hands often, if at all. They turned left at the top of the stairs and he led her to the room at the end of the hall. Alannah breathed a little easier when the door closed behind her and she heard him locking it. And then she saw her next problem.

There was only one bed.

Amare's words ran through Alannah's head and Alannah her face grew hot. She was not sharing a bed with Odhran. Not now. Not ever. *Experimenting?* How many people did he bring here? Alannah pressed her cold palms to her cheeks. This wasn't happening.

A queen-sized bed covered in a wine-colored bedspread—the color reminded her of Amare's lips—took up most of the room. Two small wooden tables sat on either side of the bed. The dark wood had taken a beating over the years. Cracks ran through the wood like a river cut through terrain. Chunks were missing. One of the drawers didn't have a handle. The windows sat side by side. Odhran crossed the room and pulled the thick black drapes closed. He tossed a key down on the small table in front of the windows. The fireplace in front of the bed roared to life and Alannah jumped. In front of the bed was a fireplace. Odhran's cough tried and failed to cover a chuckle.

"You might want to change out of your wet clothes," he said, bringing her attention back to him.

"I'm not changing in front of you."

He sighed and stood up. "I'm going down to get us something to eat. You will have the room to yourself."

"Good."

He stopped beside her. "What I asked before…it was a mistake. A blunder. I have no intention of doing anything untoward."

He left—shutting the door tight behind him—before she could answer or argue. The lock clicked once more and her shoulders dropped. Alannah pulled her backpack from her shoulders. She carried it to the small table by the window and set it down. She rifled through for dry clothes. There weren't many options. Almost everything was dirty by now. She couldn't wait to go home and do laundry. Something she never thought she'd be excited for, but after this trip, a normal chore would be nice.

She undid the cloak and draped it over the chair to dry. Wet clothes followed, hitting the wood floor with a plop. Alannah changed into her last pair of black leggings and a plain forest green long-sleeved shirt. She laid out her wet clothes to dry. Rain pattered against the windows. A roaring fire and rain would be perfect for sleep if she wasn't so keyed up. She couldn't believe she was here. In a room. With him. And she would have to sleep near him. It wasn't like sleeping near Elliot. She trusted Elliot. He was open and honest. Odhran was not.

When Odhran returned, she sat cross-legged in front of the fire. He set two plates of food down in front of her and sat beside her. Wet hair clung to his cheek. He nudged one of the plates towards her and took the other. Alannah picked up the sandwich, the bread was soft and warm, and bit into it. Salty sweet ham and smoky cheese exploded on her tongue. The tang of mustard lingered as she swallowed. *Delicious.* She sighed.

She was keenly aware of Odhran staring at her. "What?" she asked.

He shook his head. "Nothing."

"You're staring."

He looked away.

Alannah took another bite and chewed thoughtfully. This time she looked at him. Her eyes followed the sharpness of his jaw up to his equally sharp cheekbones. Her gaze stopped at his antlers. "Were you born with those?"

"No."

"Did they just grow one day?"

He sighed and set down his sandwich. His fingers sank into his hair and he slowly pulled the antlers off. They were attached to a band. He set the piece down on the floor beside them.

She certainly didn't expect that. "Oh."

"They were a gift from my father. He gave them to me before he left."

"I see." Alannah grabbed a grape from the plate and popped it in her mouth. "Where did he go?"

"He left. Just like Selanna's and Meralith's fathers."

"Why?"

"Would you want to stay with my mother?"

"Ah..." she trailed off. "Why...why leave you behind?"

Odhran's shoulders tensed.

"You don't have to answer that," she quickly added, noting his discomfort. "I was just curious."

"It's fine," he said, but his tone was guarded, cautious. "Valeria is possessive. And even if she weren't, he had little interest in being a parent. One day he was there and the next he was gone and this is all I have left." He tapped the antlers with his forefinger.

"I'm sorry, Odhran."

"You don't have to pity me."

She snorted and he turned to look at her. "I don't pity you. I feel bad that you were dealt terrible parents."

"Sounds like pity to me."

"It's not the same thing. Your poor upbringing certainly doesn't excuse your actions."

Odhran was silent. She expected him to snap back or deny it. But he took her words with no argument. Strange. Alannah shrugged and finished her sandwich in the quiet. Odhran did the same while staring at the flames flickering in the fireplace. Was he always so quiet? He seemed lost in thought. Contemplative. She wanted to know what he was thinking. *Why?*

"Why the hunt?" she asked.

"What?"

"You don't seem like a hunter, so why were you leading the hunt?"

Odhran leaned forward, resting his elbows on his knees. He picked at the seam of his black leather pants with his fingers. "I thought it would be a way to get away from my mother. A way to garner some respect and live outside of her shadow. It was going well…"

"Until me."

"I certainly didn't plan for you."

"Do you wish you would've killed me then?"

"No."

"Why?"

"You are very interesting, Alannah. It would've been a shame to miss out."

She didn't know what to say to that. When he labelled her interesting, she couldn't help but feel that he considered her an experiment of sorts. A factor to mess with his mother instead of an interesting person in her own right. Alannah finished the fruit on her plate before pushing it away.

"Do you want anything else? The menu is limited, but I can find any—"

She shook her head. "No thanks. It was good, thank you."

Odhran blinked at her. "You're...uh...you're welcome." He stood and gathered their plates, leaving her sitting alone. Why did gratitude fluster him?

Alannah stifled a yawn with her fist. She pushed herself up and stretched her arms over her head. The day had crept up on her and despite her nap earlier, she was ready to sleep again. She chose a side of the bed and turned down the covers. They hadn't discussed the sleeping arrangements. Perhaps Odhran would sleep on the floor and she wouldn't have to say anything. She didn't want to ask him to since he was the one paying for the room.

"Where—"

She looked up and choked on her words. He stood in front of the window, his shirt in his hand, and now he was looking at her because she spoke. *Oh, goddess.* She blushed, the heat spread across her face and down her neck. Hardly the first time seeing someone shirtless, but she couldn't tear her eyes away. He was tall and lean and willowy. Yet underneath it all, he had musculature, and a soft stomach, and...scars. So many scars. That sobered her. This is what Valeria did to him. Her hands curled into fists. Just when she thought she couldn't hate the woman more.

"Yes?" he asked.

Her eyes snapped back to his face. "I was going to... I..." What was she going to say again? Oh. Right. She was going to ask him to sleep on the floor. Instead, Alannah grabbed one of the pillows on the bed and slammed it down in the middle. "You can sleep on that side. Just stay on that side."

He blinked at her. "Right…"

Alannah sat down on the bed with her back to him. She wanted the floor to open up and swallow her. Almost thirty and she acted like she had never seen a half-naked person before. And she didn't even like him. *Are you sure about that?* The bed dipped behind her and her heart thudded in her chest. Maybe she should sleep on the floor.

Without looking at him, she laid down on the bed and pulled the covers to her chin. The fire died down to a smolder, keeping the room warm, but extinguishing the light. The darkness hid her flushed face. How on earth would she be able to sleep with him right there?

She cleared her throat. "How often do you come here?"

"Often enough."

"That's not much of an answer."

"I know."

She huffed. "The woman at the door knows you well."

"She owns the place."

"I see."

"What is it you want to ask me, Alannah?"

"What she said at the door…she implied that you…you know…"

"That I bring people here? Sometimes."

Alannah's ears burned. "Oh."

"Would you like details?"

"N-no! Why would I…I'm not—"

He chuckled. "I'm teasing you." She felt him shift

behind her. "Goodnight, Alannah."

Alannah pressed her face into her pillow, muffling her reply. "Goodnight, Odhran."

***

Odhran stared at the ceiling. Rain pelting the windows would be soothing under any other circumstance, but not the one where Alannah lay fast asleep beside him. He kept glancing over at her. She faced him with her face buried in the pillow she had placed in between them. *And she worried about me encroaching on her side.* The corner of his mouth lifted.

The end of the journey drew closer and closer. Tomorrow they would be back at the court and she would face Valeria. If his mother lifted the curse what would Alannah do then? What would he do? Odhran rolled onto his side to face her. After tomorrow, they would have no reason to see each other again.

You're an idiot. She doesn't want anything to do with you.

Odhran should let her walk away and be done with him, but he selfishly didn't want to. No one challenged him the way she did. *Selanna doesn't count.* No one had stood in his mother's court and demanded to be spoken to as if she existed. Alannah was brave and kind and he didn't want to let her slip through his fingers even if he couldn't entirely understand why. He wanted to take the time to understand.

Her lips parted and she mumbled something. He couldn't make it out, but her hand crossed the pillow and she patted the dwindling space between them. Whatever she searched for, she didn't find, and she huffed in frustration. Her hand moved closer and closer. Odhran froze when her fingers grazed his face. Soft fingers traced his jawline and trailed up his cheek. When her hand landed on his hair she sighed. She began to slowly pet the top of his head. Her fingers threaded through his hair and lightly scratched his scalp. Did she think he was the cat?

Odhran pressed his lips together to silence his laughter.

But his laughter ceased when she wrapped her arm around the back of his neck and yanked him closer. The separation pillow became a distant memory. She pulled his head to her chest until his ear pressed against her sternum. Her fingers kept carding through his hair. Wet earth and lavender and smoke filled his nostrils. Her heartbeat—steady and pure—thumped under his ear.

"Alannah," he murmured her name to wake her. She didn't stir and he repeated her name a few more times. Nothing. He relaxed, resigned to his fate. Although, he didn't hate it. She was soft and warm. Her chest rose and fell under his cheek. Odhran's bones turned to mush and his eyes fluttered closed. He couldn't remember the last time he had been this relaxed and he knew it was because of her. A simple, sleep-induced mistake on her part helped him decide.

There was no way he was going to walk away from her after tomorrow.

Chapter 31

Odhran pulled the horse up to the front steps. Alannah swung her leg over and lowered herself down without his help. The last thing she wanted to do was touch him more than necessary. She stepped back to allow him room to dismount. Her fingers plucked at the hem of her green shirt

"You haven't looked at me all morning," he said, landing beside her. "Something wrong?"

"No," she grumbled, looking at the front door instead of him. .

He sighed. "It's not a big deal, Alannah."

She held up her hand. "We don't have to talk about it."

Out of the corner of her eye, he shook his head, but he didn't mention it again. She had woken up with him pressed to her chest and she couldn't even be mad at him because it was her fault. Apparently, she had mistaken him for Mr. Pinkus. How? She didn't know. But she would never live down holding him to her chest, and then questioning whether or not she actually wanted to let him go.

He had stared up at her with parted lips and sleepy eyes and she had wanted to kiss him!

What's happening to me?

Alannah had never fostered feelings for anyone

before. No one real at least, the characters in novels weren't real and didn't count. But now there she had Elliot and Odhran and her attraction to the latter baffled her. Perhaps she could chalk her feelings up to stress. A way to think about something other than the looming building in front of her and the bitch that lived inside.

"Alannah?"

She jumped. He lingered beside her, his hand touching her elbow, and he looked nervous. "What?" she asked, struggling to keep her voice even and unaffected.

"Before we go in, I wanted to say..." He let go of her arm and dropped his gaze. "I don't apologize for things. Ever. I rarely feel sorry for the things I've done. I always find ways to justify my actions." Odhran shook his head as if shaking his thoughts back into their proper place and drew in a breath. "You may not believe me, and I understand if you don't, but I am sorry, Alannah."

That was the thing. She did believe him. Did she forgive him? She wasn't sure. "Thank you."

Odhran drew himself back up and squared his shoulders. "Are you ready?"

Alannah's eyes strayed back to the front door and she nodded. "Yes."

They left the horse and walked up the front steps. Odhran pushed open the door to reveal an empty foyer. Muffled bits of conversation drifted down the stairs. The throne room sounded packed and they were there for her. Alannah's heart raced and her hands shook. This was it. The end. The beginning. The moment she thought would never come. She was terrified, but ready. Odhran led her up the stairs, his hand hovering behind her back but not touching her.

Alannah placed her palms on the throne room

doors and took a deep breath. *You can do this. It's almost over. Then you can go home.* She pushed.

Fair Folk were packed into the throne room—clambering over each other to get a glimpse of Alannah—their voices buzzing around her. The hunters mingled in groups closer to Valeria and leered at Alannah. Some of the Fae stared at her in disgust while others looked at her with open curiosity. They had come for a show. They had come to watch Alannah's failure. Something feral within her laughed at how disappointed they were going to be when Alannah revealed the truth.

Alannah's gaze traveled over the sea of faces and limbs, looking for the one face that mattered most to her.

Elliot stood to the left of Valeria. She didn't like that he was so close to the wretched woman, but Senna had placed herself between him and Valeria. Even Mr. Pinkus waited for Alannah in the throne room despite his protests about entering Valeria's court. He wove himself around Elliot's legs, his tail twitching back and forth and his eyes darting between the Fae. Elliot met her gaze and he took a step forward, but Senna put a hand on his arm to stop him. Selanna and woman Alannah didn't recognize, kept the Fair Folk away from Elliot. The other woman was shorter than both Odhran and Selanna and had the same white hair. Some of it covered her face, but Alannah still saw scars peeking out from the fringe. Her visible eye darted back and forth.

"I'm surprised she came out," Odhran murmured, guiding Alannah through the crowd with a hand on her elbow.

"Who?"

"Meralith. My younger sister."

"Is it because of the scars?"

"Yes. Please don't bring it up."

"I wasn't raised by wolves, Odhran."

Alannah shoved her way to the front and stopped in front of Valeria. The woman stared down at her from her throne, her lips curved in a genuine, albeit malicious, smile. Alannah had returned empty-handed and Valeria believed herself victorious. So did the Fae. They murmured amongst themselves, but their words reached her. Many wondered how Valeria would kill her. They reveled in the idea of her punishment.

The joke was on them.

"I see you were unsuccessful," Valeria said, her ringing through the hall, silencing everyone. "I am surprised you returned with nothing."

"I returned with everything. I found exactly what you asked for," Alannah corrected.

The Fae drew in a collective breath.

Valeria's eyes narrowed. "And yet I see no one with you."

Alannah shrugged off her backpack and unzipped it. Her fingers found the soft fabric of the blouse the journal was wrapped in. Fabric unraveled and she pulled out the journal, flipping it open to her family tree and holding it out to Valeria. "See for yourself."

Silence stretched between them, like a rubber band being pulled taut, ready to snap at a any moment. Valeria's hands gripped her chair so tight the metal warped under her fingers with a screech.

"You knew, didn't you? That's why you tried to have me killed," Alannah broke the silence.

But Valeria didn't answer. She hadn't torn her eyes

away from the page.

"Oh." Alannah lowered the journal. "You didn't know."

Valeria looked as if she was having trouble breathing. Her chest stilled and red crept up from her chest. She was a ticking time bomb. One of the hunters—Percivus, if Alannah remembered correctly—stepped forward to set her off.

"This has gone on long enough," he said. "Let us finish what was—"

"Get out."

He cocked his head to the side. "I beg your pardon?"

"Get out!" Valeria shrieked. "All of you! Get out!"

"This is—"

"Oh, stuff it you pretentious buffoon! I have had to listen to you whine and bitch and moan for the better part of a month and I am sick of it!"

The Fae filed out of the doors, grumbling under breath about the abrupt dismissal. The hunters were the last to leave, their leader shocked and offended at being treated in such a way. Alannah bit back a smug smile. The doors slammed shut behind them, sealing her in with Valeria. She wasn't alone. Her companions, old and new friends, stayed in the room. Odhran remained behind her.

Valeria stood from her throne and descended the steps, the fabric of her stark white gown whispering against the floor. Alannah took a step back as Valeria grew closer. Valeria's hand shot out and gripped Alannah's chin. Silver-tipped fingers dug into her cheek but didn't draw blood. She pulled Alannah's face close. "The moment you walked into my court I should've killed you," she hissed.

Odhran grabbed his mother's wrist. "Let her go, mother."

Valeria sneered at her son but didn't let Alannah go. "And you even turned my own children against me."

"It wouldn't be hard to do," Alannah shot back.

Valeria shoved her, sending Alannah stumbling back into Odhran's chest. "You look so much like her. I hate it."

Alannah straightened. "Moirne?"

"Yes." She turned her back to Alannah. "We were friends you know. Once. Me, Elauthin, and Moirne."

"How?"

"Moirne never cared for boundaries. She snuck into Morthilas often. That's how we met." Valeria straightened her long sleeves. "I didn't have any friends really. My father was a particularly cruel man. I was written off the moment I was born, but Moirne didn't know that and it was so easy to be friends with her. But introducing her to my betrothed, my beloved Elauthin, was a mistake."

Alannah closed the journal and held it to her chest. "They fell in love."

"Moirne was everything I wasn't. Carefree. Open. Loving. I'm sure it was easy for him to love her in a way that he couldn't love me." Valeria tapped the ruby pendant resting against her throat. "They made a mockery of me. Those that knew, laughed at me behind my back. Do you have any idea how that feels?" The question was rhetorical. "I had to do something."

"You cursed her entire bloodline. Did that truly feel right to you?" Alannah asked.

Valeria stared at her, her eyebrows nearly disappearing into her hairline. "Of course."

Alannah shook her head. "No wonder no one liked you. You're horrible."

"I am what others have made me," Valeria said. "Perhaps if Moirne had chosen death then you wouldn't be here, begging for me to remove the curse. Perhaps if two people I loved hadn't snuck behind my back, we wouldn't be here at all this very moment." A tear dripped down her cheek—staining her porcelain skin red—where it hardened and fell to the ground as a ruby.

A small part of Alannah felt bad, but not enough that she would ever forgive Valeria. Her family didn't deserve this. She didn't deserve it. And now she was going to be rid of it. "We had a deal," Alannah said. "I found a person of Fae and witch blood. You will remove my curse."

Valeria cocked her head to the side and regarded Alannah with a smug smirk. "Are you certain? You will no longer have the safety of the fringe. With the coming days, you may wish you still had that safety."

"What is that supposed to mean?" Alannah demanded.

"It means, dear Alannah, Underhill is not the place you imagine it to be. Removing this curse will not grant you the freedom you desire." Valeria leaned closer and lowered her voice. "In fact, this place just might kill you."

If that curse doesn't kill you, the other will.

Alannah stepped closer. "You know something."

"Perhaps."

"She's goading you, Alannah," Selanna snapped. "A deal is a deal, mother. You should stop delaying and hold up your end of the bargain."

Alannah couldn't put her finger on why she felt like

Valeria knew something. Teasing aside, Valeria stared at Alannah as if waiting for her to ask the right question. Waiting for a chance to crush Alannah's notion of what life would be like without the curse. A final barb before Valeria had to fulfill her promise.

"What do you know of my future?" Alannah asked, unsure if it was the correct question, but she didn't know where else to start.

"You are going to have to be more specific than that."

"This is ridiculous," Odhran snarled. "Stop toying with her, Mother."

"What makes Moirne and I similar?" Alannah asked. "You said we looked alike, but that isn't all, is it?"

"No," Valeria said. "Your role in this life is what makes you and Moirne one and the same. You could say my curse saved her life in order to give rise to yours and if I lift the curse, you will fulfill the purpose she abandoned."

Alannah huffed and looked up at the ceiling in annoyance. "You don't know anything."

"I do."

"Then stop speaking in riddles and tell me!" Alannah crossed her arms over her chest, her fingers digging into her arm. "Otherwise, this is all a ruse to scare me into complacency because you can't handle that you've lost."

Valeria's eyes lit up and her smug smile turned into something more facetious. "The only one who is going to lose Alannah, is you. If you keep the curse, you lose. If I remove the curse, you still lose. Because you see, your life doesn't belong to you. In the end, it will either belong to me or the Morrigan."

"What do you know about the Morrigan?" Alannah snapped.

"What do *you* know about the Morrigan, Alannah?" Valeria shot back. "Stories are nice but they are hardly ever the truth and you have been lied to your whole life. Riona lied to you. Your "goddesses" lied to you."

"How do you—"

"The spell the Morrigan used to stop Reluvethel is incomplete. She didn't have the power to completely freeze time and when she relied on her friends to help her, they betrayed her and kept their power. So much for the witches being better than us," Valeria teased, walking back and forth as she spoke, but her eyes never left Alannah.

"You're lying," Alannah said.

Valeria waved a hand at Alannah. "You and I both know I cannot."

"Why are you telling me this?"

"Let it go, Alannah," Mr. Pinkus warned, finally speaking up.

"She can't," Valeria said. "Because she needs to know and I will be more than happy to tell her that the only way the spell remains is because every hundred years three children are born with the mark of the Morrigan. Three powerful children that grow and mature until the Morrigan calls on them and siphons their power to keep Reluvethel at bay. Every hundred years until I cursed Moirne and destroyed the balance." She touched Alannah's cheek, the silver point of her forefinger dragging across Alannah's skin. "You were born to be sacrificed, Alannah, just as Moirne was. I gave her a gift. A lineage she wouldn't have had if I hadn't cursed her."

"A gift!" Alannah exploded. "And what? You're giving me a gift of knowledge now? How would you even know any of this?"

"Like I said, Moirne was my friend once. There was a time where I tried to help her solve how she could help the Morrigan and still live." Valeria leaned down. "There is no solution, Alannah. Your life will end. How many of them will you drag down with you?" she whispered, turning her gaze to Elliot and her children and Mr. Pinkus.

The puzzle pieces clicked into place. Eleanor's warning. Telling Alannah that Alannah never belonged to her mother. Riona's dismissal of Eleanor. She probably knew. Perhaps Makenna was one of the others and that's why Riona had said nothing to Alannah. The dream. Her mother's words. Valeria had handed Alannah the missing pieces knowing the misery it would cause. Alannah had fought her way to the truth and back and she still lost.

Not fair.

What was the point of any of it? The point of Mr. Pinkus' encouragement and friendship. The point of her blossoming feelings for Elliot and, possibly, Odhran. The friendships. Eletha. Senna. Selanna. Makenna.

Not fair.

Alannah hadn't even realized she started crying until Valeria withdrew her hand and the teardrops clung to her fingers. "Oh dear. Poor, poor Alannah—"

"That's enough, Mother," Odhran's low and threatening voice stopped Valeria midsentence. "You have said more than enough and I won't hear another word from you that doesn't involve lifting her curse as you have promised."

"You are far too involved, my son. You are betting on a dead woman."

"I would rather bet on a dead woman than a pathetic, sorry excuse for a mother," he shot back, his hand coming down to rest on Alannah's shoulder. "It's time to accept your defeat with grace so Alannah and her companions may return home."

Valeria sighed. "But does she even want me to now that she knows the truth?"

Having heard enough, Elliot pushed past Senna before he could stop them. He ignored Valeria—stepping in front of her to block Alannah from her view—and cupped Alannah's face. "She's fucking with you. Trying to get inside your head. Don't let her," he whispered.

Alannah shook her head. "She's not lying, Elliot. I knew this was too good to be true," she hissed. "What am I going to do?"

"You're going to demand that she remove the curse and then we're going to figure everything else out later."

"Later," Alannah spat. "You'll be free, Elliot, why would you stay?"

"Because I care about you," he murmured, brushing hair away from her face. "Because I'm not going to abandon you to figure this out on your own."

"Elliot, I—"

"This is very touching, but you have a decision to make Alannah," Valeria interrupted. "I can remove your curse and send you on your way to die or you can return to your home and live your short miserable life until you die naturally. I'll even let you keep him." She gestured to Elliot. "And I'll return his friends as bargained. The curse will remain and you will never step foot in Underhill again." Valeria outstretched her right hand, fingers wrapped around a dagger, and pointed it Alannah. "If you wish to remove the curse, all you need to do is allow the dagger to pierce you. If you want to return home, you need only to leave and never come back. What is your choice?"

Alannah reached up and gently pulled Elliot's hands from her face. She held them briefly in between her hands before letting them go.

"Alannah," Elliot whispered her name. Nothing followed.

Alannah had made her choice. Only one route made sense. Only one gave her a chance at a life she wanted. "You...the Morrigan..." Alannah said, shaking her head. She wrapped a shaking hand around Valeria's wrist. "I don't belong to any of you."

In a swift motion, she plunged the dagger into her chest.

Chapter 32

Alannah woke in a cloud of softness. Her fingers trailed over the familiar quilted surface of her bedspread. She rolled over and sniffed her lavender scented pillow. *Finally.* She had found her way back to her own bed. Unless everything had been a terrible and wonderful dream. A dream in which she had traveled with companions and made friends and broke her curse and—

Her death loomed over her, waiting for the Morrigan to call upon her.

She pushed the covers to the side and pushed herself up on her elbows. She looked down at her feet and recoiled at the blisters and bruises that covered her feet. *I definitely wasn't dreaming.* She still wore the clothes from before. A hole where the dagger had sliced through the fabric bared a smooth patch of skin. She didn't even have a scar.

A clattering from downstairs drew her attention and shot up. *Elliot?* Was he still here? Alannah didn't remember anything after the dagger. She must've passed out. Did he learn about his friends? Were they alive? She swung her feet to the floor and winced when they touched the wood floor. The door to her room slowly opened and she paused. The pattering of little feet made her smile.

Mr. Pinkus jumped on her bed and immediately headbutted her arm. "You're finally awake."

"How long?" she asked, her voice raspy.

"A day." He stared at her with his owlish yellow eyes and blinked. "How are you feeling?"

"I don't feel very different."

"I'm sure that will change."

She shrugged. "Maybe. I suppose we'll find out when I try to leave again."

Mr. Pinkus rubbed his cheek against her hand. "Wherever you go, Alannah, I will follow."

He might regret that.

She scratched between his ears. "So, what did I miss?"

"You passed out and luckily Odhran was there to catch you. We were all swiftly dismissed from the court, and in case it was in question, you are not welcome to return."

Alannah snorted. She had no doubt about that.

"Then Odhran and Elliot argued over who would be carrying you back, at which point Selanna intervened and fulfilled the rest of the bargain you had made—"

"His friends?"

"Alive. Relatively unharmed. They're sleeping in the guestroom."

Her heart sank. "That's great. I'm sure he's relieved." She rubbed her palms against her thighs. "How are they doing with everything?"

"They've had their memories wiped. It was Senna's suggestion, and Elliot agreed."

"It's for the best, I'm sure."

"I believe so." Mr. Pinkus' tail twitched. "You know... Odhran offered to wipe Elliot's memories as well."

Her fingernails cut into her palms. "And?"

"I believe Elliot called Odhran an idiot and then

walked away."

Alannah heaved a sigh of relief. "Where is Elliot?" she asked. She wanted to see him.

"Downstairs."

She stood up, wincing from the pain, and walked out of her room with Mr. Pinkus right on her heels. The door to his friend's room was ajar and she heard soft snores from within. She was glad they were alive even though she knew that meant Elliot would be leaving, and she would be lying if she said she wouldn't miss him.

From the smells and the sounds, Alannah went straight to the kitchen. Elliot stood over the stove, scraping a dark brown pancake from the skillet.

"I think you overcooked it," she said from the doorway.

He whirled around, the spatula clattering to the floor. One moment, he stood across the room and the next he had his arms wrapped around her so tightly she had trouble breathing. His face pressed into the crook of her neck. Her skin felt damp.

"Thank god, you're alright," he murmured, his voice thick.

"Indeed," Mr. Pinkus said, jumping up onto the kitchen table. "I was afraid I would have to keep eating Elliot's cooking."

Elliot chuckled and pulled away. He cupped her face. "Are you okay?"

"Are you?" she asked.

"I asked first."

"I'm fine," She lied, reaching up and curling her fingers around his hands. "I thought I had dreamed everything at first."

"Trust me, none of what happened was a dream."

"It will seem like it. Especially when you leave," she whispered.

He can't stay. I can't put him through this.

"Alannah—"

"I'm so happy your friends are alive. How are they?" she asked, cutting him off and stepping back out of his reach.

Elliot frowned. "Confused. I had to come up with a story. I'm not sure if they believe me, but they don't seem interested in questioning what I've told them."

"That's to be expected. Their mind is probably wanting to block out what happened and it's easier for them to accept something else as the truth." She wiped her hands down the front of her shirt. "What did you tell them?"

"That we got lost and disoriented and you found us and brought us back here."

"Oh?" she chuckled. "Did I manage to carry all three of you back at once? I didn't realize I had acquired super strength."

"I didn't say it was great. It was all I could come up with on the fly."

"It's fine, Elliot. I'm teasing you." Her smile dropped. "I suppose you'll be leaving soon then."

"I'm not going anywhere, Alannah."

"Why?" she whispered.

"I told you, Alannah. I meant it." He reached for her hand and held it between his own. "I care about you. I want to stay here with you. I want to help you break however many curses you have—"

Her short laugh turned into a sob and she pressed her lips together.

"Even if you just want to be friends, I want to be here," he continued.

"You have a life, Elliot," she said, her voice wobbly. *Don't cry.* "You don't have to give that up to help me figure out mine."

He curled his fingers under her chin and tilted her face up to his. She couldn't look away even if she wanted to. "What if I want to?" he asked.

"Elliot, I—"

"I like *you*, Alannah. I want to stay." He withdrew his hand. "If you'll have me—"

I don't want to lose him. Alannah gripped his collar and popped up onto the balls of her feet. Surprise flitted across his face as she pulled him down to meet her. His lips were soft and warm and slightly chapped. Elliot barely had the chance to kiss her back before she pulled away, her face burning.

She nervously cleared her throat. "So…breakfast?"

The laugh strangled in his throat. "I was…um…I was trying. I may have overcooked some of them."

"More like burned," Mr. Pinkus added.

"They're not that bad. Just a little dark. And dry."

"Nothing a little butter and syrup won't fix," Alannah said, staring at his mouth again. Before she could think about stealing another kiss, there came a knocking at the door.

"I'll…uh, get that," she said, backing away from Elliot and into the counter. Mr. Pinkus snorted. With her cheeks aflame, Alannah exited the kitchen—without running into anything else—and walked to the front door.

Elliot followed her and lingered in the entrance to the kitchen. Her fingers curled around the knob. She didn't expect company. And she certainly didn't expect Odhran and Selanna standing on her porch.

Selanna held one hand up in greeting, a box tucked under her other arm. "Hello."

"Hi," Alannah said, staring at them.

"May we come in?" Selanna asked.

"Oh! Yes, please." Alannah stepped to the side to let them enter and closed the door behind them. "Sorry, I'm a little surprised to see you."

"We wanted to check on you. And bring you this." Selanna held the box out to Alannah. "A witch was rather insistent we get it to you."

Alannah took the box and set it on the back of the couch. She pulled at the purple ribbon that held the box closed and took off the top. The moment she touched the fabric she knew what it was. Alannah pulled out the dress she had worn on Samhain, freshly cleaned and smelling like honey and freshly baked bread. She held it to her chest. She would have to thank Makenna. In person.

Something fell from the dress and landed at her feet. Alannah looked down at the wolf necklace that Eleanor had given her. She hadn't even realized she forgot it. She bent over and picked it up, holding the warm metal in her palm. The necklace, once Moirne's, bounced on the wood surface and settled face side up when Alannah tossed it. She didn't want to wear it.

Not now.

"Would you like to stay for breakfast?" Alannah asked, draping the dress over the back of the couch.

Selanna nodded. "That would be nice."

Selanna nudged Odhran with her elbow, breaking him out of uncharacteristic silence. "Yes," he said. "I would like to stay."

Elliot glared at Odhran.

Odhran's shoulders tightened. "You have something you want to say?" he snarled at Elliot.

"Not at all," Elliot replied, keeping his voice even. "I'm thankful you're here."

"And why's that?"

"I thought the burned pancakes would go to waste."

"You—"

"Would you knock it off," Selanna cut him off. "The arguing is so unnecessary. We can get along long enough to eat breakfast."

"He's the one that tried to kill me," Elliot grumbled.

Odhran looked away. "I'm sorry," he mumbled.

Elliot held his hand up to his ear. "What was that?"

Odhran heaved a sigh. "I said, I'm sorry. Leading a hunt was a mistake. One I won't make again."

Elliot stared at Odhran with a contemplative look, deciding whether or not Odhran was telling the truth or playing a game. Whatever he saw, satisfied him. "It's a start, I guess. We'll see if it means anything." He turned and walked back into the kitchen and Selanna followed.

Alannah and Odhran remained in the living room. He stayed close to the door as if he might bolt at any moment. Something was different. Her eyes traveled from his feet to his...oh. *He's not wearing the antlers.* She also noticed a fresh cut on his cheek. Was it from Valeria? Alannah leaned against the back of the couch. "How is your mother?"

"Furious."

She gestured to his cheek. "Are you—"

"Do not worry about me, Alannah. I have weathered far worse from her," his tone clipped.

She didn't believe him. Not entirely. Valeria probably took her anger out on him. After all, he was the one who brought her to the court. "I'm sorry."

"For what?"

"For this whole mess. For you being in your mother's path. For hitting you."

He shrugged. "It doesn't matter."

"It does to me." She sighed. "Granted you shouldn't have kissed me without my permission, but that doesn't mean I feel good about hitting you."

He stared at her. She doubted anyone had apologized for hitting him before, and having done so, he stood in stunned silence. A feat she didn't think possible. His shoulders relaxed. He cleared his throat. "Would you have kissed me if I had asked permission?"

"Then? No."

"What about now?"

"I don't know. I'm thinking I may have been wrong."

"About?"

She tucked a piece of hair behind her ear. "About you. Perhaps your sister was right after all. Maybe there is something good in you."

"Do you truly think so?"

"It's possible." She shrugged. "But it all depends on you."

"May I show you something?" Odhran asked.

Without waiting for her answer, he gestured for him to follow her out the door. He held it open for her. A cool breeze made her arm break out in goosebumps. She shivered. Winter lurked right around the corner. Odhran walked down the stairs and moved to the flower bed, what was left of it, and stopped in front of it. He gazed down at it and she followed his gaze. Right in the middle sat a lone, and rather wilted, Gerber daisy. Somehow alive and hanging on by a thread, similar to how Alannah was feeling after everything, but the daisies roots clung to soil.

"How?" she asked.

"This is why I went to the village," he admitted. "Riona is well-known for her magic and I believed if anyone could salvage what I had done, it would be her."

"Salvage? They were all dead."

"The ones you threw at me that day, one still lived. I kept it—I won't have a reason for you if you ask—and when my sister told me of the hurt I caused, I endeavored to make it right."

Alannah narrowed her eyes. "She threatened you, didn't she?"

Odhran chuckled. "I won't deny it. But the idea was all mine."

"So, this is your true apology?"

He frowned. "I...I suppose it is."

"You don't seem sure."

"I'm not one to apologize to anyone but my sisters, and even then, I don't do it often. Until today." He shifted, looking unsure what to do with his hands until he settled on clasping them behind his back. "I am not sure of many things around you."

"What do you mean?"

"I mean..." he sighed. "Being Valeria's son, even when I am not liked, I am still given deference. Respect. Sometimes it borders on ass-kissing. Only my sisters take me to task. Until you."

"Maybe people should do it more often. Then you'd be used to it."

Odhran turned his head to hide his smirk. "Perhaps

you're right. But they don't. And I have found that I don't know how to act around you. Any of the usual tactics and threats don't work. You don't back down. I... you unsteady me."

"And yet you keep seeking me out."

He looked at her then, his eyes flicking up and down in appraisal. "I am just as confused."

Alannah sank down to her knees. She reached for his hand. With a gentle tug, she coaxed him into kneeling beside her. If he had any complaints about her touching him, he kept them to himself. But he grimaced when she shoved their hands into the dirt. She snorted. It wasn't surprising that he wasn't the type to get his hands dirty.

The magic came as easily as it did in Witches End. *Is this what it's going to be like now?* Her fingertips were conduits and she sank the magic into the earth. Odhran's eyes focused on the side of her face, but she focused on the flower. The stem straightened and the petals perked up.

She could've stopped there. One flower saved was more than she hoped for. But Alannah pushed a little further. She breathed out and the roots sank deeper in the dirt. Green buds sprang up around the flower. They took over the bed until the soil was full. One by one, buds opened, revealing petals of all different colors. An orange that reminded her of Mr. Pinkus' fur. A gold that reminded her of Senna's eyes. A pale peach that reminded her of Elliot's lips. And a silver with blue flecks that looked suspiciously like Odhran's eyes.

Not only her mother's flowers, but now hers. Brought alive by her magic. She withdrew their hands from the dirt.

"Apology accepted," she murmured.

Epilogue

Alannah stared at the blank page in the journal until she felt her vision grew blurry. Candlelight flickered in her peripheral. The low light threw shadows across the desk, once her grandmother's, but now it hers. Alannah sighed and rubbed her eyes. No matter how much she stared at the journal, nothing showed up on the page. She even tried the trick the goddesses used to reveal her family tree. But it didn't matter how many times she sliced her finger and swiped it over a blank page. Nothing happened. What would make the other pages reveal themselves? Or were they well and truly blank. Her grandmother didn't leave an instruction manual for the journal. Alannah would have to keep trying until she figured out how to reveal its secrets.

"Still going at it?"

She turned to face Elliot. He leaned against a bookshelf. "I think I'm going to give up for the night," she answered, sighing.

"I'm positive you'll figure it out." He crossed the room to stand behind her chair.

She looked up at him. "How did seeing them off go?" she asked.

Elliot sighed. "I was sad to see them go, but I promised to check in with them. Oh! That reminds me." He reached into his pocket and fished out his phone, practically vibrating with excitement. "I wanted to show you something."

Alannah leaned close, watching him swipe his finger over the screen. He tapped an icon and it opened up. While he seemed excited, she had no idea what he was showing her. "I don't understand."

"It's internet!" He grinned. "You remember when you asked me to ask the house nicely and maybe we would get it. I did it! Well, I actually asked the wall beside my bed because I didn't know how exactly I was supposed to ask and I was super nice about it, and now we have internet! Do you know what this means?"

"Not at all," she said, but she was thrilled that he was happy about it.

"I can show you pictures and we can listen to music and oh! Television and movies. All of the information right at our fingertips, Alannah. I can show you everything."

She loved when something excited him. "I can't wait, Elliot."

"And speaking of new things," –he shoved his phone back in his pocket— "I brought home dinner."

"Oh?"

"There was a pizza place in town and I figured it was time for you to try it."

"Well, you have spoken so highly of it," she teased.

"Pizza is an experience. Even bad pizza is good pizza." He ran his fingers through his hair. "I should also tell you that I may have invited Odhran for dinner."

"Did you?"

He shrugged.

"Why? He did try to kill you."

"Yeah, he did. But he saved you when it came down

to it so I figured maybe he isn't all bad and..." he trailed off and sighed. "This sounded better in my head."

Alannah stood up and curled her fingers in his shirt to draw him closer. "What did?"

"I look at him and see the person I could've been. Not like a killer, but a person that took his anger and hurt on everyone else because he doesn't think there is any other way to be." Elliot shrugged. "Maybe if he sees that there's another way to be, he can change. Or maybe he won't and I'm an—"

Alannah kissed his cheek. "You're very kind, Elliot. If you want to reach out, it's certainly worth a try."

He turned his head and kissed her. "Thank you," he murmured against her lips, backing her up against the desk.

The wood dug into her hip but she didn't care. Kissing was still new, but Alannah liked it. Better than she had imagined from reading. But that had more to do with Elliot being the person she was kissing than her having a lackluster imagination. She shifted, her hip bumping against the desk.

A candle fell over onto the journal.

Elliot broke away. "Oh shit, shit, shit!"

The flame blazed across the page. Alannah's heart dropped. They moved at the same time using their sleeves to stamp out of the flames. Fear seized her chest and squeezed. Fire and paper never mixed well and some of the pages would be singed at the very least. She squeezed her eyes shut. *Please don't be destroyed.* She pleaded with whatever would listen.

"Alannah, look," Elliot whispered.

Her eyes opened. The journal was unharmed. The page wasn't burned, but also wasn't blank anymore. Her fingers moved across the words.

The mother's journey marks the beginning. The maiden's unveils the truth. The crone is the end.

Find the crone before he does.

"Is it supposed to be a riddle?" Elliot asked.

"I don't know..." Her finger tapped the page. "The Maiden, the Mother, and the Crone could be the three Valeria mentioned. I would be one, Makenna the other, and then whoever the Crone is. I'm going to guess that we have to find them before Reluvethel does."

He squeezed her shoulder. "We'll find—"

Multiple clocks chimed at once.

Alannah slammed the journal shut and held it to her chest as she and Elliot ran down the stairs and out of her grandmother's room. All of the clocks—the ones in the hallways and on the landing of the stairs and even the ones downstairs—were all set the midnight. They had never been the same time before. The chimes echoed through the house. Elliot clapped his hands over his ears. But as quickly as they started, they stopped.

They stood in the living room, both of them trying to catch their breath. A scratching sound came from under the couch and Alannah's heartrate spiked, but it was Mr. Pinkus pulling himself out from under the couch.

"What on earth was that?" he asked, his tail fluffy and twitching

"The clocks, they all struck midnight," Alannah said. "Right after we found a new entry in the journal."

"What did it—"

"Look, it's moving again" Elliot interrupted and pointed at the grandfather clock. The seconds hand ticked counterclockwise and then stopped. "Is it...

broken?"

"It seems to be counting down," a new voice made them all jump.

Elliot clutched his chest and leaned against the back of the couch. "Jesus fucking Christ, Odhran! Wear a damn bell next time."

Odhran stood in the entryway; the door open behind him. "Apologies. I heard the noise and I...I had a strange feeling."

"What could it be counting down to?" Alannah asked, but she knew the answer before the words left her mouth.

Find the crone before he does.

Acknowledgements

First and foremost, I want to thank my support system. My mother, my friends Kyle, Bryan Nicole, Nat, and Cory, and my friends in the multiple Discord servers I'm in. You've listened to me complain and pop out ideas at all times of the day and pushed me to put my heart and soul into it. Nat, thank you for beta'ing multiple times and helping me create a story I am proud of.

I want to thank my former instructors Cindy Skaggs for her continued support as I navigate through the process. Paul Witcover for pushing me to think beyond my original ideas and asking me to give Mr. Pinkus a voice.

Thank you all.

About the Author

DeAnna Jackson is an author from Eastern North Carolina. She's dreamed of other worlds since she was a child making potions out of mud, sticks, and roly-polys. When she isn't writing, she is playing in video game worlds, corralling her small zoo of four cats and two St. Bernards, and lamenting about how time always slips through her fingers. You can find her on Instagram and Twitter for updates on what comes next.

Instagram: dejauthor
Twitter: JacksonDe13

Made in the USA
Columbia, SC
15 April 2022